POSTCARDS FROM PINSK

A NOVEL

LARRY DUBERSTEIN

℗

THE PERMANENT PRESS

to Marty and Judith

Library of Congress Cataloging-in-Publication Data

Duberstein, Larry.
    Postcards from Pinsk / by Larry Duberstein.
      p.   cm.
    ISBN 1-877946-04-4 : $20.95
    I. Title.
    PS3554.U253P6   1991
    813'.54—dc20   90-43907
                                        CIP

Manufactured in the United States of America

THE PERMANENT PRESS
Noyac Road
Sag Harbor, NY 11963

So the sense of possibility might be defined outright as the capacity to think how everything could 'just as easily' be, and to attach no more importance to what is than to what is not. It will be seen that the consequences of such a creative disposition may be remarkable, and unfortunately they not infrequently make the things that other people admire appear wrong and the things that other people prohibit permissible, or even make both appear a matter of indifference.

—MUSIL

I

EXPERIENCE

It is true that in all fields a person may
repeat the same mistake for innumerable
years and call it experience.

—OBERNDORF

1

The Labor Day traffic was legendary, bumper to bumper from the Chinatown ramp in Boston to Hyannisport on Cape Cod. As though in atonement for the sins of the past, all the Boston drivers would suffer together the terrible beauty of gridlock evacuation.

On this hot Friday afternoon, sipping iced whiskey at his bay window and writing some long overdue letters, Orrin Summers had felt relieved to be out of it—to be the lone survivor, last bastion of sanity. He was still breathing easy at six o'clock when he tuned in The Jack-and-Liz Show and saw from the NewsCopter a gleaming sheet-metal convoy three lanes wide and a hundred thousand cars long; it might have been tape of an ongoing nuclear meltdown.

The change in him started as the sun slid to the visible hilltops of Arlington. By now, Orrin knew, a few of the early birds had already unpacked their bags and were standing barefoot in the tide, contemplating a restaurant dinner. By now, even the stragglers would have cleared Quincy with realistic hope of something better. And by now too, he was getting sentimental, for after all it was only last summer that he and Gail had been part of the annual televised traffic jam, still in the mainstream. Six hours of crawling torture in exchange for three lovely days in Truro? He would make the deal again, if Satan would make the offer.

Orrin had begun to panic. With night falling fast, sentiment on the rise, and too *much* iced whiskey in his warm

3

dark inside cupboards, he suddenly could not bear to be here alone. His instinct, even now, was to try Gail first, but of course Gail had gone west, headed for the desert and not to take advantage of the off-season rates, either. It was her goal in sunny Reno to become his ex-wife. One year ago in Truro, Gail had given no clue to this impending change. To Orrin, she had seemed at peace, and lovelier at fifty-six than in what she liked to call her "prime."

He tried his son Clyde. Clyde wasn't home either, but at least he could never be an ex-son. And wherever he was, Orrin felt sure it could not be anyplace half so forlorn as Reno, Nevada. Working his way down the list of friends, dialing number after number, Orrin knew it was only growing darker.

Then a real long shot, a miracle. On the second runthrough, he collared Ted Neff at "The Switchboard," Ted's electronic playstation in the basement. As a rule, if Ted's phone wasn't busy, it meant that Ted was not home. He passed hours, no *years* on the line, despite the best efforts of May, his wife, his telephone Cerberus.

"Theo, I'm so glad you're still around. I need to talk."

"I can't just now, Orrin. Honestly, I just popped back inside for ten seconds—the car is loaded—"

"Of course, but before you go. It's really vital."

"I just have no time at all. We're late as it is."

"You don't have two minutes, Theo? You really don't?"

Orrin almost winced as he laid this bit of psychological shake-and-bake on Ted. Unfortunately it was needed.

"Well what is it, Orrin? Tell me what it's about, at least."

"On the *telephone*? Come by, it's on your way. Two minutes, and I'll send you both off with a nice drink. But I *need* to see you."

Orrin was calmer now, waiting for them. It was full dark, the last brilliant trail of salmon and mauve extinguished in the western sky, but help was on the way. Then he saw Ted and knew better, for if Ted was up the stairs alone, he wasn't really there at all. He would hold the line at two measly minutes, five at the outside.

"Where's May?"

"Waiting in the car."

"But that's silly."

"She's double-parked, old man, it's the only way. Just relax and tell me what's up."

"She can't be double-parked, every car has left the city. Look here—"

Orrin flicked on the TV for Ted's edification, but they had replaced the holiday convoy with a chorus line of teen queens in skin-tight bluejeans, thrusting their branded backsides at the camera for legibility. Chix? Orrin squinted to catch the word.

"Come, Orrin, out with it. I really haven't time to watch any television now, or take a drink when I'm about to drive three hours. I'm only here because you said it was urgent."

"And it is urgent. It just isn't terribly *specific,* you know. I needed a hand, the hand of friendship, that's what it was. Is. I needed company, Theo. What I really need is my wife."

"Ex-wife," Ted corrected.

"Et tu, Brute! She isn't that yet. She told me she would call when it was official, and she hasn't called yet."

He realized as he spoke that for the last hour he'd had the phone line tied up; he might already be divorced and simply unaware of the development. It was possible, heaven knows, to be *dead* and not know it, and this thought caused Orrin to break into song, all the while motioning for Ted to join in,

McTavish is dead and his brother don't know it,
His brother is dead and McTavish don't know it,
The two of them lying there in the same bed
And neither one knows that the other one's dead.

Ted sighed extravagantly and checked his watch. "Orrin, do you mean to say you are just lonely?"

"Just lonely! Christ, counselor, what does it take? Flood and famine? Agonies in the bone marrow?"

"Stop dramatizing yourself, old man. You're the one who should have that drink."

Smiling, Orrin waved at the file of empties soldiered up on the mantelpiece. "Esteemed counselor, I have anticipated your advice and followed it, yet stand before you not quite cured of loneliness. I want my wife."

"Don't be a child."

"Child is father to the man, child is father to the man."

"Gobbledy-gook. Listen, May is downstairs—"

"That's *her* fault, Theo. Invite her up, at my insistence. I'll start pouring her drink. I'll finish pouring it, even."

"Goodbye, Orrin."

"Theo, don't you see? I adore her. I *need* her."

"You *hit* her, Orrin."

"Once, for God's sake. In thirty-five years just once. If that."

"You hit her more than once. A lot more. In the old office you waved a bottle at her. And that time in the restaurant? In Providence?"

"How do you know all this?"

"You told me. Or Gail did, some of it. Or Gail told May and May told me. It adds up, old man."

"Well she hit me plenty too, and in plenty of places. Providence, hell. She hit me in the heart, in the soul. There are many ways of doing violence, counselor, you needn't assail and batter a person to do him violence."

"Shrink me not, Orrin, I didn't say anything about assault and battery. I'm sure the situation is complex on both sides, but now is not the time for me to hash it over. You said two minutes."

"I know, but I meant an hour, Theo—honestly I did."

"I haven't an hour to give you, honestly I don't. I'm off. I'll check with you in the a.m., when you're sobered up."

"I'm perfectly sober and now is the time. In the morning, Theo, sunshine will be beaming down."

"Believe me, I hope so. Why not try Jack? Or Barry? Barry might take the job on."

"No answer. You answered, Theo, you're the lucky winner! Take me with you to Truro—I'm the last human in town."

"You are not."

"The last man on Beacon Hill, then. You incur a moral obligation to take me along. I won't eat much and you know I'm not messy—"

"You'll hear from me in the morning, old man, that's my best offer, I'm afraid."

"But wait, you haven't even heard what I asked you to come over and hear. You owe me that much. If you won't take me with you, at least give me one more minute."

"But I have heard it, haven't I?"

"Actually you may have. Just let me grab a sip of whiskey and I can be much clearer on this point. Ice in yours, Theo?"

"Sorry, Orrin, I'm gone."

"Sorry? Not good enough. Friendship demands you hear me out."

"Friendship demands you *let* me out, right now. Seriously, my friend, I'm not Gail. I can't fill the space. You're just going to have to tough it out for a few months, that's all."

"A few *decades,* you mean."

"Whatever it takes."

Now the horn was blaring below the open windows. Orrin leaned out and saw May waving—waving Ted down—so he waved back, waving her up with an ostentatious display of drink, an offering. She countered by shaking her head no, pantomiming a glance at her wrist, and spreading her arms to mime impatience.

Oh there were shenanigans, and plays within plays, but really, watching them drive away, Orrin could almost smile at the honesty they managed with one another. As a psychotherapist, he could know the difference between health and happiness, and damn if this wasn't health! That alone was worth a toast or two, even if he had to drink them up solo, settling in to await The News At Ten. The bald fact was that he had nothing better to do until, gawd, Tuesday morning at ten.

He was stuck, grimly awaiting the news of divorce, partly because it would have been unjust to plan any fun when Gail was having none and partly because he had been unable to imagine any fun for the having. But his Friday and Monday people had imagined their share and called in across the board to cancel. Bad enough to be so available over the holiday weekend, worse still not to be needed.

Four days as blank as a dead fish in profile, and what if Gail *was* having fun! Orrin had envisioned her barely enduring the endless flight, sweltering airless desert nights, the wrenching chore of dissolving a lifelong union of the heart via a spate of offhand anonymous paperwork. But what if instead she had got herself thoroughly lit on that long flight (drinking scotch from those thin plastic tumblers with nary a false bottom to them) and had fallen among parvenu high-tech businessmen who winkingly guaranteed her they knew where the good parties were in sunny Reno? What if she were acting *irresponsibly?*

Mulling such matters brought Orrin up to The News At Ten, where it was fated he should learn the temperature was holding around 79. There was definitely too much Weather. Orrin preferred the company of the anchor teams, Jack-and-Liz when possible but even this fellow, Jay, and his Julie were pleasant enough. They were like friends, and their patter was friendly chat, not news really; they knew how to include you in. Orrin had every intention of taking a drink with Jack-and-Liz at eleven and to prove it he took one now, with Bill, at The Sports Desk.

It did not faze him to learn that the Red Sox had

smacked six solo homers to win by nine so that they now trailed by twenty-two with nineteen to go and stood in a three-way tie for fifth with a couple of those nondescript midwestern troupes, maybe Cleveland and Milwaukee.

But there was an idea, what about heading to Fenway Park this weekend to take in a game, even the Labor Day doubleheader? After all, the Socks were caught up in a dogfight for fifth place! He could bring Clyde's boys and make the most of this skeleton-crew city. Not be jostled, for a change. Dine off Fenway Franks . . .

Orrin sipped to elbow room, and to grandfatherhood, and now a final toast to Jack-and-Liz, who had hung in there this Friday night, staying in town to bring us The News. But to visit with Jack-and-Liz was to underwrite the absolute worst of the Weatherbabies and here he came now, wildly dissimulating as always. Brimming with absurd enthusiasm, he rolled a few confusing maps and charts across the screen, and those garbled things he called satellite pictures, and then he cast a neat rotating beam of light out from the epicenter of New England, and still in the end the little devil was caught—he had to admit it was warm and nothing much else really. Fine Boating Weather.

Orrin was thinking of Bobby Dinsmore, a boy from his distant high-school days who had loved the weather. Not the weather itself of course, the observation and quantification of it through all the instrumentaria of the day. It was a true calling too, for Dinsmore turned up later here in Boston doing just this, TV Weather with all the requisite verve and twinkle. So strange to watch him, a face from the Schenectady days, still boyish yet apologizing for rain over Beantown, promising at least a "smattering" of sunshine for tomorrow. After a period of initial fascination, Orrin had switched newscasts until Dinsmore was gone, about a year later, gone off to apologize for the mist outside Pittsburgh, presumably, or the dark coming down on Atlanta.

Orrin feared he might by now be a divorced man, yet had no way of checking up on the matter. Far afield as they had gone for their stories (the rabid bats in Taunton, then droning along about MART, the Mothers Against Rude Teens) Jack-and-Liz had made no reference to it. If a divorce falls in the desert and there is no one around to hear it, does it make a sound? Is it a divorce?

If a soldier died in Vietnam and his wife never knew it for certain, he would still be dead wouldn't he? Not to her maybe, but on some level dead?

It seemed only moments later when the phone started ringing on Saturday morning. Nine hours had passed. Orrin covered his ears. If I don't hear it, he reasoned, then maybe I am not divorced. But it kept after him, honing in, until he knew he must either pick it up or flee the apartment at once, stark naked.

"Good morning. This is your attorney calling."

"Of course it is. Good morning, Theo. How's your weather down there?"

"Couldn't be better. But I didn't call to give you the weather report."

"True true, it's the one thing I already have in ample supply. I guess I went a little silly on you last night."

"Well why not, really. It is one tough chore, slogging through a business like this. Hear from Gail?"

"Not yet. Do you suppose she got wet feet and decided divorce was not for her after all? It's a possibility at least, until she does call."

"Yes, well, in the meantime, you know where to find me."

"Last man on the beach at Normandy, first man on the beach at Nauset?"

"That's my line. Call anytime."

"Thanks, Ted. I appreciate your thoughtfulness. Please give my love to May, and my apologies for keeping you last night. And enjoy your week."

Orrin's better side: gentle, self-effacing, almost courtly. Gail, for whom the isolated hitting incident apparently stood out, must have lost track of it. Yet squeezing the juice oranges and timing the coffee, opening the bay windows and laying a fresh white cloth, Orrin felt very optimistic. The night had passed, the blessed day was newborn beautiful, and Gail was still his companion-in-life.

And even if she went through with this divorce idea (which admittedly she might, if only to protect her investment in time and travel) she could be as much. Were these not informal modern times? He could easily picture them reunited, right here in fact, in his "bachelor quarters," innocently perusing the newspaper while all the time living in sin. And he would serve her, not the other way around: poached on toast and fresh-squeezed juice, and no trouble between them anymore.

2

It was spoken in jest, all of it, and even then had only come about because Orrin took an uncharacteristic second drink with his lunch.

"I just don't know if I am being helped at this point," Alice Harris had said—no more than that, the usual prompting for Orrin to prop her up a bit. Any of a dozen fillers would have done the trick. It wasn't as though Orrin subscribed to the Great Wall of China approach to analysis, as Derek Travers did, or Bill Krickstein. He liked a little by-play, for it soothed them both, doctor and patient, and you could do it all with voice. The voice was the thing, as calming as a mantra; the voice by now refined to stage-perfection—meandering stream of honey, slow-winding and confiding, and utterly absent the critical note. He would stay within that voice.

Except that he didn't. The two o'clock was always tough, of course, there was always the risk of dozing off after a big lunch. Now, up against the brace of Bushmills and the dry office heat of late October, struggling for wakefulness, Orrin might have cued himself up a trace too sharply in the effort to achieve it.

"You could just drop it," he had said, though that was just the beginning.

"Drop it?"

"You know—cut your losses, get out. The way it looks now, it's either good money after bad, or you drop it."

Harris could not have looked more stunned if he had hit her between the eyes with a club.

"Drop it?" she finally managed. "Isn't there anything else you can say, Doctor?"

"We could try upping your rate. That often does help—you'd be surprised."

Insofar as Alice Harris could conceive of Man Joking, she believed that Orrin was joking with her now. Even so, it was in the worst of taste. And though Orrin had in fact noted a slight stumble and stood ready to correct it, it was in his particular business no more than a commonplace, shop talk, that someone in for a buck and a half a throw had one helluva motivation to get the most out of every session.

"Doctor, I wish you wouldn't. You know how I rely on you, and to think you might consider any of it a joking matter . . ."

"Hardly, my dear. I am sorry, Alice. I'm not quite myself today, and the truth is I should probably give you a *cut* rate. But—" And he had to wave her off.

Orrin had realized only yesterday, weeks en retard, that he and Gail had for the first time in sixteen years missed their annual Foliage à Deux Weekend at the Fitzwilliam Inn in New Hampshire. That fact alone spoke volumes to him of the change in their relations. But here poor Harris had gone so abruptly hangdog sympathetic on him that he had to slam it quickly into reverse. Had he not seen her face droop in unintended parody, Orrin might have gone ahead and spilled out his own troubles, physician-heal-thy-selfishly.

A few stuttersteps got them back on line, however, and soon the Harris Express was rolling full speed ahead; unfortunately for Orrin, it came back too soon to the sticking-point, the unanswerable Harris Despair, and from there to the malpractice.

"I just know it's all a waste of time," Harris was saying. "We have tried it all. I sometimes worry we may have tried everything. What else is there, really?"

"Well, there *is* always lethal injection," said Orrin, and at once they separately registered that here was error. Clearly overcompensating for all those sleep-inducing elements in the room (not least among them the Harris Lament itself), Orrin had cued himself up with a stroke or two of humor, simple as that. He had meant of course to keep such tidbits to himself but, frankly, he had failed. Might as well face up to that. Failure too is part of the human scheme, to deny it would be foolish.

The damnedest aspect was that he had really almost made it. This magnum error, the one for which no ready correction existed, came with a minute to go in Regulation Time. (Orrin always saved out two minutes of Overtime, as a concession to reality.) And the irony was that he would have been better off in the end had he simply dozed off—fatigue being one thing and malpractice, surely, another.

Asprawl atop his coverlet that night with an abridged snifter, a fractional indulgence, Orrin reflected on how much of his private time and energy he gave to every patient. In the evening, during his meals, or even in bed (waking to a care and then drifting back), he would concern himself with their concerns. And that was what made one-fifty a fair rate to charge, since you could hit them only for the office hour.

Ted Neff could keep a fine clock in his head (and a General Electric geared to his phone and God knows a microscopic Swiss chip inside the cake of soap in his showerstall, where he did his best thinking) and if ever he gave the slightest consideration to a client's problem, Bingo!, the meter was off and running. In fact it was likely that at this very moment Ted was hitting *him* up for some serious overtime, as Orrin had naturally alerted him earlier in the evening to the malpractice.

"I'm sure it will blow over, Orrin," Ted told him. "Yes I

understand she spoke the word malpractice, but these days that's just a part of speech. Very few people follow through."

"She gave me her personal guarantee."

"In a moment of extreme shock, yes. By now she'll have forgotten all about it, and be picking over her shrimp cocktail."

"But *is* it malpractice, Theo? If she did go ahead, would she prevail in court? I want you to answer that."

"Trust me, old man, they have to throw it out."

"They do?"

"Certainly they do. You simply and flatly deny it ever took place. What could sound more delusional than a charge like this one? Your record is impeccable. In fact, I'd wager you could convince the woman herself it never happened, the very next time you see her."

"What if I don't deny it, though? Would they still toss it out?"

"Cop to it? That's crazy, Orrin. There is no way on earth they can prove it happened. Your word against hers. It isn't *med*ical—there isn't an incriminating x-ray, or a scar that shows up on her CAT-scans. It's just an allegation."

"Except that the allegation is true, of course."

"Orrin." Ted was getting impatient (there would be the personal inconvenience surcharge soon) but Orrin held loosely firm.

"I do have professional ethics, you know. She is my patient. In the past year she has handed over about six thousand dollars American. I owe her something in return."

"This is not a discussion about ethics, this is a discussion about your insurance premiums. Six thousand dollars won't get you halfway to Hartford if you go and cop to malpractice. And suppose she *takes* a lethal injection, for that matter, and is barely rescued from death. Sees the light and *then* she sues. My God, man, what then? Ten million?

Twenty billion? You stonewall it and sprint on down to the confessional, that's what you do."

"Maybe you're right, Theo. Maybe she won't follow through. If I call her up and apologize—"

"Listen to me, will you. You cannot apologize for something you did not do, if you will please take my meaning. I have got to get off the line now, Orrin, but do me a favor. If you must call her, to sound her out, have Sarah do it in the guise of confirming the next appointment or something. Making *no mention* of any odd behavior on your part, whether real or imagined. Understood?"

"I could tell her the whole episode was meant as a wakeup call, a sort of misguided shock therapy—"

"Schlock-therapy-*forget*-it. I warn you, Orrin. And another thing. I do want you to relax, but how's about relaxing without relying quite so much on the distilled essence? Know what I mean?"

"Oh just a little gargle now and then, to tide me over."

"You will get yourself in real trouble."

"And you will be there to get me out of it. But do you want to hear about real trouble? Get this; Gail refuses to speak with me on the telephone. Did you know that?"

"No, I didn't know that. But I am afraid I have to do the same thing myself at the moment. Time to get off the line."

"Is she there, Ted? Is Gail at your place right now?"

"Of course she isn't. What would make you think so?"

"Let me speak with her. Please! For just one minute."

"Not here, Orrin. Can't speak with her if she's not here?"

"Let me speak with May, then. May can't lie. And you can. You even want me to lie under oath in a court of law! Why should I put any stock in your denial?"

"Orrin, my porridge is getting cold. I won't put May on because she is about to erupt on the subject of cold porridges as it is. Just a word, my friend. Relax?"

"Easy for you to say."

Hours had passed since they spoke, but Orrin was no-where close to relaxation. He stood at the bay window for the twentieth time, looking out. At dusk he had watched gray fog float right past his windows and transform the Boston Common into a great swirling bowl of smoke. Now it looked like an ocean, like a black sea spattered with the white light of many small craft, and he was drawn to it in spite of the hour.

He rallied his bones into sweater and coat and rushed out, only to find that the sea had receded, and the black-ness, leaving behind a wake of drab gray streets and the inevitable cordon of parked cars on either side. A sur-prisingly chill wind flew down off the bare hills of the Common. This was just Halloween week, yet already the swan-boats were in drydock and all the flowerbeds were smothered under mulch. In no time, the low waters of the lagoon would be stretched over with skins of ice.

An analyst should not shoot off his mouth, Orrin mused as he made his way. To do so was no different, no better, than performing trial-and-error surgery. It was silence that made you safe and rich, and in all likelihood kept you from making a bad situation worse. And it was absurd for anyone to suppose you might *improve* a situation, for who were *you,* really? Orrin sometimes had a genuine humility in the matter. Shrink $\neq$ God was his formula. If you went to Shrink $=$ God, well then soon enough you were probably just fucking them, like Harold Bamford.

On the other hand—and the other hand was literally elaborated in his purview by a couple on a nearby bench, the young lady offering an ungrammatical though possibly first-rate reading of the young man's palm—what the hell. Because if people were going to select their behaviors from information in the tabloid horrorscope, or from situation comedies on the television, or from fortune cookies at cut-rate Chinese lunchrooms where the fortune was always mis-spelled (if otherwise quite palatable), or from Dear Abby and Ask Aunt Nelly, then why the hell *not* play God!

At least we do enjoy a familiarity with the human condition and have our clients in a clear objective light. Perhaps there was a mandate to play God after all, though Orrin could hear Ted Neff's crystalline rejoinder: relax, cork up the old quart bottle, we are not discussing religion here we are discussing *insu*rance premiums. . .

But were we? Orrin might not be halfway to Hartford but what about Heaven—was he halfway there? Maybe he would be able to restrain it (for he was far from home and, liking the walk, walking farther) but he had a powerful impulse to phone Alice Harris right now, midnight be damned, and tell her the whole truth and nothing but. Why apologize for calling to her attention the lethal injection option? Better apologize for *failing* to call to her attention all the possibilities for joy; for failing to shake that awful solipsistic self-pity out of her.

Silence be damned! Tell her she was simply dead wrong about her mother (*and* about her son) and that she was obviously paranoid about the poor cleaning-woman. Tell her moreover that she was *fired,* he had no use for such incompetent clients. Why not give the girl her money's worth? Tell her she was *depressing!* Put *that* in your fortune-cookie, lady!

```
You are a most depresing
pirson and it would be
best you hide under yor
bed the rest of yor
natural life  ☺
```

Halfway to Hyde Park by now, on a wide expanse of Washington traversed only by taxicabs and cocaine-laden conversion vans with blackout windows, he started back home. It all came to nothing anyway. You could not hope to revolutionize the fortune-cookie industry overnight. And Orrin knew perfectly well that this was all his fault, and no one else's; that he ought not play God, or even Man Joking with Alice Harris, and that he was only in the swamp because he had too much to drink with his lunch.

Even God did not play God so *openly*—telling people what to do. He had known that in the past and he would know it again by tomorrow morning, when the dull October sun washed the dry unfallen leaves with soft Etruscan color. Mornings did that for people, where the evenings could be so confusing. (Especially now, without Gail, Orrin was disoriented, and was never sure what to make of them.) In the morning you knew what to do, knew where to *go*. Really, wasn't that all one could ask?

3

When he considered the members of his once-nuclear family as individuals (a fair enough proposition ontologically), Orrin could see no reason why each should prove unwilling to speak with him on the phone. He had loved them all for decades, and supported them handsomely for decades too. He would be happy to support them still, except they did not want that from him, nor his love anymore. They wouldn't even come to the phone.

Perhaps this was overstating the case. What actually happened was that he called Clyde during office hours and Clyde wanted to put him on Hold.

"I don't do Hold."

"Then I'll have to get back to you, Dad. Sorry."

"But I don't do I'll-have-to-get-back-to-you either."

"Well then, you'll have to get back to me. Why don't we plan to talk this evening, after the boys are in bed. Then we'll have a nice clear field."

So it was not so bad with Clyde. A college professor might well be busy during his morning office hours, and they would indeed have a long talk that evening. Clyde was a reasonable human being (too much so, Orrin had feared at times) whereas his sister Elspeth insisted on keeping her life in utter Bohemian disrepair and furthermore on glorifying the squalor under a shroud of secrecy. El was disconnected in every way; her alleged phonelessness was really the least of it. But Orrin did not buy the story that no one in the family knew her address in the South End. He guessed both Gail and Clyde knew it, just as each of them had met the mysterious "Hickey" and he, Orrin, had never had the pleasure.

Hickey, Christian name unknown (or maybe Christian name Hickey, patronymic unknown—for who could know or unknow, nowadays), was Elspeth's boyfriend. A tall pale man with three beards, deposited, or isolated upon his face like correctly spaced shrubberies and a curling row of beebees that defined his left ear like a constellation. Clyde's description, of course. They had showed up at Clyde and Phyll's in Lexington looking for forty dollars of the needful and fast, though Hickey had taken the trouble to frame a little joke: "Worse luck, locked out of the Mercedes again, and all my Magic Money Cards inside with the gloves!"

This Hickey would talk to him on the phone, thought Orrin, hobnob for half an hour, in exchange for a little Magic Money, or a few lines of cocaine. Did it come in "lines"? Well, between the lines, if not, or in baggies, or boxies. Whatever it took, he would be able to grab Hickey's attention because Hickey had needs. Elspeth apparently did not need, or want, anything Orrin could offer her.

But his pain from El was nothing new. The real problem at hand was Gail. Orrin had been dialing her number for a month, every day right after breakfast and just before dinner, and had never reached her once. Preternatural in so many ways, could she somehow know his ring? The Information Girl confirmed the number was good and when Orrin complained it was no good to *him,* the Girl did not even pretend to sympathize. Finally, two weeks ago, there was a slip-up at Gail's end: she lifted the receiver and spoke the one-word greeting. But when—in the face of treatment that might have soured a saint—he greeted her back as sweetly and lovingly as ever man could, she hung up without a word of farewell. Hello yet no goodbye, he thought, the story of our life.

And the very next time he called, a scant nine hours later, a machine had answered. Talk about impulse buying! It was Orrin who had to hang up that time, and it took him two days to reorganize his emotions. Then he submitted to form—waited for the beep like a good modern boy, read off his carefully worded message of apology and devotion, and rendered the dinner invitation to which Gail would make no response.

Yes it was Gail who had sealed him off. On each of the next six days he dictated similar messages and on the seventh day he screamed. Waited for the bloody beep and was for all the world intent on reading his latest revision of the protocol, but couldn't—cutting loose instead with one long hoarse primal scream into her over-industrialized ear.

This was not good lobbying, he realized as he let 'er rip, it would scarcely serve to advance his position with Gail, but what was a person *supposed* to do?

"I'm very glad to hear from you, Doctor Summers," said Orrin to his son, who did call after nine. "I have to apologize for my boorishness earlier . . ."

"Quite all right, Doctor Summers. No one should have to hold a dead line. If I had my way, we'd change back to the old phones."

"The good old hello-and-how-are-you single party line!"

"That's right. So tell me how you're getting on."

Haven't been getting on for ye-e-ears, Orrin drawled silently, in his best W. C. Fields. To Clyde he said: "Very well, actually. And you, Clydie?"

"Phyll wants you Friday—" (Would that it were so-o-o, went Fields again) "—for dinner. Any chance? I realized the boys haven't seen you since the summer."

"Haven't seen them either," said Fields, aloud this time.

"Friday sounds fine—delightful, in fact. What time and what wine, my dear lad?"

"Why don't we say seven. And we'll have you choose the wine from our own ample cellars. No sense bringing coals to Newcastle. Let me play the squire and you play the sated guest."

"The sated guest it will be, then. So good to hear from you. I never hear from your sister, you know."

"Of course not, Dad. She's living out on The Edge. You must realize one can't call in from The Edge?"

"I suppose not. But *why* is she living there? What's with her?"

"She tells me that it's a time of raging action for women."

"She said something like that to me once, too. You don't suppose she really believes it?"

"Oh and it's true."

"It's agitate agitate—that's what she said. It's all out there, Dad, tough times for a girl to settle down. *I* say she's gone a little silly on us."

"Elspeth is living it, Dad, that's all. Out there on—"

"The Precipice."

"That's right."

"Well you, Clyde, are a good man, truly you are. To call me up and compel your best wife to invite me for dinner—"

"Nonsense, we all want you here. You know how the boys love you. And we're an awful long way from The Precipice ourselves, so we may as well take the time to enjoy some good wine with our loved ones."

"You haven't heard from her?"

"El? Not since they came to pay back the last loaner. They always do, by the way, and with a nice Pouilly-Fuissé for the vigorish last time."

"Oh honourable Hickey."

"It's all a question of cycles," said Clyde, who was after all an historian by trade. "Ten years from now, El will be settled on a farm someplace raising pigs and triplets, and Hickey will be riding the commuter train in a gray flannel suit with his brimming attaché. And I will be sailing to Byzantium with a mossy beard."

"And where will I be, ten years from now?"

"Now that is a question which warrants significant discourse on Friday, over the rare roast beast."

"At the Clyde F. Summers Symposium."

"That's right. And we can propose toasts to your future *whatever* it holds. I want to hear your plans."

"Well, you know, a great deal does depend on your mother."

"I really don't think so, Dad. To be frank, that is."

"Oh don't worry, I know how she feels at the moment. But why don't we save it for the Symposium. I'll plan on seven, and maybe I'll bring a little something for the boys."

"Look at it this way, Dad," said Clyde, and launched a paragraph more convoluted than concise about Orrin's future prospects as compared to those of "tomorrow's high school hero, only just being born tonight and yet likely to die a scant nineteen years from now in some slimy distant jungle."

"Is this what you mean?" said Orrin to his sometimes verbose son, and handed over this hasty scribble:

```
 Today is the first day
 of the rest of yor life
                     ☺
```

"That's right," said Clyde. "I couldn't have put it better myself."

"*You* couldn't have put it any worse, dear," grinned Phyllis. "But we simply mean the obvious, Orrin. That you are not old—you don't look old or seem old—and we hope to keep up your youth and strength with a good square meal."

"Well thank you, Phyll, I appreciate it."

"Grandpa is *so* old," said Jethro. "If *he* isn't old, then who is?"

Orrin didn't mind any of it. Clyde and His Bride were not out to prove anything, they were simply talented in these areas—food and drink, furniture and music—and their home was a comfortable place. Clyde's Gregorian Bluefish, a last-minute replacement for the roast beast, made the best meal Orrin had eaten in months and the half-hour he passed with Jethro and then Corey in their respective lairs was easily the highlight of his fall social season. When Corey wanted to go through the stamp album page by page, Clyde assumed a rescue was in order, but Orrin would not have missed a single Andalusian, Bora Boran, or Manitoban commemorative. He loved the boy's eagerness, so small and so close to him on the bed, and he even loved the stamps, for here apparently was the last residue of fine print design in an allegedly visual age.

And when he was finally pressed for some semblance of a plan, a new approach to life, he made it into a game with the boys. On a blank sheet, each was invited to propose a new job for his grandfather, a trip to anywhere in the world, and a second wife—this last to be illustrated.

"Read mine first," said Corey, and Phyllis did:

"He's got you managing the Red Sox, spending the winter in Hawaii, and marrying Alyssa Milano. Alyssa Milano?"

"I don't know her either, but the first two suggestions are so good, she must be too. Let's hear Jethro."

"I've got his. Nothing wrong with your old job, no

place like home, and never marry again seems to be the
message here! Looks as though we have a conservative in
the house."

"Well I'm a conservative too," said Orrin, hugging both
of his grandchildren. "But let me see the illustration of this
Milano woman."

Orrin enjoyed every minute and yet was strangely relieved when the festivities concluded around ten o'clock.
Odd though it might seem, he felt no need of a social life,
whether out on the town or at The Club, which he had not
visited in weeks. His need was to be at home, this new
home on Filbert Street, and to know that he could contact
what he increasingly thought of as "the outside world" via
the telephone. Of course one could not expect to conduct a
proper life on the telephone (especially if no one ever
answered the sucker) but Orrin knew he was in for something other than a proper life just now.

Phyllis drove him back to town and insisted on coming
upstairs for a look at the apartment.

"So do I pass the test?"

"It's quite nice, isn't it. Cozy. But I hope you won't
mind my being a little blunt with you, Orrin?"

"Oh no, Phyll, be any way you want."

"All I mean is that you must know Clyde can't. Be blunt,
or quite truthful. He's uncomfortable about hurting you,
naturally . . ."

"You do it, Phyll. You hurt me—go on."

"Someone needs to say to you that two months have
gone by and you are just here waiting for Gail to change
her mind, I think. And she isn't going to. You need to hear
that from someone, Orrin, and I guess I'm the nominee."

"The villainess! Look, I understand, dear girl, and I
appreciate your concern. I even appreciate a kick in the
seat."

"*Do* you understand? I wonder if you could analyze
yourself half as well, see yourself half as clearly, as you can
see your clients."

"Even half as well might help, eh?"

"I think so. I think it's time for a toughminded self-analysis, if there is such a thing."

"I could bill myself out at half-price and still do all right on the deal."

"A word to the wise-ass," she said, and left it at that. Orrin gave her a hug and saw her back downstairs and into her car, noting the pleasant October air.

But perhaps she was right. Perhaps he ought to sit down with himself and a drink (two drinks, though, one for each of him) and interview himself in prospectus. That was the trend, of course, a client interviewing the therapist for suitability. Next thing you'd be compiling snap-shots of those whose burdens had been alleviated, like the old bite-plates an orthodontist dragged out to prove he could straighten teeth! No job too large or small, no charge for estimates—it could yet become as demeaning as selling a vinyl-siding job.

But it took no intake, no special screening, for Orrin to know that his strengths were the charm and intelligence God had given him plus the good teeth and eyes and a fine field of hair that God had yet to take away. He also knew his weaknesses: nostalgia, mild forms of bitterness, moderate paranoia. The exercise was a joke, and such spuriousness was a clean country away from the wellsprings of pain and neurosis.

Orrin at fifty-eight did not expect to hear a skeleton rattling in his broom-closet or the slither of ghosts unrequited in his attic eaves. To him the problem was terribly prosaic and altogether current—Gail had stuffed him—and it called for plainspoken pragmatic advice. He had lost the habit of bearing down anyway. With all these clinical psychos inching in on the practice of analysis (not to mention the vast clientele being siphoned off into New Age booshwah rackets that could all but promise heavy petting in their street leaflets), Orrin had gone to a fairly watery mix himself.

How many times had he urged some poor soul to take up a hobby, the old Balsa Wood Therapy? Or recommended getting outside one's personal pain by seeing to the greater pain of others: take up a Cause. Or fed them the line about dining out with a friend of the opposite sex—"Nothing sexual, but you get back a sexual identity, you know." One had to marvel at such expertise as that.

He replaced the puddle of whiskey in his glass with another one every bit as piddling; the first had apparently evaporated, the second he whacked down, since it was time for his constitutional. Now *there* was therapy, just to get the feet going on a nice October night.

A winter sky, with soft gauze wrapped loosely round a three-quarter moon and fragments of light shattered like tempered glass below it. Down along Charles, every gaslight mimicked the aurora moon, shroud and fraglight, and late strollers hurried through the wind. Crossing the Gardens, Orrin saw romance in the over-arching beeches: lit from within the tentative embrace of huge limbs, the trees took on a theatrical lustre, as though Shakespearean assignations might soon ensue there, Orlando and Rosalind in the forest of Arden. . .

By day a profuse foot-traffic, cross-section of society, crisscrossed the Boston Common. Late at night motion slowed and commotion halted, and the turf fell into the hands of a vague underclass, Dickensian riffraff, the denizens of an "edge" which Elspeth might not find so alluring. If it was your pattern to travel home from the bank to Belmont on an afternoon train, or even to climb the stairs on Acorn Street at dusk (as Orrin had done for so many years) you could easily fail to realize that this society existed, or believe its members were apparitions from the Depression past, or from far lands where democratic ideals had never taken root—the damp back alleys of Bombay or the teeming ditches of Mexico City.

But Orrin knew they were there. On the ledge of the fountain of course, in the shadows round every tree-trunk, two or three to every bench, plus the rather substantial group by the intermittent fire in the drained pool basin, a spot so safe that the constabs simply allowed it.

"Establish a scholarship, sir, in your name? Send this young man on to the University of Life?"

Orrin must have stood too long by the cluttered bench near Tremont Street. He saw there was nothing young about the would-be student, a stocky round-eyed man, but there was something likable, and something arresting in the voice. Of course it was just a hook culled from the textbook on cadging and turned to a fine phraseology, Anonymous. Still, even without an overtly messianic rush, Orrin did suppose he might help here.

"Do I take it you want to drink?"

"Wellsir, I am thirsty. What would you do if you were thirsty, sir?"

"As it happens I *am* thirsty, and I would be happy to buy you a drink or two."

"Step right this way, then. We've got this round covered and probably the next, so we can drop your contribution right into the vault."

He indicated a large wool purse, a satchel almost, with bamboo flanges, stowed below their bench. Introducing himself as P. Jones and his companion, mistress of the pursestrings, as Marie LeBlanc, he urged Orrin to call them Pigford and Sad Mary if he liked.

"Welcome to the Dog-and-Cat," said Mary.

"Cheapest tavern in the town," said Pigford. (Clearly it was something of a routine they did.)

"The Dog-and-Cat?" Orrin almost expected to see a hand-carved brightly-painted wooden sign swinging from the oak branch overhead.

"Well you can see it isn't exactly The Bull and Finch."

"Or The Lion and the Unicorn."

"And it does rain dogs and cats in this particular inn, at this particular time of the year."

"Now tell him the truth, you old liar," said Mary.

"All right. Mary had a cat when I first met her—"

"Not a little lamb?" said Orrin.

"No, a cat. And I had a dog. So there you are. When we teamed, we would always do our tippling at the Dog-and-Cat, or so we said. Simple as that."

Thus the rest of the routine. The pair took their liquor in paper shot-glasses, the three-ounce toothbrushing size, from the Stop & Shop. Mary shook a third cup loose from the satchel and P. Jones poured. Then, because the night was young and so were they, they drank the first of many healths.

4

Orrin was trying to recollect the circumstances which had led to his sheltering the man P. Jones. For Pigford, who had in that first burst of accessibility invited Orrin to call him as his friends did, was still deep in the sofa snoring and Orrin could not quite pretend to be thrilled by the sight of him.

He recalled leaving The Dog-and-Cat at "closing time" and making a pit stop at a packie on Tremont. From there they had proceeded down a narrow alleyway between brick tenements to the trashcan hearth where Pigford and Sad Mary had carved out a comicbook hobo existence, almost snug under a sheet-metal canopy bridging two sealed-off delivery doors. When Orrin, in an access of charity (and basically shitfaced) had offered them both a night's respite from the cold, Mary had perhaps misunderstood him and taken offense, standing on her honor and virginity.

"At sixty-five? Come on, Mary, fess up," he had smiled, but Mary stood firm: "Truth is truth, governor, and I turn forty-three this month and that's the truth, too."

She had in any case declined the indoors absolutely. Jones, however, agreed it might be an "experience worth having" and what with the mention of another nightcapper assented to extend their companionship a few hours further. Now Orrin remembered their journey over the lawns of the Common, ebullient and philosophical by turns. His friend had craved the chance to display his mastery of "current events" and begged Orrin to quiz him; and because Orrin could not manage the feat, Jones was left to volunteer his insights into world affairs scattershot.

By moonlight, Jones had seemed a gentleman, bright and clearspoken, a man of some ideas and of high moral standard. Sleeping in the sunlight now, he looked decidedly soiled at the cuff and Orrin could not overlook the analogue: it was as though he had brought home some aged street-witch in a blind and searing lust, only to see her laid bare in the cruel sobriety of morning light; and himself laid bare, besides.

More than willing to nurture Jones through the night, willing even now to ensure him a large and wholesome breakfast, Orrin knew that basically he needed to unload his new friend. Jones must go. And because he had Alice Harris coming to the office in her new morning slot, Jones must go with some expedition. So Orrin pushed at his guest, and pulled, and tweaked the face-hair until finally the dear fellow did stir in a brief hail of spittle and sat up like a shot with both hands over his head in an attitude of surrender. Then subsided in shivers, registered his surround, and politely requested the "dog's hair in a glass."

"I would accommodate you at once, my friend, if supplies had outlasted you in the night. As it is, my best offer is breakfast at The Paramount. Black coffee and the lot."

"A plate of eggs? Sounds fine, Orry, just the thing. And if Big Ben over there is even close to the mark, we can replenish our supplies in short order."

"As to that, I hope you'll allow me to stand you a round or two in absentia," said Orrin, who found himself sliding into the hyperflated erudition associated with stage drunks, or perhaps hearkening back to his W. C. Fields stint of the previous week. "The thing is, I have a ten o'clock appointment for which I cannot afford to be one second late."

"You really a headshrinker, like you said?"

"Truth is truth, as Sad Mary says."

"But then isn't the truth that you can afford any god-damn thing in the world? It would be."

"Put it this way, P. If by chance I am one second late for my ten o'clock appointment—and if my tardiness has a certain effect on a certain client—it could end up costing me fourteen trillion dollars, according to my attorney. And I have only thirteen."

"Thirteen trillion!"

"I know it sounds like a lot. But to fall even one trillion in arrears—look at it that way. Imagine yourself coming back to that mark."

"You are a funny one, Orry. I enjoy your company. And I thank you for all your hospitality. Did I tell you anything about myself last night?"

"Quite a lot. But the only thread I could see winding through your checkered career, was thirst."

"That's putting a fine finger on it! You cancel out my thirst, Orry, and I swear to you I would be in the U.S. Government Post Office still today. And eligible for a lovely pension too, at an early date. There's the bitch of it."

"You kind of blew it, P."

"That's hitting the nail smack on the head! I swear you would make one *hell* of a headshrinker. What's the hour charge over there, anyway?"

"Well there's a sliding scale."

"Once again? I'm not much on the musical side."

"The hourly charge is on a sliding scale—from low to high, according to one's ability to pay."

"Now I get you. So then what's the low side of it?"

"One hundred dollars per session."

"Service com-pree!" Pigford burst out, with sur-prisingly international enthusiasm. "Talk about your bar-

gains! I won't dare ask after the high side. But who are
these poor buggers can only afford the hundred dollar rate?
Car parkers?"

"You may be a man of the street, Pigford, but you are
also a man of parts. I'm frankly embarrassed to be discussing such numbers with you."

"Don't be, *I* don't care. I made my bed. And anyone can
pay the hundred for a well-disposed ear, by all means let
him pay it. It's not like you're charging at that rate for his
hamburgers or whiskey."

"The essentials, you mean."

"I do. You never want to overcharge the essentials, but
why not make em dig deep for luxury. Isn't that best?"

"Damn if you don't make me feel better already. But I'm
afraid we better step on it, if we want to catch a good
breakfast. There might be time for a shave, if you like."

"Oh no. Mary likes some growth on me."

"The Virgin Mary? What would it matter, if she tells the
gospel truth?" Orrin tossed in a wink, to disarm against
any possible offense here.

"She is no snuggle of mine, nor anyone else's, and that *is*
gospel. But she is partners with me and she does have to
look at me, as I do her. It's an appearance thing, Orry. Just
the same way she won't wax her mouth because I hate the
look of it."

"Because it reminds you of your wife? Or your mother?
What?"

"Cause it reminds me of an Indian chief, such as slew my
great Aunt Maisie. And if you believe that, you'll believe
anything."

Asleep he had been almost disgusting, but conversing
Pigford was once more affable. Like many drinkers, he
could not help making unsolicited excuses for himself, or
making the business of drink his recurring topic. No
doubt, therefore, his society would pale in time. Also he

continued to shiver very gently, even in the steamy warmth of The Paramount, with a stack of hotcakes and two mugs of coffee inside him. Only the dog's hair could quiet this, Orrin supposed, and with a complicity mitigated by inevitability he did stake Pigford to a fresh supply.

"So what will you do today? What is a typical day for you?"

"Typical day in the life of P. Jones? Well, for starters I'll tell you any day is a piece of cake. It's the nights."

"I couldn't agree more," said Orrin, frankly alarmed by this irrefutable brotherhood of issues. "But still, what will you do? How will you pass the time?"

"Milk and honey, nothing but. We'll eat at the McDonald's, three or four meals usually—"

"Can you afford that, then?"

"We can afford anything that's free. Didn't you know they pitch out perfect burgers all day long? Lest they be un*fresh*, you see."

"I didn't know. So they run a soup kitchen out the back."

"It comes to that. Soup kitchen hold the soup. I'll tell you, Orry, in the daytime there are windows of opportunity everywhere. Take the Boston Public. The Library over there. Newspapers and magazines, all there, sometimes a movie—and *they* pay the heat bill."

"It makes me proud to be a taxpayer."

"Oh me too. Gladly."

"But Pigford, you know that as a doctor I have to tell you this existence will kill you. Not the cold fresh air, which is largely to the good, and you do seem to manage cheerfully with your bills—but drink itself will kill you."

"I suppose something was bound to."

"That's just talk and you know it."

"They say alcohol is a disease, I know that. But thirst

can make you helpless too. Thirst can distract you so much
you will do nothing right, and never care either."

"You said last night you were almost ten years on the
street. Do you think you will last ten more?"

"I will if you will, Orry. Just because I like your company."

Considering how much Pigford enjoyed his company,
Orrin had to be slightly relieved not to see his friend again
that same evening, or in the weeks to follow. It could easily
have become a *situation,* he realized, and so had been careless on his part. He felt a twinge of guilt for having taken
Pigford up and dropped him, though it was consoling to
think that Pigford had not done badly on the deal.

Nor had Orrin. True he went back to his lowgrade
pleasure-poor existence, eating Celeste Pizza-For-One and
watching the News, and it did make for a downcasting
regimen. Yet he did not feel so cast down as he had before;
something had changed. And though he could not quite
identify it, he was already reaping some benefits. Once or
twice he slipped into The Club on sleety afternoons, to
make a few brisk sallies and slip back out in good face.
Twice he ran into Ted Neff there and on neither occasion
did he pry after details concerning Gail Summers, a sign of
strengthening will. And he did in fact escort a woman to
dinner: nothing sexual (nothing much gastronomical
either—just the mildewed snapper) but you get back a
sexual identity. . . .

The woman was Amy Sugar, whose status as the only
woman with whom he had gone to bed during his long
marriage to Gail only served to certify the "nothing sexual." With Amy, Orrin had experienced the curious chemical change that can take place when lovers cease to meet
and are very much relieved to do so. Whatever had

brought them together in raw physical collision became an archaism so abruptly that Orrin could neither recall nor imagine it the moment they had concluded. And now (some eighteen years later) Amy Sugar was like a boyhood chum. They could exchange their annual life-summaries with genuine pleasure, some nostalgia, and far more comfort than emotion.

Orrin had definitely felt better since his evening with Pigford but it was well along in December before he managed to grasp the nature of his breakthrough. It was not that he had seen the Other Half living out the back door of McDonald's, or tallied up his blessings in a tricky and difficult world. It was simply the notion of boon companionship.

He needed a friend and he saw now that it did not have to be a woman. Indeed it *could* not be a woman, for two good reasons. It could not be Gail without her consent and it could be no other woman because he loved Gail. Moreover, the complexities of *getting* a woman were mind-boggling, life-draining, whereas his fellow man—some personable intelligent fellow to share the dinner converse or an occasional show—could be had with ease. A room-mate was the thing.

But perhaps fifty-eight-year-old men did not have "room-mates"? Then surely there would be other terms by which to categorize the position. Whatever Orrin chose to call it, he believed advertisement would bring him one, simple as that. If he preferred a youthful, footloose approach, he could pin up his notices in the laundromats and bookshops along Charles. If he preferred safety, there were the snob-housing bureaus and university bulletin boards.

He could be brutally specific, write his own ticket. Did he wish to require tidiness and reliability, or would he prefer to harbor someone with a lengthy criminal record? Someone who eats righty but signs his name lefty? He could probably have the fellow made from scratch in the laboratory, for a fee. There had to be thousands of educated men desperate for decent affordable lodgings in the Boston area, and all he needed was one of them. Piece of cake.

5

Having no firm plans and no family (not so much as a shot of grog in prospectus until Clyde called at the last minute), it was Monday before Orrin realized that Wednesday was actually Christmas. The fact was further obscured by his own resolve to take a rest cure over the weekend, alternating sleep with TV football and plenty of *fluids,* to bounce back from a touch of influenza.

He was no enthusiast of football but there it was, on every station, at every hour, and because the play-by-play announcers had the same soothing voices employed by the news readers, he did visit with them extensively. There were also snippets from old films—the Marx Brothers on ship-board and a Gary Cooper western, plus an ad for *Miracle on 34th Street,* which he could remember, clearly and fondly, taking the children to see one winter long ago, in Baltimore.

Just once did Orrin foray out to the steep glazed sidewalks of the Hill. Tentative but upright, taking baby-steps, he fetched back more fluids from McCallister's (the purely medicinal Bushmills) plus a clutch of magazines to read. True he still held to the postulate that only the desperately bored or the deeply fatuous take magazines, but this rule of thumb had always been waived in time of illness. Besides, he wanted a cultural leavening: immersed in the waters of our time, he might emerge a better, an updated man.

And a healthier one. For he was very strict with his rest cure. His thermometer might be insensitive (continually registering only the first 98.6 degrees of his fever) but

Orrin Summers was not. He knew when the joke was on him, he knew about the bootlegged degrees. From within his own skin, from the merest touch of cheek or forehead, he knew he was running closer to a hundred-and-one around the clock.

Bed rest and fluids did the trick, though. By Monday morning his strength had returned. The sun bore through briefly and there were runnels of water carving trenches in the ice as he again inched downhill for breakfast. At The Paramount he ordered his regular, the Hessian Eggs, which was Greek apparently for hash-and-eggs and which they prepared with the same charm that infused their pro-
nunciation. Cottage warmth and steamy windows, the privacy to peruse one's paper at length, and *they* washed the dishes! Versus breakfast at home? Versus Rice Krinkies that were soggy and toast that was always cold by the time you had your coffee, coffee that was always cold by the time you found the cream and sugar? Nolo contendere, on all counts.

At the office he consulted with Sarah on Gail's present, in keeping with Christmas tradition. "I think it's so sweet you're getting her a gift this year," said Sarah.

"But I get her a gift every year," he said.

Of course Sarah was making reference to the divorce, and in her narrow way presuming it definitive. But divorce no more sundered the bond than the legal fact of marriage confirmed it; the true weld was in the relation and Orrin had every hope that when all the smog had cleared, Gail would see her way back to him.

"I was going to say a week in Miami—that's what every-one wants right about now—but no . . ."

"No?"

"Well Gail won't appreciate your planning out her time, if you see what I mean. You did ask, Orrin."

"By all means," he said, rescinding the scowl that had crept across his features.

"But what about a membership? The Fine Arts or the Ballet. Something that gets her going without tying her down."

"Oh you are brilliant at this, Sarah, you really are. I will do exactly as you suggest. And I'll only have a handful of things to shop for this afternoon."

"Mine's done. I even have it all wrapped, and my turkey is in the fridge."

"Efficiency like that, dear lady, is the reason I love you, and so I am never surprised when you exhibit it. I wish I could send you to Miami for your gift but how would I manage next week without you? So I am only sending you as far as Worcester as it happens."

"Worcester?"

"Julio Iglésias tickets!" he said, brandishing the pair. He had snapped them up downstairs at the Starr Agency twenty minutes ago in a moment of inspiration.

"How could you know?"

"Well I'm not as obtuse as you think, dear. After all, we are in here to pay close attention to the species."

"I *never* talk about music with you. Not a word."

"But you sing. You play the radio, very softly, and you sing along. And then you keep singing after the radio goes off."

"Do I?" He indicated the tickets in her palm as proof. "I guess I must. Thank you, Orrin. It's a lovely gift, Worcester. Shall I give you yours now too?"

"By all means. Though on second thought better wait. It may be the only package under my tree on Wednesday. If I get a tree, that is."

Right after Trudy Pavenstadt's hour, Orrin dashed over to the Downtown Crossing, where he picked out a watch for Corey and, for Jethro, a hockey game so large and elaborate that he had to taxi it home between rounds of shopping. Clyde and Elspeth were not so easy. The shopping itself was far from simple, for the stores were so jampacked with bodies (and the bodies so swollen with winter gear) that one had to alter one's stance more often that Dewey Evans.

In a glorified knickknack shop he saw a sign offering STOCKING STUFFERS FOR $10 AND UNDER and sensed there had been real change from the days of walnuts and oranges. Were people really investing a week's pay in the Christmas stockings alone? He thought of Catholic families and of Finnish Lutherans, sixteen offspring strong, and he thought My God even the most extravagant person must have pause!

Badly disoriented in a mackerel-crowded haberdashery, he bulldozed a standing mirror and found himself ankle-deep in jagged triangles and trapezoids that crazily, collectively, composed the ceiling. The mirror had loomed as a passageway, a lovely trompe l'oeil, and Orrin had simply "run to daylight" like all those scatbacks over the weekend. But now he saw that every shop was a maze of baffling mirrors, that every rack and cranny, every wall and hall only served to return one's own sickly smile. Were Pinkertons peering through from the other side?

Or was this a subtle inducement to buy? Something carefully studied by those who study such things carefully? By putting you self-conscious, and therefore defensive, they impose an obligation to buy? Well, Orrin Summers bought nothing and felt they would be lucky he didn't sue them after the attempt on his life.

But the Christmas spirit never came to him and worse, for the first time since he was eleven in Schenectady, Orrin pinched something from a store. This was Elspeth's gift, a slim gold bracelet from Eckersley's, and he had logged twenty brutal minutes in a line trying to win the privilege of purchasing the thing. There were still six souls ahead of him, each one generating extensive paperwork, when a gigantic tide of thirst washed over him. Pigford's kind; thirst as emotion.

To make matters worse, a sharp pain came clawing at his left chest and he could see himself needing to drop dead on the quarry tile yet lacking the room to fall. This is not your heart, he told himself, not your heart. An obvious anxiety attack—but why always the left chest, why can't anxiety ever attack the right?

Meantime he inched gingerly past half a dozen mirrors (not in concealment, but rather fear of further carnage) and fled the jeweler's eye. Orrin Summers was of course no common thief, he was simply a good man circumventing the Christmas rush, and at the same time guarding his delicately restructured health. Indeed he scratched down the street number of the shop with a mind to mailing them the full cost of the trinket plus *tax and interest* when he did the next check-writing at his desk.

, That he did not get to it, that afternoon or any time thereafter, owed more to the general disorder of his days than to any attempt at meanness on his part. When he came across this unfinished business weeks later—too late to act on it, unfortunately—Orrin had to console himself with the knowledge that it was only the thought which counted.

Clyde had been kind, and yet his Christmas dinner proved to be largely a departmental affair—three faculty couples—and for the most part Orrin had enjoyed his lowgrade virus more. Plus it had to be conceded that the boys lost much of their charm whenever their sensors picked up a package of any kind. (Clyde and Phyll were either immune to this horror, or simply felt safest looking the other way.) In his discouragement, Orrin did take a lot of grog that day, though perhaps no more than was necessary to offset an apparent manufacturing error in its proportions.

He got his true Christmas wish, or seemed to, six days

later, when sitting up in bed he heard a bell, was momentarily confused by it, and then realized the sound was
coming from inside his telephone. Someone has called me
up!

And the someone was Gail, a storybook ending to the
bleak holiday saga he had undergone. For fourteen roaring
seconds, tintinnabulation and salutation, the blues was
history. His soul swam in the vortex of a loud hurricane of
happiness. Hearing her lovely voice in the dim, Gail-less
room, Orrin had no sense of having ever known sadness,
or loneliness, or any emotion at all save joy. For those
fourteen glad ticks in time, he was a blissfully married man
with a blissfully rich past (which he had somehow mis-
placed, briefly) and a blissfully proper future which could
obviously take care of itself.

"I knew you'd call, really. Even though you never took
my messages seriously, I knew you would call."

"I took your messages seriously, Orrin."

Something in Gail's voice, some new element, less
lovely, gave him slight pause. Though she did not elaborate, it did distinctly seem any elaboration might prove a
downer. But this was only a tone, and possibly an imagined tone at that. Orrin could ignore it.

"So will it be New Year's Eve?" he said brightly. "Auld
lang syne after all, my dear? Remember the time we
walked out on the frozen harbor with two of Derek's
champagne glasses. And you said we were literally on the
rocks—meaning the ice, you know, not our marriage—
and—"

"Orrin, I called because Dummer is very eager to close
on the house today or tomorrow. It's about taxes, I think.
And we both must sign."

"Fine, when do we do it? We can continue this talk then,
over a nice cup of coffee. It is just so good to hear your
voice—"

"I've actually signed it already. You should go anytime

today or by tomorrow morning at the latest. He'll leave it with the secretary in case he's out of the office."

"But you called me. He didn't call me. His secretary didn't call me, *you* called, Gail. You *must* want to have a drink together, for auld lang syne."

"I really don't. It's just that Dummer feels you dislike him and back off all his suggestions. Anyway, he says he sent this to you in the mail and you didn't send it back. So he thinks you're stalling him."

"Of course I am. And naturally I dislike Dummer, he's a bloody *realtor* for Christ's sake, Gail. I never wanted to sell that house in the first place. I love it. It's my home."

"It *is* sold. We both save money if we sign by tomorrow, that's all. There's no point in being obtuse."

"Oh surely there must be *some* point in being obtuse. Do you realize, Gail, that I put up those shelves in the front hallway with my own hands?"

"Not with someone else's hands, Orrin?"

"Aha! You see, you *do* have back your sense of humor. I knew it was only a matter of time. Listen, Gail, are you sure you aren't ready to come back?"

In the ensuing dead air, Orrin could see her compressing her lips, see the critical narrowing of her eyes: not ready.

"Well then let's at least have some dinner tonight. After the signing." More silence on the line. "Breakfast, then. Start the New Year off right with your basic Hessian Eggs. Gail, for Christ's sake after thirty-five years we could at least have a goddamned cup of coffee!"

"Thirty-six. We could, yes, but we would be happier if we didn't. Please go sign it, Orrin. If you don't, you don't. I honestly don't care that much, although Ted says I could sue you for the lost gain—"

"What? Ted said that, about the lost gain? What nonsense. And for my friend to encourage you to sue me. My *lawyer!* I could sue *him,* for conflict of interest."

"He didn't encourage me in the least. Dummer said it

and I simply called Ted up to get the legal reaction, if that's what it's called. Isn't it pointless to lose thousands over just a stubborn reluctance to face reality? I mean, you're the analyst, Orrin."

It was unbelievable but somehow she felt *no guilt*. None. It left him very little to work with.

"Gail, I have not seen you in months, *literally*. It's so absurd. You have become a figment of my imagination. In fact today is the first time in two months that I have even heard your voice, unrecorded."

"I did want to tell you something that I read last week, in somebody's memoirs—I can't remember who. Anyway, in Russia just after the Revolution, the marriage laws apparently became quite informal. In Pinsk, in 1929, the only requirement for divorce was a postcard. Either party could send one, to the other, and the marriage was done for. Just like that."

"This isn't Pinsk or 1929, it's here and now. And it's *us*, Gail."

"It's you, Orrin. I'm out of there, as they say. I don't want to hurt you, Orrin, honestly I don't. But I don't want to see you either. I've said what I called to say, and now I'm going."

"Only on one condition!" he blurted out, but she stuffed him anyway.

He sagged. The dead telephone was a lump of lead in his hands. It was as though he had spent months nursing a client up to a breakthrough and then, just as the change was palpably coming, she slipped down and slid all the way back to Square One, where she would for a time of course be unreachable. Gail had dangled the carrot; now he felt more helpless and out of touch than ever. But the little bugger started ringing again!

"Okay I'll bite," said Gail. "What was the one condition?" She was not even trying to hide the playful smile in her voice. Orrin's heart rose to the bait.

"The condition? Yes! That you must respond to my next

recorded message. No—my next *three* recorded messages."

"No."

"All right, all right—just the one, then."

"No."

And before he could sally back, she slam-dunked on him
again.

Gail was angry, no question. Not about the state of
things currently, but angry about the past. Angrier, admittedly, than he could have guessed. (Months now, after all,
with zero softening.) But she would ring again shortly, she
would never leave him twisting in the wind this way—"I
don't want to hurt you," she had said, with apparent
sincerity—and when she did Orrin would have the Right
Words ready to say.

But what were they? He worked up a quick draft. I still
have your Christmas gift here, he would tell her. Gail
loved presents, enjoyed suspense. She would say "No" (in
keeping with her new style of discourse) and he would
simply say, "It's nice, though, a very nice gift that you are
sure to enjoy," and he would make no mention of The Lost
Gain, not a shadow of a syllable, even though the nasty
absurdity of it did keep circling back on him as he was
drafting The Right Words.

By now he had rinsed the jellyglass, the one with Elmer
Fudd leveling his blunderbuss at an implied wabbit, and
had filled it right up to Fudd's eyeballs with whiskey. He
had drained it back down to Fudd's *lederhosen* when the
phone did in fact ring again.

"Hello!" he said, jovial as a two-martini nurse. And he
was trying to recollect the perfect hook that would get The
Right Words rolling, when he perceived the voice was
male. Not lovely and not Gail.

"Hello," the voice was saying. "It's about the room you
listed—educated male hetero and what all. I'm wondering
if the position is still open."

6

Eli Paperman stood before him so tall and young and vital that it made Orrin slightly faint. And Paperman saw this, for his very first words were, "Are you feeling all right, Doctor Summers? You look a little shaky."

Orrin's impulse was naturally to lie, to offer up a touch of the flu or something. It wasn't Paperman's imposing physical presence that had shaken him really, or his obvious command; it was simply the fact of him. Below Orrin's bed (itself a welter of tangled, mismatched linens) were socks, three or four pair he guessed—nine socks, he would later find, or 4.5 pair—and around each sock would have clustered a soft gray nest of dust, magnetically drawn. Had he been in his right mind to conceive of a roomer?

For here stood a perfect stranger (the very phrase never had meaning until now) yet someone who could be sharing his life, intimately, by tomorrow. You warned your children off strangers, as your parents had done with you, but the actual strangers in your life were generally pleasant and of little significance. And they were people briefly glimpsed, like the retired Army man who had shared a seat with Orrin on the train out to Lexington, or the bespectacled fellow who had slid the ketchup down the counter to him at breakfast. People who *remained* strangers.

That was comfortable and gave you a nice feeling, sometimes, about the world community. This was potentially uncomfortable and even risky, in the same way it was risky to take a mail-order bride in the Yukon. Pot luck and yet you had to make it work, you had to live with it. And now here stood this fellow Paperman, the raw fact of him for Orrin to digest.

For until Orrin pulled the door open and actually saw him there, the whole idea of a room-mate had continued whimsical. It *was* a whimsy, a joke of displacement and consolation, and maybe a subtle nose-thumbing toward Gail. He had written it off anyway by this time—not a single response to the deadly syntax of his advertisement— and though he had once imagined the benefits of such an arrangement, Orrin had never begun to assess the burdens.

He could scarcely take the time to conjure them up now, but the most obvious was impressed upon him willynilly: that he had been alone, on his own recognizance, blissfully unconscious of his face, of his posture and grooming habits, freed of any call on attitude or expostulation or reply, and now instead he was arranging his face and preparing to lie to a perfect stranger about his state of mind.

He was so stunned, however, that he had yet to speak at all. And during the ten seconds in which Paperman's rote solicitude hung in the air, Orrin had time for a hundred decisions and revisions of his opening statement. Oddly enough, he settled upon the truth:

"Well yes, I *am* a little shaky. I really wasn't expecting you."

"I'm sorry. I thought we said six o'clock."

"Oh I'm sure we did. We did in *fact*. I mean that I wasn't expecting . . ."

"Go ahead, tell me. I'm not that sensitive. If I'm the wrong category in some way, I do understand we may decide not to go ahead—"

"It's not that. It's that I wasn't expecting *anything,* you know. I had placed the ad without contemplating the results, and then for days there *were* no results. And I somehow forgot there might yet be . . . I'm not expressing it at all, am I. Let me at least offer you a drink, if I may?"

"Sure, thanks. Would you have a beer?"

"I think so, but it would just be some cans of Budweiser that have been in the fridge since last summer. Are you sure you wouldn't rather have a whiskey?"

"Bud in a can is fine—it's the tangy taste of can that gives it zest."

"Zest, is it? A little alloy leeching into the brew? All right, but let me pour it into a glass for you. Have a seat and we'll talk things over."

Orrin's panic had subsided in the face of Paperman's easy demeanor. He was glad to be giving Paperman a drink and sitting him down for a chat: looking ahead to what Paperman might have to say. Already he had moved from the impulsive, What is this bozo doing at my doorstep? to the slightly defensive, What can this tall fellow make of *me*?

But it was just talk about the glass. Orrin's sink was in such disarray that although there might very well be unbroken glasses down in there (and no reason to suppose otherwise) it would take an archaeologist to get one out intact. The lone vessel on the countertop was Orrin's own jellyglass, which he now reinstated to Fudd's Eye level (sometimes he would aim for the very pupil, and hold it up to the light like a thermometer to calibrate his marksmanship) before rejoining his applicant in the living room.

"Are you sure about the can?" said Orrin.

Paperman looked to be about thirty-five years old, with uncombed waves of red-brown hair, clean-shaven cheeks, and an expression of clear intelligence. "Believe it or not, I actually prefer the can."

"And I'm sure you're right to. Trouble is you can't get whiskey in a can, so I have to make do with an occasional F.E.—Fudd's Eyeball, that is."

"I can see that. But then you can never ask for your 'usual' in a bar."

"Not quite, no. It does save money to drink at home."

"You could have some fun making a scene, though.

Demand to see the innkeeper. What do you mean you don't serve F.E., what the hell kind of joint is this?"

"I'm much too shy to enjoy making any scenes, I'm afraid. I suppose as a courtroom lawyer—isn't that what you said?—you don't have that problem."

"No, I'm not shy. But I'd guess you're not either, if you don't mind my impeaching your witness."

"Are you calling me a liar in my own home, Eli?"

"I am saying you don't strike me as shy. And it may be my home too, after all. I do need one."

"Tell me, where are you staying right now?"

"I had been staying with friends, a week here and a week there. The last two weeks I've been in a room at the Oxford Guest House. In Cambridge?"

"So you're not among the heating-grate homeless, anyway. Are you new to the area?"

"No, I was in a house in J. P. for more than a year. Until quite recently. To be frank with you, my lady friend kicked me out into the street."

"Is that so? So did mine, as it happens—last summer. I have only had this place since July. But what went wrong with yours, if I may be so 'bold'?"

Orrin gave a flourish to the word, both to disarm against any possible offense and to play upon the question of shyness. He had given that round—with pleasure, actually—to Paperman. It was a relief to be forestalled against falsehood by simple unadorned insight.

"Oh it was a gradual thing. I came into a situation where four people were sharing a large house. Gradually I became involved with one of them and gradually she became a little more involved than I could be. So gradually it got bitter until about a month ago when, suddenly, I felt her foot."

"The boot! And nothing gradual about it."

"That's it."

"Well it's all very reasonable, I'm sure. Mine was more painful, you know—a long marriage dismantled unilaterally. It's the unilateral aspect that pains one, you know. I suppose I should sympathize with your friend the placekicker, on those grounds."

"I wouldn't bother. She has already replaced me with something better. She is a woman who goes after what she wants and generally gets it."

"Something better, though?"

"He's very well off. They go skiing in Aspen for weekends and I had to struggle to provide her one rent-a-wreck trip to Mount Tom last year."

"An attorney who is not well off? Isn't that unheard of, a contradiction in terms?"

"Are you calling me a liar in my own home?"

"You know, I think I am, Paperman. Yes, I'm quite certain of it."

"Good, then, I'm pleased. But it isn't a lie. I do a lot of *pro bono* work, and community work. I'm a liberal or a radical or something. An idealist, let's say."

"But are you so strapped that I should worry about the rent?"

"Definitely not. Worry can take a real toll on people."

"As can rent, however."

"Well, as you say, I'm not exactly heating-grate homeless. Though I should ask what the rent *is*. 'Moderate' sounds good, but what does it come to in round numbers?"

"Three hundred a month, your share. The place costs me eleven but I plan to keep the study, and it's more like a boarder than a straight split. So three hundred was what I thought."

Paperman spread his arms and smiled. "Show me to my room," he said.

Orrin's grocery shopping had lately fallen off to the

point where he suspected himself of having skipped some
meals entirely; certainly there were several he could not
recollect. One night the dinner had been dry toast and
whiskey, though more typically he would slide a frozen
Pizza-For-One into the toaster-oven during the early Jack-
and-Liz. There simply was never much else to choose
from, for when he ventured down to DeLuca's Market to
stock up, he found everything priced to the sky and
nothing that appealed to him anyway. Occasionally he
took home, more from a sense of obligation to his earthly
corporeal husk than from appetite, some tiny cut of expensive steak and either cooked it and nibbled a bit or put it
straight into the freezer from whence it would never return, but gradually became a gray knob of frozen cellophane the transformation of which into dinner stood
well beyond his culinary reach.

Tonight's occasion, however, called for a good restaurant meal, he and Eli Paperman readily agreed. (Indeed
they had thus far disagreed on only one point: Paperman
would move nothing in for a week, yet insisted on paying
for the entire month of January.) They settled upon a
favorite place of Paperman's, a Cajun room on Boylston,
called the Blue Bayou. Rope nets of nylon drooped to
conceal a messy ceiling and large red shells had been
mounted on the walls; their very best energies, Paperman
reassured him, went into the food.

"You're a bit out of shape, it seems, Orrin," Paperman
was grinning as they settled in. Paperman had taken the
park in vast, unflagging Olympian strides while Orrin
scurried to keep up, falling short of breath in the damp
freezing air.

"I hope you aren't a reformer, Paperman. I'm not seeking reformation, you know, just a little help with the rent. I
should have asked: Are you now, or have you ever been, a
jogger?"

"Not me. I confess to being a reformer, but never of individuals, least of all myself. And no, I do not choose to run."

"Thank Christ for that much. Here you have conned me into sharing my house with you and I haven't even done the full Inquisition."

Orrin did fear the Runner's Mentality and the baggage it brought along. During the one year Ted Neff had taken it up, had worn the uniform and spoken the language, he had hardly seemed the same man. It was as though they had lost him to a wacky religious cult, or to serious drugs.

But Orrin didn't have to care what Eli Paperman did, that was the whole point, and in any case he didn't care. He *approved* of Eli in some odd way; maybe liked him was the truer word. Trusted him? Orrin had somehow gone from shock and recoil to complete habituation, in the space of sixty minutes. "I'd have a bottle of Bud," said Paperman, "and my friend would like an F.E. whiskey, neat. And can we get more rolls?"

Eli was already working on his second of the sweet airy popovers. Orrin smiled, like a foreign dignitary with great faith but little English, as the waiter confessed the house did not carry F.E. Now Paperman was sporting: "Well, just bring him the closest to an F.E. you've got, and then we'll order."

The man withdrew, abashed, and was seen in conference with the bartender, after which he reappeared with Eli's beer and a shot of V.O.

"The two letters, I guess," said Paperman, as Orrin choked down a swallow. "The low common denominator."

"Fire in a bottle! They have caught it for sure. But I like the place, Paperman, the rolls are excellent. Will this be authentic Cajun food?"

"Absolutely. They keep an authentic Cajun in a cage back there, and he blesses every dish before they bring it out. But look, how's about a toast now—to my landlord!"

"Room-mate," Orrin corrected him democratically.

"Well let's say landlord when you're pissed off at me and room-mate when you're pleased. That's how it usually goes. But now I'm ready for the Inquisition. Shall I make a preliminary statement to the court?"

"Oh I would."

"I am thirty-eight years of age, raised in Palo Alto, California, graduated U.C. Berkeley and ten years thereafter from a small law school in Philadelphia that you never heard of. And I have never served in the Armed Forces. Your witness."

"Your statement raises two good questions right off the bat, doesn't it?"

"If you say so."

"It does. One: what did you do in the ten years between college and the anonymous law school? Other than not serve in the Armed Forces, that is."

"I don't know, really. Nothing I can pin down. All kinds of work, travelled. Almost chose a path in life two or three times, almost chose a wife once . . ."

"But?"

"But I wasn't up to any such choosing and for some reason I was lucky enough to know it. I decided at one point that life was like poker—the longer you could stay in the game without paying out, the better chance you had of winning in the end."

"It takes courage to sit tight, though."

"It takes something. Immaturity, strength, paralysis. Sort of a combination of virtues and defects. Anyway, what was the second question raised?"

"Just that I understood people went *to* California, never the other way round. By the way, did you know that Dreiser and Tom Mix are buried alongside one another in Hollywood?"

"I should have guessed. I did know they were buried. Or at least that they were dead."

"All right it's a little obscure. But it is a good example."

"Of what, though?"

"It's an example of California."

They ordered dinner. Two green salads, two beers, something called a blackened redfish for Paperman and for Orrin the seafood gumbo. Paperman urged Orrin to be extravagant, as this would be his treat, while Orrin protested *he* should be the host. It was therefore resolved that each would pay for the other's bill of fare, so that each could reap the benefits of both guest and host. Orrin took a second popover and declared he had not been so hungry in months.

"And I'm half Jewish," said Paperman, resuming and concluding the thumbnail autobiography.

"Which half?"

"That's a tough call, since the left side of the brain controls the right side of the body, and vice-versa."

"Your father, obviously. Is he a professor in Palo Alto?"

"No, he writes insurance, as he likes to put it. He doesn't ever *sell* any insurance, you understand, he writes it. As though he were Tolstoy or something."

"And your mother? Do forgive my natural curiosity and feel free to take the Fifth Amendment if you'd rather talk about the Celtics."

"My mother has done some part-time book-keeping, on and off. But her main work was four kids, plus of course my father the writer, who is also my father the eater."

"Siblings?"

"No thanks." They both smiled. It was true that Orrin's office manner, spare and inviting, could sound in the restaurant setting like an offer to pass the appetizers, or some unlikely condiment in a monkey-dish. "My sister is married, with two kids, in Redwood City. Her husband works for the state of California. He's a planner. You won't really remember any of this junk, will you?"

"Every word, Eli. What does he plan?"

"As near as I can tell, he plans plans. But they pay him very well."

"And the two brothers?" said Orrin, after a brief spate of subtraction.

"Both younger. Bill played baseball, one year of minor league, and got himself killed in Vietnam. Norm is dying a slower death in L.A., waiting to be Paul Newman the Second."

"Looks like Newman?"

"A little bit. You might have seen him in *Caribou Summer*, under the name of Tad Randall."

"I'm afraid I missed *Caribou Summer*. You were closer to the sad one?"

"The dead one, you mean. I love them all, my whole ridiculous family. But it's been a long time—childhood, really—since I was close to any of them. What about you, Orrin. Your parents."

"Well of course I *am* a parent, son and a daughter, so there's that. My own were both schoolteachers, in upstate New York. Good quiet gentle people. Both have been dead some time now, you know."

Orrin frequently employed the verbal bridge 'you know' and though he was vaguely aware of the tendency (rather attached to it, in fact) he did not always notice. Here, because of context, he did and so smilingly appended: "I guess you *don't* know, do you. But this is really delicious, Eli, a very enjoyable meal."

Paperman agreed, and taking the shift to indicate a liking for some silence, or for less intimate talk, he passed a few minutes eating fish and salad. Orrin also ate, hauling large shrimps and chunks of flavored fish up out of the gumbo, and mused about his way with conversation, the role he generally took. He was an interrogator and a listener—as though life was for others to live and then report back to him on what it had been like. There was a chicken/egg aspect to his choice of profession: a shrink because he was that way, or that way because he was a shrink? But he had not been that way with Gail, or with the children, had he?

"I'm sorry if I made you think of your folks unhappily," said Paperman, who was above all, it seemed, a *direct* person.

"Not a bit, Paperman. As a matter of fact, I was thinking about my children. One of whom is very nearly your age. But I was thinking of a time he and I were riding in a car on a sunny Saturday morning, just the two of us, and it was very cold, and some bigtime gangster had just been shot to death in a barber's chair in New York. Clyde asked me dozens of questions about it—he was clearly fascinated—and I told him about bootleggers, and Al Capone, and Legs Diamond. The Mob, you know. And we got onto criminals: why some people are criminals and some aren't. I don't know what made me think of it, to tell you the truth."

He could have known, for he had been delving back in time, trying to reconstruct the way he had behaved with them at different ages. How had he seemed to them? False, withdrawn, cold? Surely not in the moments he was able to reclaim—that Saturday with Clyde in the blue DeSoto, or the night they came home tipsy and caught Elspeth, then nine, squatting in the liquor closet. Never the defensive sort, El complained she had tried every bottle and found nothing she liked to drink.

Those times, that night, he had been fine. Gentle, like his own father, charmed by them really, and always happy to be the fount of information. *Fatherly* no doubt, though perhaps (like his own father, again) ever so slightly impersonal.

Backtracking through the Public Gardens, Orrin and Eli Paperman stepped down onto the frozen lagoon and slid across to the steep little island where ducks nested in warm weather. The Christmas storm had cracked a big alder branch right near the trunk and it dangled in the thrall of wet black ice. Beyond it, up through the web of smaller branches, a white moon seemed very tame and close by.

Something in this image reminded him of childhood—his own? Clyde and El's?—of some distant happy emotion that was no less pleasant for remaining obscure.

II

The Germ of Corruption

"Funny position, wasn't it? The boredom came later, when we lived together on board his ship. I had, in a moment of inadvertence, created for myself a tie. How to define it precisely I don't know. One gets attached in a way to people one has done something for. But is that friendship? I am not sure what it was. I only know that he who forms a tie is lost. The germ of corruption has entered into his soul."

—CONRAD

7

Business was bad, but Orrin felt comfortable with it. You could hardly take a bill before the Congress, on behalf of the psychotherapist's lobby, saying there is insufficient neurosis and let's start doing more to *induce* it. For Orrin's money, life itself was crazier than ever—the trouble was that most people were perfectly well-adjusted to it.

Even at this low ebb, Orrin had thirteen clients on the books. You could say this was unlucky, but he said it was better than twelve. Besides, it wasn't a case of the more the merrier. If he went to twenty, if business picked up to that extent, he would be overwhelmed—especially if two or three were the kind that Beekman called "full-time help," the ones who came five days a week. It seemed to Orrin the days were full enough, when you added to work the inevitable errands, the transit time and the squandered time, small pleasures like eating, plus all the incidental erosions of a society where several layers of government and a hundred outfits in 1-800-Land had your profile in their accursed computers.

How anyone found the time for squash, or swimming, or all this *weight* training that went on was a mystery to Orrin. Perhaps he had become low energy without noticing it, from vitamin deficiency or emotional disorder. Or perhaps it was the comparison with Eli that made it seem so. Eli was, of course, a much younger man, but he was also a true phenom, who expended the energy of three men each day and never showed a trace of fatigue.

Paperman careened through the streets before breakfast

(he called it "walking") when the city was just stirring. In still cold January air, dull washy sun on the dewblacked macadam, he moved among stray cats, bread trucks, and a faction Orrin had yet to pin down, which Eli called "The Donut Crowd." Then it was a counter breakfast with both papers before he bolted to the courthouse for a full morning.

Eli shared office space in Cambridge, where he worked afternoons and early evenings, yet he managed to squeeze in an hour of basketball every day at the Y.M.C.A., frequent movies (virtual private screenings in the daytime, at discount prices) and sundry assignations for coffee, beer, luncheon, and dinner, with friends both male and female. It was an awesome humbling program; Orrin was just as glad to have a little leisure.

For he had come into a sort of intellectual renaissance. He found himself making notes and beginnings on a variety of topics, turning ideas into theories, theories into potential papers. He had not written anything in ten years—had in fact defaulted on a book contract after blowing the advance on a junket to Berlin—but was now considering a full-length treatment (or more realistically in light of his current energy level, a paper) on the psychological fallout from altered family structures.

Orrin Summers the intellectual had pretty much foresworn News and Weather. Moreover, in the weeks since Eli's arrival, he had placed but a single phone call from Filbert Street. He had been thinking of Ted, and specifically of how he had badgered Ted in those desperate moments after Gail left. That was all right in a way, to call a friend in time of need, so long as he also called in milder times, to say hello or offer a less refusable sip of whiskey.

So he phoned on a Sunday afternoon of sunlit snowflurries, with the vague idea they might join up later for a plate of spaghetti in the North End, to visit at leisure by red winelight. But Ted was more than usually frantic.

"Orrin, for God's sake. It's Super Sunday."

"Of course it is. I'll be right over."

"No! Stay!"

"I'm not a dog, Theo."

"Sorry, please excuse. It's just the excitement."

"So shall I join you?"

"Sure, why not? Come ahead if you like."

"Thanks, but I think I'll pass. I appreciate the invite, though. I really do, Theo."

"Testing me!"

"No, not at all. I just called to say hello. And to thank you for all your patience and kindness these past—"

"Testing me," repeated Ted, but hollowly. He was gone. Orrin could picture his attorney, absently clutching the receiver, his gaze locked on the screenful of behemoths.

"Well, at least you passed the test," Orrin consoled him.

"Fuck you, Orrin, it's third and seven," said Ted, and Orrin took his hanging up to signify a "no" to the unmentioned dinner scheme. In a way it was good to be hung up on again; it reminded Orrin of how far he had come.

That afternoon he took a note from Paperman (who was out of town for the weekend) and went to a matinée. And because everyone else was doing the Super Bowl Shuffle, he had the theatre to himself for a film called *Colonel Redl,* a lovely sunless disjointed boring portrait of political man in the web of classbound Europe before the first World War. An Austrian named Brandauer (Marlon Brandauer?) played the title role with some genius and still Orrin kept losing focus. Twice he snapped awake in the small over- heated screening room.

By the end he was experiencing a terrible but very specific thirst—for Coca-Cola with ice cubes—and drained a tall one, absurdly delicious, at the concessionaire before stepping out to the further refreshment of an ear-biting wind. The foot journey home was nevertheless welcome. After sitting so long staring at a sheet of light, the blurred

Whistlerian half-dark of the dimming Boston skyline (the Pru looming above the Paine) seemed a vast yet highly personal work of art.

Back home, feeling at peace and almost complacent, Orrin was about to launch a Pizza-For-One into the toaster oven when Eli stormed in and ridiculed the notion.

"Frozen pizza for one? Why don't we get a real pizza, for two? It'll taste better, boss. Some fresh peppers, onions, a little sausage if you like?"

"Why not just pop in two Pizza-For-Ones. It's so easy."

"Don't you touch that toaster oven. Fetch your pipe and slippers, and I'll be back in twenty minutes with the real thing."

"Pepperoni, then."

"Done. All you have to do is not unplug the fridge by accident, so the Bud stays cold."

"I'll take care of it, Eli. Count on me."

And Eli was off again, after a working weekend plus six hours of travel on Sunday, spilling out the door like a kid shedding the confines of the schoolhouse for the first big storm of winter.

Paperman was not a reformer, not really, and he was not always around. Far from it. He was gone for days at a time, pursuing justice for Puerto Rican housemaids in Connecticut, nuclear energy workers in Oklahoma, unwed fathers in Washington State. It seemed he left no legal stone unturned.

Still it was indisputable that Orrin Summers *was* a reformed man, and that the change was tied to the advent of Paperman. Orrin imbibed no more alcohol now than the supplicants at an Episcopalian service. One small drink at the hour of transition—the stereotypical cocktail reinstated—and that was it. Orrin drank as his friend Pigford drank, to gratify a thirst, and these days he was not so thirsty. When he was, in the depleted oxygen of a badly subdivided movie room, the thirst had been for soda.

He had cut back his News to Jack-and-Liz at six. They were at their best then anyway; at eleven they often looked sleepy, soft and furry at the edges. And as to Weather, Orrin had gone existential, taking his weather as it came. He might register a personal impression at the window, or even stand a moment on the little balcony if serious questions of apparel hung in the balance, but no more did he consult The Little Lost Boys.

All this reform made room for work, and work had become his richest vein. His clients were charged with new interest, they came alive for him again, and he continued to elaborate his dialectical outcroppings every night. It had been a long time since Orrin believed the world might be enlightened en masse, or that he might be the man for the job. He did not go that far now, but could again acknowledge the value of rendering the best thought in all fields, including his own.

Brisk walks, better food, and yes, less of the wet stuff did restore his energy. That was a point. It might not kill him, but it did leave him unshakably sluggish on too many mornings. Now he slept well and woke clear-eyed, ready for the light. If Gail could see him now, she might retract everything she had said and done.

Meanwhile he had his finest day at the office in years, losing a client for the best of reasons ("cured") and gaining two new ones from the recommendations of former clients, always a welcome and valid tribute. Orrin felt competent, and his success had cost him nothing. This was an aspect of psychotherapy that Eli had questioned: especially in the carriage trade, did not an analyst have more vested in the illness than in the cure? The Hippocratic Oath one thing, the wolf at the door another?

Opening two files, closing one, Orrin was outside the range of any conflict of interest, though the truth was he would miss seeing Lynn Warburton. He had liked her from the start. It had taken eighteen months to smooth her way back to self-esteem and it had brought Orrin at one point, a low water day in late November, within a camel's hair of his first in-office indiscretion.

Sarah had left early that day, and all the constellations were in place for a quickie on the couch or a segue to one of Bamford's famous Phase One Dinners. (Phase One: dinner. Phase Two: the bed.) It was not the impropriety which had stopped him either, for he had already finished calculating the odds against humiliation just like a teenager in a car.

But he had envisioned an entire night with her, in the reality dimension—indeed on his home court at Filbert— and there was no place for Warburton there, in that downcast chaos, in sheets last laundered around Labor Day. *That* had brought him back to the mark. That plus the recognition that Warburton's self-esteem, on the rise, had crossed orbits with his own, still descending.

"I helped her," he bragged to Eli that evening, the night of Warburton's graduation. "I helped a fellow human! Don't you agree that's quite wonderful at my age?"

"The woman was seriously depressed?"

"Oh yes. Suicidal for months." Warburton aglow, inner light dancing in her blue eyes, made it hard to summon back Warburton as waxwork, eyes drained of all color, like cellophane. "She had everything but the nerve to do it."

"But isn't that always true? Isn't cowardice all that keeps anyone alive, in one way or another?"

"Is it?"

"It keeps us all behind the lines, away from the danger. Fear is everyone's best protection—and the best weapon of the reactionary party."

"I wasn't invited to that one, Eli. But really, how dangerous is political action in this country? Physically dangerous, I mean. Not very."

"Oh you take your life in your hands any time you cross the power, believe it. A hell of a lot of black people have been murdered. Native-Americans too, and I don't mean back in the days of Daniel Boone only. Then you have your Karen Silkwoods . . ."

"Do you fear for your own life, then?"

"No, but only because I'm a coward. I wear the uniform and I play by the rules."

"But you probably decided playing by the rules would be more effective."

"Yes I did. But it's still frustrating to do it. Don't you think Martin Luther King would have felt just terrific if he could somehow—just once—have nailed J. Edgar Hoover with one huge left hook?"

"I'm getting confused here between cowardice and restraint."

"Yeah. Well anyway, I'm glad for your client, Orrin. And for you."

"I was rather attracted to her, actually. Which is very rare for me. I'm really quite a one-woman man."

"It's the next best thing to no woman at all."

"Come on. You? You must have them coming at you from all angles."

"Well I'm single and pushing forty, so I have had a few girlfriends—"

"I thought there might have been an accumulation."

"—but no, Orrin, I'm no Don Juan. To tell you the truth, I've always thought—and this is serious, Orrin, I'm being honest—that you have to choose between love and life."

"That's hardly the most romantic of testimonials, Eli."

"With real love, and marriage and family, your best energies have to go into all those petty cares. And you find it impossible to work for anything larger than your own little life provides you. I've seen it happen so many times, to the loveliest people."

"But not to you, yet."

"Damn it, Orrin, I can't stay straight with you. I keep remembering that you're a shrink and then I start to feel I'm revealing some terribly obvious flaw in my story. In my character."

"Let's chuck it then. I don't want to worry you. And please don't ever think I'm judgmental, or that I'm looking to break anyone down into psychological categories. I'm really not like that."

"Fair enough. I got uptight. And probably that means I *was* revealing my flaws. But it needn't be blamed on you."

"Thank you, Paperman, that's damned generous of you."

"So what were we talking about before all that stuff came spilling out?"

"Suicide, I think."

"No wonder we changed the subject, in that case. But no, it wasn't really that, it was your client—the one you have a crush on . . ."

"It looks like I am the one who revealed too much! I'm afraid we will have to change the subject again."

8

The first week of February there was a severe ice-storm and the power was out on Beacon Hill all evening. In the whipping ice of twilight, Orrin had ventured from the flat for no better reason than that he found it unpleasant sitting indoors as the darkness thickened and spread. A brief hit of the old sinking feeling. He would try for candles at the Seven-Eleven store, and maybe grab a tin of popcorn too, to "improve the occasion" as his parents had always done with blackouts at the Grand Avenue house in Schenectady.

That house—a farmhouse originally, lopped off a generation earlier from the land which had once been sown around it and standing now barnless and alone on an acre with two Macintosh apple-trees and a weed-smothered tin-rust shed—was Orrin's first childhood home and he had loved his young life there. During the Depression there were friends who felt the pinch. Albert Hageman's family, and then Billy Dornhoeffer's, had picked up and moved away, though their foreclosed homes stood empty and useless for years after, until the cardboard bank signs became faded, and delaminated at the curling edges. Orrin's parents both kept working, which made them "rich." When many families were desperate for a single paycheck, they had two, and although teachers did make low salaries it was also an inexpensive life. Their one modest luxury, a Model A Ford now six years old, was all paid up and still running.

They were so rich that in 1936, right in the midst of the trouble, they bought a larger house outside town and

moved, against the children's wishes. Orrin's father explained that the move was *for* them—they needed more
space to grow and they needed more of The Great Outdoors—but each of them protested his premises. They
loved the older house (all three had been born in it) and
The Great Outdoors was right at the foot of Grand Avenue
anyway, in the form of a limitless wetland, with bending
birches and a swamp pond for ice-skating. Even beyond
that lay a nine-hole golf course that only children used, for
toad hunting, football, hide-and-seek. You didn't have to
own The Great Outdoors, explained Barney (who at thirteen was necessarily the spokesman), but their parents
wanted to own it, so they all went.

The new house never measured up. For one thing it was
literally new and so lacked all the farmhouse fragrances;
pantry suffused with the pleasant must of decades, basement of damp earth and worn softened duck-board. This
basement was concrete and always smelled slightly sour;
its walls were sheer gray, with no wood or earth visible
anywhere. The children called it The Dungeon and they
never went down into the "playroom" that had been a big
part of What They Needed.

The Grand Avenue house became Orrin's paragon of
comfort and home, yet he had never come close to duplicating it, having slid into a profession that called for
urban trappings and having married a wife who preferred
them as well. He never even got as far out as a suburb; it
had been Providence, Baltimore and, for twenty years
now, Boston. He had disembarked forty-nine years back
and still there were occasions, like a storm and a power
outage, that could summon up the very odors and textures
of that undistinguished much-beloved manse.

In those days the lights frequently went off for a few
hours, summer and winter alike. People managed easily
enough, since not much was plugged in, though a dependence on the radio was rapidly forming. Orrin's mother

kept their set babbling and scratching throughout her four-to-seven spate in the kitchen. It was the way of things that after working the exact same hours as Orrin's father (in the same schoolhouse too, and after travelling home with him in the same car), Elizabeth Summers would then clean house, prepare the dinner, and tidy up afterward with help from the children.

But only when there was a big blow, the late summer gales or a fourteen-inch snow-howler in January, would the lights stay out all night, all weekend, or all *week* twice or three times. Then they cooked their meals over a log fire—beans warmed right in the can, frankfurters on a crooked stick—and lit the evening's reading with plumber's candles, the stout white wax like a foundation under wind-wavering flames in the drafty kitchen. Elizabeth might play the piano, sometimes four hands with Orrin's sister Jessica, in lieu of radio entertainment, and they would each take a turn at popping the corn. They were not an exuberant family, not one where humor ran high, but they would all loosen up and laugh wildly at the startling explosions of corn inside the covered pan. Popping the corn was an entertainment, and a treat, and to Orrin it was also emblematic of the house itself. It was the house that symbolized the rest for him: childhood innocence, family happiness, security.

Scaling the hill now with candles and popping-corn in hand after the unlikely triumph of finding the Seven-Eleven open (bravely serving the community by Coleman lantern-light, even with their registers "down"), Orrin must have caught an odd slant of gaslight, because one second he was merely executing an errand and the very next he was experiencing a rush of physical joy—pure, airy, and unselfconscious. Almost delirious. His heart up-swept in the bristling wind, it was as though he had reinhabited the soul of an eight-year-old.

Wholly innocent of liquor, Orrin almost started skip-

ping in the snow, wearing the heedless grin of the drunk-
ard (or the happy child), brimming over with the riches of
this world. But it was cold out. Head down now, plough-
ing through a rippling curtain of flailing ice, he was soon
delighted to regain the selfsame portal he had so recently
fled.

He fashioned crude candelabra for the kitchen and the
living room, soldering each candle with its own drippings
to the saucers. Then he jiggled the flue, tested the draft
with the wisp of smoke from a match, and set about laying
his first Filbert Street fire. As he packed pages of the
morning paper and stuffed them under chunks of wood on
the grate, Orrin did feel a mighty distance from popcorn
heaven, but at the same time determined to give it a good
try. Simply to introduce the aroma of popcorn into the
room would be gratifying. If he actually got that far he
would happily give up the rest; read a chapter or two by
candlelight and be sound asleep early. Power would be
restored by morning, and white sun would glare handsomely off the frozen steppe.

And then the telephone intruded quite shockingly into
this pre-industrial quietude. Long dormant, all but forgotten—a fossil really—the device was unlikely to sound even
without a crippling storm. To hear it intact, raging bells in
the flickering dark, was actually scary, a show of black
magic from Ma Bell, allegedly moribund. Orrin was almost afraid to touch it, for at the very least it seemed an
omen, heralding bad news.

"Orrin, I'm glad you're all right."

"Eli! My God you gave me a fright."

"I did?"

"The phone, I mean. You do know it's a blackout? And
so incredibly silent here, I was lost in my own thoughts so
completely . . ."

"Well I'm just checking because people are stranded here
and there. I tried a while ago and I called your office, too."

"I appreciate the concern, but all's well. I had cancellations and came home early. It's kind of exciting in a way, don't you think?"

"I wouldn't go that far. I'm stuck at the office myself. A couple of us are just going to sleep here, on the couches."

"Do you have a supply of coffee, and some food?"

"Believe it or not the restaurant downstairs is open. The lights aren't gone yet and we just finished a meal there. It's more that the busses and trains have stopped, so we voted what the hell. I wasn't too tempted to start off on my bike in this."

"Too bad for you, Eli, you are missing a real treat. I'm making a batch of popcorn."

"I thought you said the power was off—"

"In the fireplace. It works. Although I'm afraid I had to feed your little chair to it to build the fire up. Hope you don't mind . . ."

"I hope you are kidding. I better not say keep the home fires burning. But why don't you give it those cartons full of paper in the back hall instead?"

"My life's work! Listen, Eli, thanks for calling. I'm glad you're settled nicely over there."

Orrin had given up hope of getting the chunks to do anything but sizzle, wet and black, and had begun to wonder which of Eli's associates were stranded in the office with him ("too sexy for mere sex," he had described one of the women) when the phone went off again. Paperman had started a trend.

"So you're good there?" said Clyde.

"No problems at all. You?"

"We're fine. They actually got us back on somehow. Can you imagine going out in this weather to repair power lines?"

"Well Clydie, you and I don't quite fit the mould but there are men with a hero mentality. Who *like* a chance to battle the elements, you know, high seas and raging fires."

"That's right. Injustice, too. The moral equivalent of war."

"William James?"

"Very good! It is a blessing to have a father who is as overeducated as I am. So you're surviving?"

"Better than that. Thriving. I had a lovely walk in the wind and now I'm back here making popcorn in the fireplace and reading by candlelight. Improving the occasion, as your grandmother used to say."

"You make it sound idyllic."

"It is, really. Don't worry about me. But did you manage to check on your mother?"

"I tracked her to Ellen Brody's, where the two of them have improved the occasion by laying in a gallon of wine and two old Hitchcock tapes. And the wine will work even if the V.C.R. doesn't. So I guess everyone's covered."

"And we'll all get a day off tomorrow. Enjoy it while it lasts."

So Clyde had called his mother first. Could Orrin feel so petty that he wished the reverse had been true? Could he, moreover, long to be curling up with Gail and the Hitchcock films and the wine, as they ought by rights to be doing?

He could and yet decided (sweeping the cold soft paper-ash from the hearth and stowing the unpopped corn) that on balance he felt just fine, as advertised. He did not feel alone, or lonely. Indeed he considered the possibility that he might feel *popular* as these phonecalls kept rolling in. But no, popular was not the word for it. Orrin could in the end be quite precise: what he felt was *alive* again.

"Not me," Paperman was saying. "I try to steer clear of the freedom-of-speech freaks. I don't want to end up defending the K.K.K. or the porn industry. Not my trip."

"No."

"Justice isn't abstract to me, or even relative. It's absolute, obvious, moral."

"But of course that's fascist."

"Of course."

This was a morning on which Orrin accompanied Paperman on the dawn foray, all the way to the wharves where business was nearly concluded and back to Copley Square where it was just getting underway. Now they sat over plain rolls and coffee on Newbury Street because Paperman was up in arms about cholesterol after a fourteen egg week, and about nitrates after seven matching scoops of hash.

"I'm not a health nut. I just like to portion out my poisons," he explained.

"I agree with you. Keep the body off balance so it won't know *how* to deteriorate."

"I think it's true, though. That's why I'm so pleased to see you off the sauce."

"I have always been a moderate tippler, Eli, though you may have met me at the height of my thirst and taken a wrong impression. Spending the past week with you, for instance, I might conclude you were formed entirely of Hessian Eggs. But it was a passing moment in time, one turn of the crop so to speak."

"Rest your case. I'm certainly no reformer," Eli grinned.

"Getting back to free speech, though—you were about to say why you did take this particular case?"

"Because it isn't really free speech that's at issue. Free speech provides the occasion, that's all. Listen, why don't you come to the courthouse if you like and eavesdrop. You can analyze the motivation of all the key players."

"Oh I can do that sight unseen, from this chair. You've got financial gain, the quest for personal power, and sexual self-promotion. And of course the over-riding desire to be loved in shameless comfort."

"The dim view, eh?"

"Just so. But not you, Eli. Your motives stand apart."

"Go on. Do me, then."

"Dawn air, aluminum beer, and precise justice for all."

"You are some bullshitter, Orrin. You should have been a lawyer. But why don't you come. You might find it interesting."

Something had changed in the relation between them and it had happened a week earlier, the night of the storm, though Orrin had not identified it until yesterday, in the office with Sue Roth. "If he would only *call*," Sue had pleaded, not for the first time. "I know he's busy. But he could still be a friend, be in *touch*. Is that so much to ask?"

It was not so much to ask, Orrin allowed, yet was still too much, for this simple reason: either the man called or he did not. The matter was beyond her control, especially as she had made this point to her husband time and again without effect.

Give up! That's what Ann Landers would have told Roth, free of charge. But beyond the obvious (that one must be one's own best provider) Orrin saw the momentous element of *dumb luck* in life.

"He knows I am in agony from the migraines," poor Sue continued spinning her wheels, "but by the time this man is out the door and in the car—what, ten seconds?—my head is healed. By then I don't *have* a head, I don't exist."

True, her husband might have been a habitual caller, a polite inquirer. With so little more, a brief even insincere toot of sympathy, his wife might be twice as happy. Maybe happy *enough,* although naturally she would have held different, higher standards had he been less of a shit-heel. Still there was luck involved and no one was invulnerable to the fallout, from good luck and bad—least of all Orrin himself.

Rejected by Gail, stuffed and left staring at black curtainless windows, Orrin had become motionless on every level of his being. *It did not have to happen,* and yet once it had, he was stuck with it, defenseless. None of his training could avail him, nor could intellect, nor humor, though it helped, as did the few friends who would tolerate his heartfelt shenanigans.

And then came Eli. He could take some credit for Eli, at least generically, but so much more was sheer luck, and timing. Like the business of Eli phoning in the night of the blackout—luck and timing. It was only a gesture of course, a mannerism as it were, yet wasn't it also the call that Dick Roth never made to his wife? It was "nothing," but like the sweet nothings a lover might whisper, it was everything as well. And the sheerest luck of it was manifest in the unlikelihood the phone would even function on such a wild night.

Actually, Orrin's luck had been running since Christmas. Optimism beset him. This was chemical change. Orrin, who knew the human emotions for a chemical laboratory, could hardly be surprised intellectually. He was surprised emotionally, though, because emotions never carry with them a sense of their own shelf-life, of what if anything might succeed them.

He was seen by friends at The Club, by Barry and Beekman and Theo, as "coming around after a trying time," so that he was again on good terms with them over restaurant lunches and afternoons at Clarendon Street. Orrin tacitly accepted their version and did not urge them to pay closer attention to his life or to their own. They were not allowing enough, he was nonetheless certain, for the element of dumb luck.

9

Having squealed like a second child all Fall for want of attention, Orrin now found himself turning away invitations. Offered the five-minute introductory to Lenke's talk at The Hancock, he passed the little plum (and the handsome honorarium for keynoting) to Jack Beekman. When Clyde came up with tickets to a Wilde farce at The Colonial, Orrin invented prior commitments. Even for Jethro's birthday, two weeks away, the best he could do was waver.

There also came a chance to philander with a "great lady" (nominated to the post by Paperman), a divorcée who turned out in a footnote to be the very one who was too sexy for mere sex. Not ready, protested Orrin Summers, try me again in five or ten years.

He was not so very busy technically, but he was working hard on Acknowledgement, among other things, and did not want to let a crowded social agenda bail him out. Better to defer re-entry, though he did accept from Eli a last-second invite to hear some Mendelssohn at the Davis Chamber Series in Cambridge.

"Tia Adams was coming, but her boy has a hundred and two."

"Isn't that my girlfriend, though? The Great Lady? I hope you aren't moving in on me, Eli."

"Tia and I are strictly pals. But wait, does this mean you are lifting your five-year embargo?"

"Not I. That's just the bark of the dog in the manger you're hearing. Anyway, I'm happy to fill in. I have never had an embargo on Mendelssohn."

So he went, and it proved another piece of pure luck. Because the night of cloud-smudged stars, the ornate old concert hall, and the playing were all just right—the venerable room like a wooden box full of melody, as high as it was deep and wide to form a perfect cube of music in which the phrasing of Mendelssohn's charming violins ricocheted rich and clear. Orrin had not seen or admired in years the gracenotes that had always set the Davis apart, the rounds of carved plaster in the dome, elaborate marquetry inlays in the mahogany panels. The dated stage lighting was all the more defining for being dim and irregular, as players flared their hands and the planes of their faces in and out of shadow simply by bending to the flight and tumble of notes.

"It does take you back in time," said Orrin, as they stood in the buzzing open concourse, sipping coffee at intermission.

"I never heard classical music as a child. In fact—I'm not sure I ever realized this before but my folks didn't listen to music at all, of any kind. Isn't that odd?"

"It is, but I didn't mean that. I meant historically. Back to the culture of Old Vienna, or evenings in Leipzig at the time of the Hapsburgs."

"Glory Days, sayeth The Boss. I don't know from Hapsburgs but it's a wonderful series and they perform well beyond my ability to criticize intelligently. I'm just a fan."

"Oh it's beautifully played, Eli. I should phone friend Mia and thank her personally for dropping out."

"It's Tia and you know it. Why not swing by with a tin of aspirin for Mickey and stay for her matchless blueberry upsidedown cake— which by the way is mine by rights."

"I expect she has some aspirin in the house."

"Prescribe something, then. Some *potion*. Hell, Orrin, I forget you're a trained physician."

"So do I, it was all so long ago. Enough of your match-

making joke, though—I can't tell if I am in supply or
demand. I'm just glad we have another hour of Mendelssohn coming to us. It may not be the most profound
music but it is very good for the soul."

"It's only Rock 'n Roll but I *like* it."

"Do you? Like rock-and-roll, that is?"

"Do *you*?"

"I'm afraid not. I was already pushing thirty when they
had Elvis, you know. But I have a daughter—believe this if
you can—who plays rock music professionally. If that's the
word."

"Is she good?"

"Who knows? I haven't heard her sing a note in years.
She's part of a group, though I gather she is the lead
singer."

"What's the group?"

"I don't even know. Isn't that terrible? I should find out,
just so you can tell me if she *is* good."

Later, after the music, they strolled into Harvard Square
and sat in a booth at the Wursthaus eating corned-beef
sandwiches and sampling unlikely beers. Orrin's brand
hailed from Australia and tasted like six-months-in-a-can,
so he left the bulk for Paperman the tang enthusiast and
switched over to a Fudd's Patella for himself.

"A very mellow scene," said Paperman.

"You know, if they hadn't driven that word from the
English language it really would do, for this."

Orrin swept the room with his arm, but he meant to
include the night as a whole: the blessed little February
thaw, the sweetness of the Violin Concerto, the easy companionship. A happy night—simply that, and that simply,
too simple to be spoken. There had been introduced into
it, though, one minor nagging matter. How was it, how
could it be, that he did not know the name of Elspeth's
singing group?

True he did not know one bunch from the next and

would likely care for none of them. If she worked at a school, however, as Clyde did, could he fail to know its name? If she was with a firm—business, law, whatever—he would surely know what that firm was called. How was this any different? Whose fault was it, whose doing? Orrin wondered how far back one would have to go for an answer, and summoned up Elspie at age eleven, her nose still stubby and her cheeks billowing like Dizzy Gillespie's around the squeaking clarinet. Her navy-blue blazer with the yellow school insignia darned onto the pocket. And they celebrated the occasion over carte-blanche sundaes at Bailey's and as a matter of fact Orrin recalled that Elspeth had ordered strawberry with strawberry sauce and jimmies. Was that a good father?

He summoned her up again at sixteen, precisely sixteen, the night they took El and her best friend Rory to the Top of the Hub for flaming chateaubriand and a defiant white wine—because red was more "correct." Rebellion! They joked about how school was stupid, boys were stupid, everything was stupid—except Orrin was still in the joke. An ally, then, at age sixteen.

When had the curtain come down on him? She grew up, of course, he and Gail were bound to become peripheral; but when had they become an outright mortification, or worse, himself a nonentity? Never to see her face, never hear her voice (however good) not even to know the name of her singing group. His own daughter and he could not summon her up at twenty-six.

With the Neffs one night, they had laughed out loud about the changes, recalling a time when young men and women were simply forbidden each other's company in college dormitories. Years later came the stream of liberalization, beginning with a trickle: short visits on Sunday, with the door wide open and four feet on the floor. More than a decade later friends in the academic community alerted them to the next phase, the door a crack ajar and three feet on the floor. Was it a joke, the three feet? An invitation to the bizarre?

It came as no surprise that the floodgates soon were loosed. In Clyde's time at Dartmouth, your door was equipped with a lock, and what you chose to do with your feet or the feet of your friends was considered purely personal. Then Elspeth went and lived in a totally coeducational dorm, sharing a bathroom with seven men, like Snow White. It seemed so abandoned, so far beyond anyone's control, that he and Gail had let it all go with a laugh. Better not to know, fruitless to keep asking, and then there was no longer any way to ask. . . .

"You know," he remarked to an uncomprehending Paperman, who was lavishly calling for dark ale from the Fiji Islands, "It never occurred to me the group might be good. I never even considered it an issue."

Eli kept on the move. He somehow managed to light down in Tarrytown, New York and Terre Haute, Indiana the same week, yet miss only one breakfast at The Paramount. Orrin, who had an agreeably irregular schedule himself, with more flexibility than most people, was stunned by Paperman's unpredictability. Eli was always going on short notice because he could not, or would not, say no to anyone. It was hardly accidental Eli was a single man—no sane woman could plan a day around him, much less a life.

As room-mates, though, he and Orrin had no need of plans and rarely made any. Procedure was to count heads at seven, then shop accordingly at the high-priced grocer on Charles Street. Then the scent of vegetables frying in oil, or the sizzle of breaded fish, to the strains of Bach or Schubert.

"It's cheaper, two people eating in," Orrin joked one

night, "than the same two eating out. I remember that from marriage."

"Like about a thousand percent cheaper. If only one of us could cook, we could be eating better too."

In truth, Eli had a flair in the kitchen and knew it. Orrin did prefer it when they could eat together. But if Eli was at large, Orrin could easily fall back on his own resources, newly expanded. Not just the work piled up on his desk in the study. He had resumed the custom of passing an hour or two at The Club, late afternoon to early evening. It trimmed the night down to a manageable size, and left him in a state of poise toward the world.

(In an early paper, he had argued that this was the precise purpose of social life—the purely social contacts that cast no shadow on the snow—to provide this poise. It was a trick of physics achieving it, not one of psychology, for alone all day or constantly among people one could never achieve it, notwithstanding the riches of solitude or the capital assets of the crowd.)

There was nothing tricky at The Club. One took one's pleasures there as fortunate men always had: choice to-bacco, good liquor, well-informed talk in ample armchairs with brass-tacked skins of leather. These same pleasures might exist in the home, pipe and slippers and a log on the fire, but they rarely had the same salubrious effect—hence The Club, throughout history. Late afternoon had been a good time for Orrin when the children were still at home, because it gave him a presence in the house, always home by six, yet braced him well for the chaos of it all.

One dark rainy Tuesday, Orrin stopped at home to nudge the thermostat (The Weatherbaby had been frankly alarmed by cold air coming down from Canada) and was headed back out in scarf and hat when Eli came galloping up the stairs, as drenched as though he'd just been swimming in his clothes. Orrin, who had not expected Eli back

before the weekend, smiled and helped to extricate him
from the soggy coat.

"Who was chasing you up the stairs?"

"No racetrack but the night, no finish line but the dawn.
How is everything, Orrin?"

"Fine, very good. I like that line of yours."

"That line of Bob Dylan's, actually."

"How was Los Angeles? Did you do all right?"

"We got the injunction—that was the main thing. And I
got to spend an hour with my brother. Otherwise I'm just
plain tired."

"Tired! You ascended the stair like the original Greek
lighting the original Olympic torch, with garlands of
flowers round your head."

"Nice to know I make a good impression. But right
about now a shower interests me more than a flower—a
nice hot one and a familiar bed. Are you coming or
going?"

It made an interesting moment for Orrin. A complex
moment. For he was going, all but gone, having just set
his evening in motion. Now he was no longer in the mood
for The Club, not of a mind to step out into the cold
silverblack drizzle which Eli was so vividly pleased to have
left behind. The hot shower and soft familiar bed, once
enunciated, smacked of heaven precisely, plus of course he
would not have been going in the first place had there been
company at home.

Still, he *was* going, and so felt obliged to *keep* going. To
whom he owed this obligation, Orrin could not have
said, as he was perfectly free to change his plan either with
or without a small white lie. As it happened, calibrated by
his reply, he was imperfectly free in fact.

"Just going. Only for an hour, though. Maybe you'll
still be around when I get back."

It was nothing. Orrin only marked the occasion because

it was the first small infelicity of luck or timing in memory. The previous day, to test it out, he had wished for sloppy weather (during his period of confinement at the office) and sleet came spinning from a lowery sky. Then, when he was set to go, he changed his order and almost at once the sweet melting rays of sun were flooding the streets. Orrin was on a major roll. Maybe it had been the same way with God, long ago, the week he said Let there be light.

There was one setback the following week, a sort of lapse. Eli had been called straight back to L.A. and in his extended absence Orrin briefly let down his guard. It wasn't easy taking a single drink at The Club, no one else did that, so this one time Orrin took two. A harmless indulgence, and certainly he arrived home sober.

He went on to heat something inside a plastic pouch, some brackish noodles and gray meat with a vaguely continental moniker, and eventually settled back to glance at the News. When the talk turned to additional air from Canada (and yes, he was again sitting still for the Weather, if not seeking it out) Orrin had gone ahead and fortified himself against the elements with a short one.

Jack-and-Liz were out sick, though, or out on the town, so he switched over to Chet-and-Nat instead (likable capable Chet, potentially beautiful Nat) and for the hell of it elected to top off the night with a tall one, a real drink of whiskey, after which he did lose consciousness briefly. And the next thing he knew he was staring at a hostile image of Alfred E. Newman.

He might have let out a scream, he might have barely suppressed it, again the details were hazy. But it wasn't Newman after all, it was Ted Fucking Koppel (as Bamford called him), pontificating through his teeth on late-night television. "Bullying people with his dead-fish eyeballs," in Hal's phrase. Orrin quickly clicked Koppel goodnight, and was left to muse on the subject of timesis.

Not everyone knew about timesis, including those who habitually favored its use. Good fucking night! you might say, before you slammed the door. Or Awful damn cold out there, as you wedged your muffler in under your chin. Timesis was simply the practice of jamming an obscenity between the adjective and its noun.

Orrin had investigated the matter because of Gail. It was a cute surprise habit of hers, to occasionally foul-mouth her delicate formal cadences and to do it just that way, timetically. Of course it was less cute when frequent, or vehement, as when toward the end it seemed she was jamming an oath into every modifier-noun occasion that arose. Orrin supposed he had stumbled onto its significance, finally, when she tucked him out.

But now he undertook a brief consideration as to whether "Ted" truly modified "Koppel" or merely preceded it, before going on to recall Auden's famous remark on the frequent use of the adjective "fucking" in the ranks of the British Army, where its only function was to signal the approach of a noun. Not long after that, he lost consciousness again, still on the sofa but this time for eight hours.

Next morning came the invoice. In the bathroom mirror, Orrin saw what might have been an ailing mole if it hadn't been himself instead. Because the thought of coffee made him shudder, he took his chances on a single soothing sip of Bushmills, but he felt like the Tin Man gone to rust, with barely the mobility to dress himself. And it was late. Someone down at the office (please God not Harris) had surely been forsaken without flowers.

Sorrow over this proved no keener than the urge to steer clear altogether, to compound the error of absence by avoidance. Though he started in the direction of the office,

Orrin was far from certain it would turn out to be his true destination. Below the footbridge in the Gardens, he paused briefly on a damp bench, with cold sweat standing at his temples. He had lost his conditioning edge with the booze; the much ballyhooed sobriety translated into a simple unfitness for drink.

Bravely he continued. He *would* face the music. He *was* coming out of it. And by the time he hit Beacon, he remembered that he and Eli were on for Davis Hall again tonight. It would be a pleasure to hear the Triple Concerto performed live. At the last light, Orrin paused again, and stood absently humming the first cello crescendo from Beethoven before some of the cold air from Canada came and slapped him along his way.

10

Odd (since Jethro was a boy) but it was Elspeth whom he most resembled. He had the Giacometti frame—knees and elbows like knobby joints in the metalwork—and the unique quality of Elspeth's hair, which could seemingly hold light, store it, and give it back at unlikely moments. Streaky brown hair, thick yet somehow loose, unclustered, it shone from within, might even glow in the dark.

Gail said that her own was the same as a child, though of course such magic never showed up in faded sepia photographs from the family's shoebox-files, where she could appear almost homely. She was in fact extremely attractive. Hal Bamford, always quickest to value the distaff, had once remarked she had a rare look among women, that of an adventuress, a co-conspirator in sensuality and action. (While Gail herself was baffled by his statement, others had assented to it and over the years she accumulated gifts that enlivened the theme: a safari hat, malacca cane, and once a diaphanous ivory blouse she would have blushed to wear in her own bedroom much less into the world.)

Orrin loved the role of Grandpa. It was only a walk-on, a short stint as a sort of good fairy, but he had a genuine rapport with Jethro and Corey that made it more than just palatable. He accepted the odd bout of fatigue or crankiness from them and they did the same for him; plus they were more in tune with his irony—his absurd humor—than were many of his older friends. Often the middle generation, Clyde and Phyll, became the butt of jokes and understandings between the first and third. ("*We* know what Mom really means, don't we, Grandpa?") It might read as a conspiracy, but in fact it served to tie them all together.

And Orrin enjoyed being lavish. Today, as always, he had taken care to bring along an unbirthday as well as a birthday package and there was never any predicting which would be reckoned the greater prize. A lifelong student of the psychology of birthdays, he had once explained himself to Phyll: "The most apt to cry at the party are the birthday child and his sibling, whose birthday it isn't. So the second box can change it all." (Actually the second box could change only half of it; Orrin had no trick for shielding the birthday child himself from tears.)

As one aged, of course, the sad note underlying a birthday needed little elucidation. But kids did not associate aging with dying, or at least they didn't feel that a year gained in youth could constitute "aging." Most were eager to be older, and claim new privileges ("When I was five, I was barely alive/ but now I am *six*. . .") and yet one also heard their pleas for stasis: "And I think I'll stay six for ever and ever."

Children treasured the specificity of their individual lives more than grown-ups knew (or remembered) and so experienced along with the fun and festivities a thoughtful regret that such a special year was ending. They lived in the present, yet on a birthday the past and present for a few hours coincided emotionally, and the regret was there as true human sadness: we will never pass this way again.

Jethro had yet to crash, though the big crash usually came late in the day, when it could easily be attributed to fatigue from "all the excitement." Of course Grandpa Orrin was the official Minister of Excitement, with something of a gift for creating frenzy. He led the whole kennel outdoors (and how like a kennel it was, all of them yipping and swarming at his heels) and urged them to hide. Then he hid too, in a large trash barrel under the car-port. When they cottoned on and found him, after a stifling five minutes in the stinking crypt, they laughed wildly, crazily, and tipped the barrel on its side to start it rolling. What did they think, he was made of rubber?

At least they did not think him ancient (Grandpa the Wrinkled) though he knew in truth they did not think at all, not just now. Nary a thought in their collective head as they spun the barrel over the macadam onto the gland-jarring gravel. "They love you," said Phyllis, rescuing him, getting him on his feet somehow. "Yes, but at what price!" said Orrin. And loving their love in spite of himself, he dashed back inside to rig up the Old Stock Pond.

For this sentimental favorite, Orrin had to crouch behind a blue paisley sheet with a box of cheap traditional toys—yoyos, balsa gliders, mazes, Chinese rings—plus a pail of water. As each child cast his string line over the top off a stick of bamboo, Orrin made splashing sounds in the pail with his hand. Then he would attach a toy to the line and give a tug.

He was uncomfortable maintaining the catcher's crouch, especially after his adventures in the rolling barrel, and he soon came to fear that Jethro's guests might have outgrown the Old Stock Pond. The kids sounded bored, and dissatisfied with their catch. What did they expect, electronic party favors or a winning ticket to the Megabucks? They were all a bit spoiled, as part of the times, he guessed. Me Me Me behavior was once met head on by the elders, but this was the Me Me Me decade, the elders had tacitly approved it.

Orrin was sorely tempted to tug on Jason's line and send it back empty, for Jason was the one who had earlier complained there were too few balloons. (Phyll had warned him they would all be named Jason, but only two of them were and the other guy was touchingly sweet.) Orrin, who had come within a pulse of bursting his heart to blow up those tight little balloons, had to stand in mute disgust as Phyll responded to the grievance by quickly inflating two more for the bad Jason, *after* ascertaining his favorite colors!

By now, he feared, his own dear Jethro was corrupted too. Just another buck in the swarming animal horde, who took from one pleasure nothing more than a manic desire for the next. This job was not merely tiring, it was disillusioning, for children were not well featured in the plural, or with prizes of any kind at stake. As different as they were, in age and gender, it had been true with Clyde and El: invariably a pleasure with either one alone, permutations of stress with two.

Meanwhile he was having trouble with his knots. His hands were not so steady, his fingers unfit for such finicky work. Fearing he would fumble with the string only made him fumble the more, until finally he spilled a box of crayons and they all started laughing and whaling away at the sheet. Orrin didn't know what to do. At first he was torn between an impulse to cut-and-run and a wildly absurd compulsion to continue the fiction, to finish the game up in good form. Then, rising up between these poles, came a brief flood of fury and he stood. And his aspect, looming over the blue paisley, must have been terrible indeed to judge by the abrupt silence of the little fisherfolk. He might have gone primal on them, chased them around the room kicking ass, had he not seen their vivid abject terror.

"The Old Stock Pond," he announced, with regained dignity, "is closed for the holiday. So sorry, you know."

"What holiday!" the Jason was in his face demanding, and others quickly echoed the challenge.

"Jethro Summers' Birthday, of course. No school today, all across this great nation of ours."

"That's cause of Abraham Lincoln," several shouted.

"You don't believe that, do you? Lincoln? They only say

that so the other kids won't be jealous of Jethro. Pond Closed, though, and anyone who didn't catch a fish yet will please come to my office right away."

"Where's your office?"

"Yeah, where's your office?"

Orrin brought three of them into the coat closet and let them tangle it out for the remaining trinkets. He smiled down on them, his crocodile smile, thinking terrible ten-fingered monsters. As they emerged from among the coats, Phyll went to the kitchen to get the phone and Clyde announced the cake and ice cream. Orrin came to table in a conical turquoise party hat, and with a dignified straightfaced reserve helped to settle them into chairs.

"It's your grandmother," Phyll hollered from the kitchen, "Come say hello," and Jethro rose from the groaning-board with a face as lumpy and elongated as a sausage. Clyde touched him gently and admonished, "Be good," as the lad went off to pay his dues.

But was it Gail on the phone, or was it Phyllis' mother Dierdre? Coming out on the train, Orrin had wondered if Gail would be at the party too, and he had felt oddly nervous of the impression he might make, as on a first date. As guests arrived, he would open the door with mixed anticipation and a carefully arranged careless face. When he learned she was not coming, he was both relieved and deeply disappointed. Crazy I am I am, he thought, either way.

Was it Gail on the line now? It doesn't matter, he told himself, doesn't make a bit of difference. And yet: that might be *her,* her voice, less than twelve feet away. My wife, Clyde's mother, Jethro's Gran—talking and I cannot hear her, she doesn't even want me to.

At last the decks were clear, although inevitably one child was abandoned forever and Phyllis ran him home.

"It's easier than calling the parents with a gentle reminder," Clyde explained, "because then you're stuck waiting. And if they're the sort that have forgotten the kid once today—"

"You don't think they *meant* to leave him?

"Well who knows. But everyone is too spent for more waiting at this point."

"I know I am—spent. I'm not in such bad condition, you know, I do a lot of walking. But *this.*"

"Birthdays are rough. And you bore the brunt of it, Dad."

"Good old Grandpa."

"Well come sit down, now that we have our house back. I'll tell you my idea for your trip next month."

"By all means. Why next month? Why a trip? Where to?"

"Next month because the weather here will still be nasty, but it gives you time to plan it. A trip because it's the best therapy for handling this sort of thing. And where, anywhere, as long as it's warm."

"The best therapy, no less! Here I, a doctor of the mind, advised by my own baby and a layman to boot."

"That's right. You disagree?"

"Oh no. It's good advice, and I've given it out enough times that I had better agree with it. When applicable. But you see, I have a number of projects going just now. And it happens I've been enjoying myself tremendously."

"So things are better. What, have you got yourself a gal?"

Orrin almost blushed. Not just at the prospect of a "gal" (so trippingly phrased) but at the source of such inquiry. His baby indeed, once a putty-soft seven-pounder in the crook of his arm, wondering aloud if Orrin had taken on a new partner in the very process which had brought him forth! Life was certainly strange. Then another thought crossed his mind.

"Clydie!"

"What? Why not, for goodness' sake. It is just a matter of time."

"Are you trying to tell me, to *prepare* me in your charming roundabout fashion, for the announcement that your mother has someone? Is that what we're working up to?"

"Not a bit, Dad, I'm not in on that secret. She may have someone, for all we know. Though to be honest, I didn't really expect her to, not so soon."

"And you did expect me. Why?"

"I don't know."

"Your mother is a very attractive woman. That isn't supposed to be so difficult for a son to imagine."

"I'm sure she is. She was a bit down on the male-female experiment, that's all. Whereas you were going to feel a need to replace her."

"That's silly, Doctor Summers. Life has much more to offer than the male-female experiment, as you call it. Especially if you are fifty-nine next month. Which you are, if you are me."

"Come on, Doctor Summers, you're hardly a fossil. Actually, now that I'm getting up there in years myself, I thought I'd stumbled onto a psychological truism—"

"Another one?"

"—which is that you never feel any different. You go along aging one day at a time, and the years do go by more quickly, yet you are the same person you were in college. On one level. You don't register the changes. You don't ever *feel* old."

"Yes, well, I remember thinking that too. But somewhere between your age and mine, one does indeed begin to register the changes. Which isn't the point. The point is you underestimate how much I *care* for your mother. It isn't simply all the years we spent together, it's that I love her. Your herrible horrible *difficult* mother I happen to love, very much."

Orrin did not ordinarily refer to his love for Gail. As he made this statement to Clyde now (and it seemed very

important both that he make it and that he address it to
Clyde) Orrin tried to recall whether he had mentioned love
to Gail herself in recent years. It did not seem likely. But
that was nothing. Given Gail's outlook on things, and her
quick untamed tongue, it might be masochistic saying love
to her. Better simply to act on it, for talk was cheap after a
certain number of times around the track anyway—either a
relationship was working or it was not.

He had definitely mentioned his love to Theo last autumn—or at least he had said more than once how much
he needed Gail, by which one surely meant the same thing.
Whiskey helped him say it then and whiskey may have
helped him say it now. Nonetheless Orrin knew whiskey
could not make him say it if it were not true.

"Speaking of my loved ones, who spurn me, how is
your sister doing these days?"

"Very well, actually, to judge from the reviews. I haven't
seen her either. In fact, whenever I think about where we
are, Phyll and I, and where Elspeth is, I am amazed that I
ever see her."

"Reviews?"

"In *The Phoenix*. She made Up-and-Coming groups for
the year, with special kudos for the songwriting."

"But that's terrific. You should tell me—I'm ashamed to
have to ask—the name of her outfit."

"Air Force Two. They are opening for Warts and All at
The Rat in a few weeks—a big gig for Up-and-Comers."

The Rat? Warts and All? It was a silly game they played,
thought Orrin, though of course it was probably great fun
for them. He felt very accepting of the whole enterprise,
especially with the award for writing songs. That was
certainly a bonus after the loud electric howling he had
imagined. He would have to hear her out, his daughter the
composer.

"What was it again, The Air Force? So military?"

"Air Force Two. It's about the kinds of force in the air,
she says, as in 'you are on the air' versus the planes of

death. That's a direct quote. And you know about Air Force One."

"The presidential plane. I do now. I'm afraid I failed to make the connection on my own. Well, it is the sort of name that becomes famous, isn't it?"

"That's right. Because of Air Force One."

"I suppose that could be it. But tell me, where is this Rat located?"

"Kenmore Square, maybe?" Clyde re-lit his pipe and shrugged again: not his territory.

"Oh well, I'm sure Eli will know."

"Eli will?"

"Didn't I tell you about Eli Paperman? I must have. He is my room-mate, believe it or not. I advertised for a room-mate and got this bright, pleasant young lawyer. In his late thirties."

"Well this does sound interesting. I'll have to meet him."

Clyde spoke matter-of-factly through a vacant smile, but he was quite taken aback. His father had a room-mate? Clyde did expect news of a girlfriend, thinking (as Orrin had said of Gail) what an attractive person his father could be. And with all of his clients women, in varying states of need and dependency . . .

"He must be single?"

"We are all single, my son. Though we join together in Holy Matrimoney, we do still remain single. But yes, Eli is a confirmed bachelor."

"You say that with a slight twist. Is he gay or something?"

"No no. His last girl booted him out. That's our common bond, you see."

"Come on, Dad, you can't see it that way, can you?"

"Oh who knows how to see anything. Let's talk about you now, Clydie. I want all the latest news from inside the ivory tower. And Phyll is back—"

"Yes I am. Free at last. I hope I didn't miss anything good. Has Orrin reported on his self-analysis yet?"

"What's this, Dad?"

"Actually, my dear, we've just finished talking about me. We're onto you two now. But Clyde can fill you in later."

Next afternoon at The Club, Orrin was sitting with the medical crowd, Jaspers and Connoly and the young one with the aviator glasses, when he spotted Ted Neff shedding his coat in the foyer. Ted had seemed evasive of late, sliding away from conversations, though of course Orrin knew that was Ted's way with everyone. As he watched Ted now, tacking backward past old Sarge, he realized that for the twenty-plus years of their friendship, Ted had been the very image of Man Backpedalling, the vanishing point of every picture.

Poor Ted never had "time." He spent much of his time strenuously protesting that he hadn't any. And yet here he came, across the room full speed, hearty handshake pre-extended:

"Orrin!"

"A pleasant surprise," said Orrin, referring to the surprise of Ted advancing on him.

"I was hoping to find you here. We're giving a party— general purposes—at the house on Saturday. Hope you can fit us in."

Party. The old crowd. Orrin enjoyed these occasions immensely, though he would never confess to such a thing. But what, he wondered, would the Neffs do about Gail?

"Oh she's invited too. Why not? If there's a problem, you can work it out between yourselves. Or come to-gether, to save on cabfare."

"I'd be delighted to come, Theo. And I hope Gail does too, I'd love to see her. Do you think she might?"

"You want the truth, Orrin?"

"Always," he flatly stated. Then reduced it, when Ted looked askance, to, "Allright—usually."

"She asked May to let her know if you would be there."

"That's clear enough, then."

Orrin kept a civil, disinterested face, though he felt hammered inside. Doubly so, for although Ted had come clean under cross-examination, he had clearly asked Gail first and pre-fabricated a plan of retreat with her.

"Why not wait and see? I did let her know you've been on a good streak."

The instant Ted spoke, he knew he had spoken too much. An uncharacteristic mis-step, and now he could but flinch as Orrin flew back at him:

"*Good* streak! The presumption!" But Orrin was sputtering a bit, giving Ted what little time he needed to regain his balance, re-align his spine. "What am I anyway, Theo— a pitcher? A designated hitter? That I should have slumps and *good* streaks!"

"But of course you do, Orrin," said Ted soothingly. "Don't you know the first thing about yourself?"

11

Eli Paperman told Orrin of the experiment he once conducted, in an attempt to cram one hundred years of living into seventy-one years of life.

Seventy-one, Eli explained, was the mean age of mortality among American males. It was when you expected to die. You could exceed the mean, of course—presumably half did—but might you not also beat the reaper at his own game (which was Time) by simply refusing to sleep?

Because a year was not just a year any more than a kiss was just a kiss. It was also 8,766 hours. A typical good burgher aimed to sleep seven hours every night, often complaining of fatigue when he managed only six. Thus, according to Eli, the man was pissing away 2,555 hours a year with nothing to show for it.

Eli had never consigned his own life away to such an extent. As a boy he feigned dependence on a night-light so that he could read to his heart's content. At fifteen he was listening to late-night radio in his room, rhythm-and-blues from Oakland and the country stations emanating from Bakersfield. In college he tried to squeeze in three or four hours of sleep, using black coffee as a chemical backup.

Then it occurred to him that by not sleeping at all, he could add thirty years to his allotment of seventy-one. Bingo. And so obvious. People were forever saying there was not enough time in the day, but the *time* was there, it was the people who weren't. They were upstairs snoozing. Remove the time pressures of a family, mix in the hours usually squandered on sleep, and there would be time enough for a man to do everything he wished to do.

"So what were the results of the experiment?" Orrin asked.

"I got tired."

Eli confessed almost sheepishly to double vision, belly aches, and a dullness of mind that devalued the waking state. Sleep was apparently a necessity, like food. Research revealed that even Superman took his rest each night. So Eli had gone back to strong coffee and four hours, while retaining the basic premise: the less you sleep, the more you must be "living."

Such a man, with such an outlook, seemed wholly admirable to Orrin and quite unlikely to be found at home in the evening, watching the animals mate on PBS. Such a man would be abroad, ever on the go, early and late. It did also prove to be the case, however, that Eli had made a new friend.

Her name was Marcy Green. Eli had neglected to mention her, perhaps thinking that she was not of direct concern to Orrin. (Because mere gossip did not interest Eli, he assumed it did not interest other men either.) But on the night when Orrin woke to the remorseless visage of Koppel, and on some of the subsequent nights where Eli's quilts went unruffled, he had been ruffling the quilts at Ms. Green's establishment over in Cambridge.

Orrin learned of her existence when he took up Paperman's offer to witness the law in action. In the two-hour hiatus between Alice Harris and Jane Liederman, he crossed the river by train and took up a pew at the Middlesex County Courthouse in East Cambridge. The neighborhood on one side of this dignified building had clearly not prospered, was barely surviving. On the other side of it, just as clearly, the land grab was on, and whole blocks were as devastated as a war zone, pending the latest phase of "development."

Inside, Eli was defending a group of protesters who had elected to recline on the broad entrance step of the Baker Laboratory, where fearless amoral chemists were devising new recipes for deadly nerve gasses. This was the case Eli had described, in which free speech was only a pretext. The issue was bad press for Baker, to conduct some public heat toward their heretofore unpublicized dabblings and possibly restrain them.

But Orrin had not really come for the issues, he had come to see some legal fireworks. To see Eli fire salvos of goodness and the evil scientists crumble under the moral force of them; to hear the wicked Attorneys For Nerve Gas chant patriotic gore in the background, like a Greek chorus. So he was a little disappointed by all the soft civil discussion between teams of young attorneys who clearly shopped for their suits together. Each team even featured two women in blue skirt-suits and Etonic running shoes.

"Your Honor," said Eli, in his closest brush with controversy, "these people are hardly criminals . . ."

"A criminal act, however . . ." said the Judge, half-heartedly, as though cueing Eli's lines at a slapdash rehearsal.

"An act of civil disobedience . . ." responded Eli in this shorthand code they spoke, and he went on to list authors, teachers, and even nuclear physicists in the congregation. "There was no harm to anyone, and no threat of harm, until the police . . ."

"Mr. Paperman . . ."

Neither the Attorneys For Nerve Gas, who sought chiefly to keep all voices as low as possible, nor the J., who required only a superficial genuflection to the postulate that there *were* laws, protested when Eli proposed community service in lieu of punishment. Perry Mason this was not. Under a sleepy guarantee that there would certainly be sentences *next* time, the Baker 27 were set free.

Marcy Green was one of them. Orrin had seen her in the

dock, noticed her: intriguing titian tresses, serene hazel eyes, strong shapely calves. He noticed her merely as a connoisseur. When she broke her first smile, at the favorable ruling, he felt it logical to assume everyone in the room was noticing her, for the smile transformed her prettiness into beauty. And then this great beauty turned out to be, well, almost *related*.

They sat in a sunny window of the Barrister, an otherwise dark bar directly across Cambridge Street from the courthouse. Eli ordered stuffed quahogs, which were served on the sort of large white half-shells that people sometimes use for ash-trays, and a pitcher of pale flat beer. To Orrin it tasted like club soda, but he drank up to be a good boyo, and to inspire the modulations of Marcy Green's smile.

"It was not high drama," he said, "but at least justice was done. Is it usually?"

"You really never know. If we got McKinnon, the hanging judge, they would all have been on bread and water for the statutory year. It also helps that no one in this bunch has old cross-references in the F.B.I. files."

"You must be joking."

"You heard Epworth. And he's by far the most decent— he might even approve of the demonstrations. But he will lock up a second offender just the same."

"Well, for now anyway, here's to jurisprudence. And to the victor go the spoils."

With his glass, he had indicated Marcy. That smile of hers must surely have launched a few ships in its time, maybe not a thousand but one or two a month anyway, set adrift on the deep blue sea of urban America. Fairly full, well-defined, curving lips—and the teeth. What were the mechanics of a smile, such that a show of teeth could alter relations? Teeth?

"But I'm the victor," she said. "This clown here is just my mouthpiece—dime a dozen."

"All right, then, to the spoils go the victor. And that

comes from a book, though I'm damned if I can remember which one. My wife would know."

He did not feel like a third wheel, but rather like an approving elder presence, for whom they could display their youthful beauty and their affection for one another. Strangely, he liked the role.

"Tell me, Marcy—what do you do, aside from reclining upon the accessway to laboratories?" They smiled at his comical, Boris Karloff enunciation of the word, for no better reason than good nature and the happiness of the moment. Beer love.

"Currently," said Marcy, "I am floundering."

"In the fishing industry, you say?"

"A wag! No, I'll tell you the whole sad story sometime."

"Why not now? I love a sad story."

"Go ahead, Marce, I've got a call to make anyway," said Paperman. "She just won't tell it in front of me, in case she needs to change a few details."

"Maybe I will tell you. A shrink? You could be just what I need."

"Would that it were so!" said Orrin, flirting outrageously under cover of Paperman's age and ascendancy. All in good fun. "You go use the telephone, Eli. We'll curl up by the fire with this saddest of stories. Page one, chapter one—"

"Chapter One, I waste my life. Ten years as a dancer . . ."

"Wasted?"

"Yes. Not good enough to cut it, and not quite bad enough to quit. Or maybe I was bad enough and just loved it too much to know. But I knew I hated teaching it."

"That was painful."

"Yes. Especially with the good ones and the very bad ones."

"You identified with the others? Who were caught in the middle?"

"If you say so, Siggy. Maybe if I'd done more—even a

few of the small prestigious halls—I could have settled into an atelier and grown old gracefully with it. You know, with my hair up in a bun."

"Your hair would certainly look lovely in a bun," Orrin said to her. Silly fool, he said to himself. But she didn't notice, or mind. "So when did this great waste conclude? Or has it?"

"A couple of years ago. Since then I've just worked at jobs."

"Goodness, girl, you make it sound like a dirty word. Jobs, and the people who do them, make the world go around, Marcy." (Silly·silly fool, he thought. Better calm yourself, quickly.) "What sort of jobs, though?"

"I've done desk. I've waitressed. Spent six months as an air hostess."

"Not really? You must have risqué tales to tell."

"Not really. Frankly, I never wanted to sleep with businessmen."

"Just never made it a goal of yours."

"No."

"So why did you fly?"

"Who knows. Maybe just to get a rise out of people like you and Eli."

"Ah. And now you are floundering."

"Currently, yes. Waiting for something to turn up, as Micawber would say. I hear the big money now is in escort prostitution, except I—"

"Never wanted to sleep with businessmen."

"You got it. Shrink, shrank, shrunk."

Marcy shrugged and knocked back a long swallow of beer. Orrin admired her way with a glass, her understated if slightly rehearsed cynicism, her smooth arching neck.

Teeth were a new consideration, but he did know about necks. As a young practitioner, he had interviewed for the state of Rhode Island a multiple strangler who was a sex fetishist of necks. Since you could not properly fuck a neck, the lad attacked his problem otherwise, but, as Judge John Epworth had pointed out in Green et al. v. Baker Laboratories, there *are* laws.

Again Orrin's admiration was aesthetic, not impassioned, deriving as though from a Degas sketch some sense of the power in a line. The connoisseur. But even the connoisseur knew that this was more than a line, it was alive and beautiful. He knew exactly what young James Hinderlie of Woonsocket, Rhode Island would have felt for this neck, and what Hinderlie would have done.

Orrin next saw his room-mate at six o'clock of the following evening, when Eli burst in the door with both arms full. Buckets of Chinese food, a six-pack of beer, and a white box with ribbon and string–cannoli from Hanover Street.

"I was all over the map of the city today, so I did a little food-gathering for the tribe. Have you eaten?"

"Oh no, I'm not even with drink yet. What a lovely idea, Eli. I'll set the table?"

"Why bother? Let's just woof it off our laps like good Americans—news and booze, if that's what you were planning."

"Irish whiskey with The Buddha's Delight?"

"Why not. And then let's watch the worst show on television—something ridiculously mindless and decadent."

"You, Eli? Even I don't need reform there."

"Oh but I want to see those catty women swaying under a thirty-pound load of makeup; I want to see Today's Man, silk-suited and desperate for a sniff of them. In fact, I can hardly wait."

Scooping the food off their laps like good Americans, drinking off the arms of their chairs, they relaxed for hours in the same way Clyde and Elspeth might have done in junior high, when they would poke fun at the shows and commercials while gnawing their way through the pantry fare like a pair of giant rats. It sometimes bothered Orrin that they always ate more between meals than they ever did at the carefully laid table, but Gail correctly argued that food was food, with those two as thin as pickets . . .

Eli made it to The News At Ten, before announcing he needed a solid eight hours. Orrin could not believe his ears.

"Sleep too? That lovely gal isn't wearing you out, is she?"

"I have these binges. About twice a year—my version of the flu. But I'll be fine in the morning, don't worry. The waterfront at five-thirty?"

"Unlikely, thank you, Eli. I did mean to tell you, she's a charming girl. Wonderful."

"Yeah, Marce has got a little tang to her."

"Is that the best you can say? To hold her roughly equal to an old can of Bud?"

"You said that."

"But such indifference, counselor. Are there really so many fish in the sea?"

"Is that the best you can do? To compare that charming creature to some slimy fish?"

"Well she did mention she was floundering, but no, I can definitely do better. Let's say a swan."

"Okay, then. And thanks, Orrin, I agree she is a good one. We get on pretty well together too, considering that we're members of completely opposite sexes. Did he say snow?"

"Who, Jerry? I didn't hear him. And you didn't either, Paperman, you're just changing the subject."

"What I'm really doing is hitting the hay, whatever Jerry said. But I'll be sure and relay Marce your compliment about her looking like a duck. She'll like that."

"A swan, as you know. But don't. You might inadvertently omit all the implicit poetry of the remark."

"And just give her the bird? Ah, enough of this. Good night, O'Summers."

Orrin's smile outlasted Eli's exit, softened and stayed as he sat recollecting a thousand college nights, jesting the night away with meaningless good nature. It was a warm time for the heart, that closed society of males. A thousand unselfconscious moments that were memorable precisely *because* they counted for absolutely nothing.

When the phone stirred him, half an hour later, he reached for it quickly—not because he thought it might count for something, but simply to guard Eli's rest. Was it a trick of the mind, though, or a valid extrasensory perception that made him so certain it would be Gail?

"I knew your ring," he said. "Really I did. Tell me how you are, my dear?"

"I'm fine, Orrin. Are you well?"

The phrase slipped past him, with its oddly formal cadence, so that he could only reach out and nudge it ahead, like a slowly floating balloon: "Quite well, thanks, and yourself?"

"Fine, I already said. Everything all right at the office?"

"What is this, Gail?" he suddenly snapped. "Have you been hearing rumors I went bricko or something? That I quit working to grow my fingernails? This has a strange sound to it. What's up?"

"You're right, of course, I was in a strange mood to call you. I can't explain. I was worried, that's all, and thought I'd better check on you."

"You thought I might be planning remarriage?"

"To be honest, I was afraid you might be dead."

"And you sought to inherit?"

"No need to get nasty, Orrin."

"Of course not. I'm sorry for that. You know how happy I am to hear from you, no matter why."

"I had a dream about your dying, and it frightened me. As I say, I can't explain it—it's irrational. I simply wanted to confirm you were all right."

"Well I'm touched, Gail, truly touched. To think you care a bit makes things almost acceptable. Maybe we'll see each other after all, at the Neffs on Saturday?"

"Fifty-fifty for me, at this point."

For several minutes Orrin could again sit basking in an afterglow, this time from Gail's newfound concern. Yet a note lingered from her tone, perhaps even more so from her having stuffed him eight months earlier. She had left him dashed, ripped, to recover on his own; now she was calling because she'd had a dream. In a weaker moment he might have taken wild heart from the anomaly, but now it seemed the lingering note was one of false hope, as though in the absence of his hectoring pestering calls she feared the loss of his pained adherence.

Keeping him on the string—wasn't that the subtext? Renewing her power over him? In settling the long emotional score, it could be part of her catharsis to see him still twisting.

The business about Theo's party—what was the angle there? Did she wish to raise false hopes there too, that she would show up and be congenial, or even loving? She could be setting him up for a harder fall if she arrived at the party under foreign sail in spite of Clyde's disclaimer. Orrin hated to think she might be plotting against him, or toying with his moods and expectations. But if she really cared about him, why not just come home and resume a proper life?

Orrin struggled, unsure of his ground here. In fairness to Gail, he had to acknowledge the many times he had begged her message-machine for mercy, assuring it they could at least still be *friends*. And though it was true she had not been friends when he most had needed her friendship, this was perhaps the way of things, the dance of moon and water, neap tide and spring tide. It was probably inevitable that the ebb and flow between two people be poorly synchronized. Certainly relationships, like everything else under the moon, turned on timing. Not on emotions themselves, but on the timing of them—on when they kicked in. On luck, again.

"Thank you so much for calling," he had closed. That way of uttering slightly absurd courtly salutations was a large part of Orrin's charm, whether deeply heartfelt, purely social, or both at the same time. "I'm so pleased you thought to do so."

So many so's, though! Perhaps what he should have done instead was give her a nice little shot of timesis, a vrai broadside. (Good fucking night, you awful damn shrew!) For she was hitting him, wasn't she—but softly, so as to make it feel almost good.

12

The day after Gail's call, Orrin had a dream of his own. Gail had sent a note on blue perfumed rice-paper, inviting him to see her new flat in the Back Bay. He went, only to find himself at an address on Thames Street in Providence, not far from the old office in the Commodore Building.

He saw a silhouette pacing back and forth across a curtained triple-casement, then watched the door fall ajar before he could touch the bell. A cool wind lifted him inside, where he stumbled onto a carpet of astonishing thickness, a silent pile of autumn leaves.

From his knees, Orrin spotted her, in a yellow negligée so short it did not cover her naked hips and thighs. She was starting up a central staircase, sexually exposed, when he now saw it was not Gail but a much larger woman with glossy black hair and laser-bright green eyes that he could see, or sense, even while watching her back.

His outcries echoed to no result and when he attempted to stand, invisible bands of steel locked the backs of his legs like terrible cramps. Pleading for help, he crawled forward to the bottom stair, but the gargantuan woman, with powerfully sculpted buttocks like a Rodin bronze, neither turned nor spoke as she kept ascending a now endless flight of wide white-carpeted stairs.

"You invited me here!" Orrin insisted. "You must help me."

"I invited you to Marlborough Street," she said, the voice sounding from far off (from inside a telephone, possibly), "not here."

Orrin awoke with a deep soreness in his neck and both legs tensely constricted, bound up in the twisted bedding. His chest was soaked inside the pajama jacket and his long moribund member was now a shaft of irreducible granite, having siphoned off the blood from the rest of his body. It took some time, and some slow steady breathing, before the effects of the dream released him.

It was old Homer who observed that many a dream is mere confusion, "a cobweb of no consequence at all." But not this one. And Orrin knew enough about dreamwork to ignore the woman's superficial appearance, for here it was Proust who had pointed out that in dreams "The person whom we love is to be recognized only by the intensity of the pain we suffer."

To come upon a dream so purely clinical was nothing new to Orrin Summers, but the intense sexuality, this rare sweat of arousal was something else again. It was annoying, no question, to know that he had dreamed of her sex, where she had dreamed of his death. That told the story! No amount of fiddling with faces, facts, or somatic stimuli could redirect such raw data as that.

He thought of Paperman's girl, in the tavern booth with that smile, and for a second wondered . . . But no. As his pulses receded, he knew it was Gail, Gail's arms and legs he could image encircling him. He could scarcely recall their last time together—two years, at least. And two years without sex (which it had been for him, no sweet substitutes) could cause a man to wonder much. Hereby apprised that both the need and the power to attend it persisted in him, he had to question the meaning of his long celibacy.

His colleague Beekman maintained that seven days without an orgasm rendered the mind at best semi-operational. And what about the Farnums—Ginny going off at sixty with a much younger man and Eliot, jilted at sixty-two only to ricochet into the bed of Wilma Robillard the

very next night? Was he, Orrin, simply an oldfashioned
fool? His celibacy had seemed tolerable and sane, but was
it?

Maybe it was. He loved Gail after all, she was the one he
wanted; should it be so easy to transfer that? His only date
since the separation had been the enchiladas verdes with
Amy Sugar, a sexual dead-end so to speak, and that had
seemed appropriate. Yes, Orrin thought, I am denying my
sexuality. And then, timetically, Big Fucking Deal. I'll stop
denying it when I want to stop.

Some people could fool Orrin Summers and Orrin
Summers could surely fool some people. He was convinced, however, that not for one minute could he ever
fool himself.

Next day, the night of the Neff's house party, Orrin was
torn between the desire to see Gail there and the wish to hit
her with a pre-emptive strike.

Possibly he could accomplish both goals, Eli suggested,
when Orrin broached the topic over breakfast at The Paramount.

"Oh no, Gail is much stronger. If I do see her, I'm the
one who will feel it."

"You should go. These are your friends—your network
of support. Isn't that a psychological term?"

"It's the old sucker play, and I refuse to play the old
sucker."

"Well but if it's gamesmanship, O'Summers, you could
go her one better. Take along a lovely. Who's the prettiest
woman you know?"

"Gail's friend Kate Walter. A real stunner. But she
loathes me, unfortunately, always has. No idea why."

"Someone new, then. Flaunt your friendship with some
new *mystery* woman to get Gail's goat."

"I have no mystery woman to flaunt, Paperman, lovely or otherwise."

"You could flaunt Marcy! She'd do it in a flash. She loves to ham it up, you saw that."

"Eli, I'm surprised at you. The rusty knife?"

"Gail shouldn't care. If she does care, we'll have helped matters. And if she really doesn't, at least you'll have learned something."

"Oh good. Who wants to learn that?"

"Come on you chickenshit, flaunt Marcy Green."

"Maybe some other time. But thanks anyway—for the network of support. The truth is I don't like my friends all that much."

This was not the truth, or if half true was not to the point. Orrin did have mixed feelings about their social circle, but he never failed to enjoy the conviviality of their gatherings. He enjoyed belonging, welcomed the stock jibes and the waxing heedlessness, swapping dance partners to the accompaniment of those stock jibes as well. Such charades might be shamelessly hollow by dispassionate standards, but Orrin was not one to shortsell mere comfort, or fun.

He sat this one out, however, alone and palely loitering on Filbert Street with a sweet old British lady on the TV who would stumble over a fresh corpse every time she left off her knitting. (Luckily she was a detective of sorts, and managed to finger the criminal.) Orrin three-fourths wished he had elected to flaunt Marcy after all. There they would be, for starters, he and Marcy, and he might like that. How much better to inspire gossip instead of pity! And the rusty knife might prove just the ticket for high and mighty Gail Summers. It *takes* a lawyer, sometimes, to locate that old killer instinct.

He one-fourth wished he had gone even without Marcy, gone alone. For he was alone now anyway and the fact was

Orrin had slipped back a centimeter or two from some of his self-imposed reforms. As his solitude had subtly expanded, he had again found it tricky selecting his behaviors. Looking down the barrel now toward a lonely slush-filled Sunday, he could foresee further slippage, to the dismal strains of trash-sports on television. So he played it safe and stayed in bed all Sunday morning. He *was* tired. He wasn't just hiding under the covers, he was *resting,* and helping to restore the balance of sleep in the world which Paperman so constantly disrupted. Such a dim, gray sloppy universe displayed itself above the half-curtained sash that he was sure it was still late morning when he rose at two to brew some coffee.

Walking out briefly for the papers, he watched the jolly legions mill about, as if this squashy mess were the softlit snow of picturebook Christmas. Rowing past him with their bundles, sometimes clasping hands—he even saw a child skipping, and decided things must not be so bad after all. The air wasn't cold, it was *refreshing,* extremely; and the Common wasn't crowded either, it was ample host to a teeming cheerful community, like those shown in paintings by Prendergast.

"Care to invest, sir? In a good man's immediate future?" Orrin looked up in amusement when he heard the music of importunity, the sound of Pigford cadging. And it was he, though the petition had not been addressed to Orrin but to the bright young couple before him.

Curious to see how much they would cough up, not wishing to hinder Pigford's undeniable style, he waited to one side with his hello. But as he audited this and the following transaction ("Allay your conscience, sir? Help the cold and homeless? Twenty-five cents lets you sleep like a baby . . .") Orrin began to doubt he would greet his friend this afternoon.

Pigford was good. ("Alms for mittens? My phalanges cry out to you, sir . . .") It might have been fun to see how

he made out over the course of an hour, chart his hits and
misadventures. Judging from early returns—all paper, no
coins—his hourly wage might well exceed that of an attorney.

But Orrin felt slightly deflated, almost betrayed. It was
idiotic to feel proprietary about a beggar and yet he found
he liked P. Jones all over again, while Jones' affection for
him was made to seem in retrospect spurious. Jones would
settle for anyone. Orrin could hope it was not so, but he
could not overcome it enough to step up and say a friendly
hello. In truth, he was afraid Pigford would not recognize
him.

Orrin spent the early evening cleaning up the flat, and
brooding over his missed connection with Pigford. It was
terribly complex for a simple and irrelevant situation. His
several collections of dust and paperclips and pennies
floated like a necklace of islands, an archipelago, on the
polished aqueous hardwood.

No use doing much in Eli's room. There the prospect
was always grim. The one window opened on an unbroken facade of blackened red brick, never a hint of
brightness. Eli was so rarely around in daytime that he
might never notice or care, but to Orrin the light and
sunlight were vital to one's frame of mind. He respected
primal clichés, was alert to facts as seemingly divergent as
bears hibernating, chickens ceasing to lay their eggs in
December, Swedes stepping blandly out of tenth floor
windows in the noontime shadows that engulfed them.

Maybe others, their lives lit strongly from within, could
afford to overlook this aspect. Clyde and Elspeth, as children, would invariably choose the darkest corners in
which to read, or absently switch on some souldraining
overhead fluorescent—all the same to them. And Orrin
would mouse around perfecting their light, stressing a
proper respect for their eyesight ("You only get one pair")
while secretly tending their mortal souls.

In Paperman's dark vacant digs, Orrin nudged a few things around and switched on the bedside lamp, just so the room would feel better to him whenever he wandered past the door. And decided against going back out to look for Pigford.

"Marcy's taken a job. With the Watertown School Department."

"Has she really?"

"Special instructor in dance and exercise, that's her title. She'll go around from school to school."

"That's odd. She told me she hated teaching dance. She really did say it with some conviction, Eli."

"Oh I know. She hates teaching serious dancers. But these are just kids, blue collar kids mostly, who have to be charmed into giving it a try. She might take a shine to that. Who knows, maybe it'll turn out to be her mission in life."

Orrin thought of Clyde, called early yet softly to a professorship; of Elspeth, hellbent for rock-and-roll; of Gail, belatedly feeling her way as a freelance editor, rather courageous of her, really.

"You seem a little subdued, Orrin. Something bad happen at the party?"

"One can only hope so, but if it did I missed it."

"I was afraid of that. Marce loved the idea, by the way."

"Oh well, I had a nice quiet evening here."

"Speaking of which, how's tomorrow for company?"

"Marcy?"

"Tia. She wants to see my new dwellingplace. And she also did mention that I owe her thirty-five dinners. So I thought we'd cook up a nice spaghetti."

"Eli, really—I'm not interested."

"Not interested in spaghetti? That's only because you just finished breakfast. Trust me, O'Summers, your appetite will return."

"I do hope that's not a play on words."

"It'll be fun for you, Orrin, I promise. She's a smart lady and you'll love her Alabama drawl. I could add that she is sexy, but I won't. Though that means I can't titillate you with detailed descriptions of her round firm silken buttocks—"

"Enough, Paperman. I can only take so much suppression of descriptive detail. The point is I am denying my sexuality. This has been decided after careful consideration of the subject in dreamwork. What is she, though, Swedish? An Alabama Swede?"

"Not Swedish, just a Dorothea who got shortened along the way. But Tia aside, Orrin, speaking generally—don't you think it's time for you to step out a little?"

"I can't tell you how reassuring it is that you see such a potential in me. It isn't easy, you know, starting life over."

"Uh-oh. I knew it wasn't just Gail."

"Well of course. What's the point, you see, at fifty-eight, really fifty-nine. It's hardly an age for getting a new life."

"Wow, I hope you don't get any middle-aged customers in your headshop! Orrin, even the Mean American Male will live to the age of seventy-one."

"You have told me all about him, Eli."

"That's thirteen years, man. And your health is perfectly good, you could easily have *thirty* years. But take the thirteen just as a figure."

"Thirteen, yes."

"Say you were twenty and someone proposes to you, Hey I can slide you right on up to thirty-three, no problem. Or you were thirty and he offers to scoot you ahead to forty-three."

"So much math!"

"Orrin, I want a better answer than that."

"You *lawyer.* Look, my dear friend, all time is not the same. Some years must weigh differently in the scheme of a psycho-biography."

"Right. And this could be the best of times for you, not the worst. Think of the freedom you have. The financial security. The knowledge."

"Oh balls."

"Don't say balls, it doesn't become a man of your years."

Orrin's eyes shot up, but he knew he'd been entrapped when he saw the Paperman grin. Caught biting off a protestation of his right to a foulmouthed youthful outlook, he could hardly go ahead with the plaint of age.

What the hell, all he really wished to do was deny his sexuality, and even a young man could do that. A young priest would have to do it, and priests were not insane. (Though actually, Orrin had seen Bamford's paper arguing the reverse—that priests were ipso facto whacko—and had found it surprisingly credible, for Bamford.)

"The point is you aren't starting life over at fifty-whatever. You are, though divorced from this particular woman, *continuing* your life. Come on, O'Summers, you must have said this to lots of people."

"Must I have?"

"It comes down to this: I owe the lady thirty-five dinners and I have to pay one of them back tomorrow night. So you get to eat my famous spaghetti for free, if you'll just agree to do a little of the shopping."

"Paperman, you wear an opponent down."

Paperman was indeed a mighty engine. What he lacked was a transmission. One required a number of forward gears to propel oneself through life, not to mention the invaluable reverse and good old *neutral,* readiest of them all. But Eli could not idle, or roll slowly forward as the emotions sorted themselves out. No place for neurosis in his automotive metaphor. Like Goose Gossage in '78, he had just the one speed.

13

After the introductions, Orrin went back to the kitchen, where he was simmering the sauce according to Eli's detailed notes—two sheets of yellow legal paper! Offset behind the crockpot, Jack-and-Liz were furtively burning on the little nine-inch TV, a trick he picked up from Gail.

Annoyed at simply missing the news, or stealing glances at it in harried fragments, Gail had finally resolved upon a tiny countertop TV for the kitchen, and had announced her resolve so stridently that Orrin was moved to bring one home for her the very next afternoon. He knew it was Gail's nature never to act on such needs, never to get around to it.

This time she fooled him, arriving an hour afterwards with the exact same set—indeed from the same store and on the same credit card. They laughed about this, and left it hanging as to which of them would return a set for credit. Jokingly Orrin suggested they keep both and when the bill arrived contend it was an obvious mistake (charged twice for the same item!) and insist the matter be straightened out at once.

But Orrin was busy and Gail, he later decided, was clinging to her own purchase as some sort of symbolic act. As a result they kept both sets, and this too was symbolic, for soon enough their existence broke in two and the little televisions parted like puppies pulled from the warmth of the litter.

"Let me take over here, Orrin—Mother Paperman's

Special Sauce after all. I should at least stir it once or twice. It smells wonderful."

Orrin leaned forward for a whiff, so he could zap Jack-and-Liz on the sly. He missed what Eli was saying—fennel?—as from the corner of his eye he watched Jack's unsuspecting face bend out of shape, then shrink down to an intense dot of white light and go to green.

"So!" he said, forced out to the living room, where Tia sat, a brownhaired woman in a tasteful white wool dress. But that was all he said.

Orrin did not *feel* perverse ever, it was just that sometimes he *was* perverse, and for a few agonizing seconds now he could only smooth the antimacassar and swirl the ice in his drink. Then, luckily, a nervous pretty smile spread across Tia's features and both of them felt the weight had lifted.

"I love your place," she said. "Though how you can bear to live with Eli Paperman is beyond my feeble powers of reasoning."

"Oh he's probably easier to put up with than I am. I can't cook and I'm a sprawler. My projects end up in all the good spots and his are forced into dusty corners—such as his room."

"I heard that," called Mother Paperman from the kitchen. "I demand a reduction on next month's rent, under the dust clause."

"Really, Eli is a delight, even with all his manic demented activities."

"I heard that!"

Tia poured them more wine. Here was a woman of middle age—a mother, an attorney, somebody's ex-wife—yet Orrin could not help classifying her as a "date", whether his or Eli's, and therefore an uncaged phenom to be fed and weighed.

"My son Mickey is very fond of Eli—wanted me to take him in. Eli threw a football to him one afternoon years ago and became, chemically somehow, a surrogate daddy right on the spot. Though I suppose I'm going out on a limb using such terminology in your presence—"

Orrin waved it away, but could not resist a brief perverse silence. This much you learned: when people spoke with a shrink, they were ever mindful of the fact.

"So why didn't you?"

"Take him in? Why because he's impossible, of course. One minute he's right there organizing the tiniest detail of your life for you—against your will, generally—and the next thing you know he has vanished from your sight for months, like a merchant marine."

"That does seem to be his pattern."

"Anyhow, he's too young for me. I am forty-four going on fifty and that boy is thirty-something going on twenty-something."

Orrin was ready to place his bet. He was neither omniscient nor clairvoyant, could not read green tea-leaves, promote the constellations, or look into a man's eyes and lay all past sins at his feet. But he had this one wired. These two had slept together years ago, two or three times at most, and because neither one had fallen hard they chose to drop it rather than involve the son under false pretenses. And now they had something rare and fine, a friendship, like brother and sister yet cleansed of the Freudian shrapnel.

They sat to dinner and the conversation flowed smoothly, though perhaps the wine did too. Tia seemed to lapse from polish, eating ravenously amid a flurry of excuses for her appetite. "It's just so delicious!" she said, as though resolving her own bafflement as to why she kept hammering down the sausage.

Orrin guessed she was tipsy, and he knew that his own kindness toward her had been inconsistent. Nonetheless he found her gluttony slightly offputting, and something in her posture now, pitched forward toward the sauce-boat, gave him alarm. For a second he was sure she would suddenly bring it all back home. Then a more charitable rush overtook him.

Tia helped here by returning from a washup transformed, with shining naked face and brown hair tousled. Humming to herself with the absentmindedness of the mentally incarcerated, she was now altogether lovely. Of course Orrin had also taken a mellowing dose, and may have been rounding up. Certainly he had compromised his own wine with very little of Paperman's hyperactive pasta, or the small bitter salad.

"Did I mention that Tia is a criminal lawyer?"

"No more so than most, surely? But you enjoy defending the innocent?"

"I'm afraid very few of my boys are innocent." For a few beats, Tia seemed to be tabulating them in her mind. "Hardly *any.*"

"You say my boys. You like them personally?"

"I do, often. I would probably have to pay you millions to find out *why* I do."

"True, my dear, except that it doesn't matter why, so long as you are happy with yourself. And that pearl comes absolutely free of charge—though the spaghetti will be nine ninety-five plus tax and tip."

As she laughed, merry eyes and flyaway hair, Orrin discovered that he had come to feel altogether uncritical regarding Tia Adams. By now Eli's phrase about her silken buttocks hung in his mind, as she shifted those very resources over the sofa cushions. He had to stifle an urge to brush one light wisp of hair from her brow. And the idea that she should travel home unaccompanied on the Red Line (as she insisted she could and would) was unthinkable to the outmoded gentleman in him.

"You will allow me, as a courtesy, to walk you to the train, at least. Call it a compromise, between your principles and mine."

"I won't for one second *allow* it," she laughed, but I will graciously accept your offer, Orrin. It will be a pleasure to walk out with you."

With her plantation-days drawl, Tia might have been satirizing his manners or merely enjoying his company; Orrin did not know which. Under the gaslights and the rivet-rattling signs on Charles Street, he was tempted to take her arm. To do so seemed only appropriate, but he resisted the temptation and she did not (as he imagined her doing) slide her own arm inside the crook of his. Indeed, she charged down a sidewalk every bit as briskly as her partner Paperman—possibly a barristerial affliction?

"Well, here we are, Dorothea."

"Oh. He told you. He isn't supposed to tell people."

"My parents did the same thing to me. My father's name was John and he always hated the plainness of it. So he came up with Jessica, Barnaby, and Geoffrey for us. Geoffrey Orrin Summers, that's me. Two 'f's' and a 'g' in the Geoffrey."

"A distinguished moniker."

"I tried to shake it in college. Left high school as Orry and resurfaced freshman year as Jeff. Jeff Summers. But it wasn't me. I never responded to it, you know."

"What's in a name."

"Whatever you say. Dorothea."

All this went on and still he did not take her arm, wrestling inwardly against his own like Doctor Strangelove. Everything about Tia seemed to inspire uncertainty in him, but uncertainty seemed to mean inaction. They shook hands—yet another ambiguous moment, faces poised—and then her train was clattering out of the shed onto the Longfellow Bridge, over the river. He watched it wind past the masonry pepperpots.

Not ready to head straight back home, Orrin turned in the direction of the Esplanade. He was glad he'd kept his head. He had fallen, but not too far, for the incarnate silk of her skin, for the soft colors nestled in the planes of her face. The sky was webbed with brittle frost, and icy slivers of wind lanced through his chest, yet Orrin felt free and safe—for the moment safe. And though it had been close with him, safety right now was more important to him than sex.

Where the delta widened at the Esplanade, the gusting wind seemed to skim a coat of ice onto the gold-lit river in one sweeping pass, then dust it over with powdery snow before veering wildly across the open plain. Orrin had reached the band-shell and climbed the granite step. Inside the curving confines of the denuded shell, the wind grew quickly hysterical.

Orrin had a brief playful fantasy of assuming the conductor's pose, gazing out over the summer evening concert-goers, but he could not physically manage it, as the wind buffeted him back. This was a little scary. He tried to sing and then to yell louder than the wind, but it was no contest; under an acoustical avalanche, Orrin no longer felt playful.

He jumped down and landed running, impressed to near panic by the power of the night. You could stay out a moment too long and be damaged, even killed, by moving air! And he had stayed too long already: breath very short and toes so numb he was stumbling inland toward the Back Bay. When at last he gained the shelter of narrow streets, he fell gratefully into the first public house he saw, a place called Tom & Viv's, with asparagus ferns in the window and blessed greenhouse warmth inside.

"Do you by any chance serve hot coffee?" he asked, managing to push the words past numb lips to a young lady in red vest over black shirt behind the bar.

"No sir we don't," she said, in the singsong voice of the phone company robot.

"Good. I'll have a double whiskey, neat, please. Bushmills?"

"We do have that."

He could barely hold onto the first glass that she brought him, but matters steadily improved to the point where he was tossing them down quite nimbly. And before his twenty was exhausted, Orrin heard himself loudly insisting the heat be turned down and a laughing woman two stools west was offering him ice cubes *au paume*. An evening of extremes, certainly.

But had that pretty girl in the red vest really asked him to leave? Doubtful. Or immaterial, as he was ready now for the wending homeward and was happily wending, if betrayed once or twice by his sense of direction. Floating upstreet, feeling fine under the stars, craving those warm heavy covers.

Finding himself on Marlborough, however, not half a block from Gail, was a coincidence too great to overlook. Indeed it would be downright rude to be this close by and not at least say hello. So he picked his way along the wrought iron to Number 232 and was about to press her bell.

Then he thought better of it. This was a first visit, coming somewhat late at night, and of course unexpected as well. Rather than jar her nerves with a sudden buzz, might it not be wiser to venture round to the fire escape, ascend, and tap gently on her glass? In the undertow of a wave of sentiment, Orrin stood ready to show any consideration, large or small.

He rose like an angel ascending, weightlessly, feet barely skimming the iron treads. Dizzy from the aggregate height of many stairs and landings (and from the aggregate hooch as well), winding past granite lintels till he all but lost count, Orrin finally stopped to catch his breath. Above the blooming stalks of brightness that lined the alley like sentinels, under winter skies that spread an umbrella of soft light, Orrin inhaled a deep peace.

Gail looked peaceful too, perfectly still beneath a thick

blue comforter just like the one they had shared so long—
the one he used still. Oddly, she had twisted some gadget-
ry into her hair, but Orrin knew better than to complain.
Strictly her business. She did something similar once before and he had asked her to stop, after he dreamed recur-
ringly of leeches slapping onto her skull. Oh she was bitter
that time! His *dreams,* she raged, could not take precedence
over her *reality.*

He had always loved her best in sleep—no, not best, but
most easily. Never saw her asleep without experiencing his
love keenly, just as it was with the children. Perhaps they
loved him too, when he lay dreaming. Perhaps they would
love him to distraction, love him endlessly, in death. So
little *conflict* among the deceased . . .

But Orrin was not considering a dramatic death. In fact
a quick glance at the ground made him grip the rail firmly
with both hands. Then a perfectly appalling sight nearly
blew him loose. Gail's blue comforter had lifted, like an
angry tide, and swinging his legs off the far side of the bed
was a large jaundiced hairy man. The back of his neck lay
in folds, like a stack of doughnuts, and his shoulders had
sprouted clumps of black hair like epaulettes. And this
man stood, as casual as Caesar rising from his throne, and
wandered out to a dimly lit plum-carpeted hallway.

It was too much to expect a man to bear this silently
(*unhealthy* for that matter to do so) yet Orrin tapped at first
with the greatest respect and delicacy. That was the point
after all, to arrive as gently as possible. But it did make
sense to have this out with Gail alone, before the ape man
returned. "Gail," he whispered, tapping more insistently,
with his house key. "Gail!"

When finally she stirred and turned a baffled squint to
the manic rattling of the two sash against the flimsy lock
that joined them, Orrin had a second shock. Her face was
grotesque, sadly altered, like a nightmare Disney witch,
the mouth set in an angry sneer, eyes narrowed in powerful

caricature of soured womanhood. Not at all like Gail, not at *all,* and indeed—he finally realized—not her in fact. Who *was* this woman, and how had she gained entrance to Gail's rooms? "You're not my wife!" he roared through the glass.

Yet through his genuine rage and confusion, Orrin began to feel a seeping relief that Gail had not been sleeping with the ape man after all. It now appeared a mistake had been made, and regardless of who had made it, the correct response was flight. Orrin fled, riding gravity down while resisting only its extremes, until near the bottom all coordination departed his limbs and he clattered down the last flight loosely, in almost a free fall. He snatched at the flowing spokes to slow this terrible momentum, but the balusters proved much too quick for him.

Though he hurt literally all over, Orrin found the strength to run again, for a police siren came rising like the wail of an animal and sent one clean stroke of terror to his racing battered heart. So quickly, though. What a wonderfully responsive police force, he couldn't help thinking with considerable civic pride, as he ran from them raggedly.

He flagged, sagging against a brick garden wall, as the sirens grew fainter. The trouble was elsewhere, apparently, nothing to do with Gail or the ape man. And as the sound drained away, Orrin thought about the scene that must be playing itself out upstairs. The woman shrieking, the ape man gallumphing in, glancing round and assuring her it was just a nightmare; if sensitive or clearheaded, recalling for her some recent experience that might have triggered the dream; and she resisting his version until at last he held her, fetched her hot milk with sugar and vanilla, and the face in the window began to seem unreal after all. . . .

On Commonwealth, in the smoky shimmering frost, Orrin hailed a cab and rode home. He crashed onto the bed like a bag of sand. Talk about hitting the wall! Even as a

youth, he had never run as he had run tonight; in the past
decade he'd scarcely run a step. Four in the morning, good
to be home.

He slept fitfully, in half-hour patches, and the oddest
dream kept intruding through a dark rainy morning.
Clyde and Elspeth, side by side in twin beds like his and
Barney's, the ones with wild west decals on the headboard.
They looked like furious munchkins, Clyde and El, faces
squashed with anger as each pounded away on a mound of
vanilla ice cream—a huge mound the size of a heavy
punching bag—whaling away with chafed fists. Their
blows would flatten the stuff, shaping it this way and that
like dough.

A bolt of sunlight, the eery luminous kind that has just
burned through a dark cloudbank, came in the bay, striking a page on the dining table. It made the words on this
unsigned mysteriogram seem a directive from God himself:

DENIAL DENIED?
AFFIRMATION AFFIRMED?
LIFE DOES GO ON?

It was not from God, of course, but from Paperman.
Pressing his case, as always, and floating out to sea on a raft
of false assumptions. Orrin had to smile. At least Eli had
washed the pots before going off and yes, in his infinite
wisdom, had left a shot of black coffee in the red pot upon
the white stove, for his room-mate.

14

Life did go on, and Orrin knew perfectly well that to deny one's sexuality was a serious business. Yet he had lived so long without one (a sexuality, that is), he could still underestimate it in the abstract. Had it remained abstract, there might have been no problem. But something had triggered him—a confluence of events, really—and left him in a state of sexual longing.

In the days following Eli's dinner party, Orrin suffered spells of harsh jealousy over Gail and her hirsute companion in the blue bed. Alice Harris looked up one morning to find him in a trance of fury, grinding his jaws. "Doctor?" she had interrupted herself to say, and Orrin swabbed on a thin smile over the inner murderous indexes. "Sorry, Alice. Gas bubbles, you know. Please go on."

Certainly she went on, for how could *gas* bubbles faze a true-life sufferer like Alice. But the gas was real, as were the injuries to knee, wrist, and kidney he had sustained on the fire escape at Gail's.

In calm hours he could excuse her behavior. A free woman, after all, residing in a free country. He was not fool enough, however, to excuse it solely on the grounds that it had been someone else in the ape man's boudoir. That would be naive, inasmuch as he had simply never found the right window. Hold her blameless because she cavorted beyond his range of vision? When she might well have a lover of her own, whether hirsute or smooth? At least Orrin was tactful and did not mention his suspicions to her phone answering device.

But it wasn't only Gail. There was Tia Adams—alternately seductive and repulsive to him, and wasn't *that* transparent to a scholar of the mind! Tia whom he had weighed so parsimoniously, turning her over in his palm like a stone of questionable worth. He had sat in smug judgment of this pleasant pretty woman, and who was he to do such a thing? A damned sight older than she was, and every bit as desperate and alone. And perhaps she wasn't desperate at all—that was just an impression, or even less, an assumption. What about her judgments on him? How did he look under unkind light?

Weighed and found wanting, yet in this curious lustridden aftermath, Orrin found himself wanting her, instead. He was jealous of her strength, jealous of Eli's confidences, jealous even of the implicit ex-husband with whom there were apt to be the shameless brief reunions taken on the wing. Jealous and more. He summoned up the unseen silken mounds of her bottom scuttling and resettling on his corduroy cushions and went on to imagine them in the privacy of her home, bared casually to the bedding, to the sunlit windowpanes—such treasure he had spurned.

Embittering too was the feeling he might have missed his chance. He somehow expected more from Tia, or from Eli on her behalf. Expected further opportunities to deny his sexuality here. (She would supplicate while he stood firm; Eli would jest while he dissembled.) To deny his sexuality in the void, against the brief and now clearly withdrawn possibility of *not* denying it, seemed especially disheartening. "The rejector experiences the feeling of rejection," he noted for cross-reference, but with little balm.

He could even daydream of young Marcy Green. Eli, with his commitment to staying uncommitted, was in effect taking advantage of Marcy. That charming young lady, thought Orrin, it could be *me* taking advantage of her instead! Such notions, carnal thoughts of Marcy, he recognized as smoke on the wind, yet he had them and so had in due course to note them, for he was denying his sexuality, not his rationality as well.

These women were suddenly vivid flesh to him, at times obscenely so, as they spun through his restless mind like temptation's wheel of fortune, now one now another and soon enough almost anyone. Women on the street, or the sweet sisterly Sarah at her desk, the deserving Bensonhurst, her calves surpassing shapely one afternoon in youthful blue tights and oxblood strollers. He experienced such a polymorphous temptress that he was forced to conclude he was horny, and that denying his sexuality at this time was a business *so* serious as to be worthy of reconsideration. Perhaps he should call Tia Adams after all—but for a *date?*

Eli was no help in the crisis. He simply wasn't there. Orrin even tried finding him at work, only to be treated to the absurd cover story, "Mr. Paperman is out of town for the week." Maybe so, if he and Marcy had ambled up to Ipswich for a bucket of clams, or slid out to Stockbridge for some cross-country skiing at cozy inns. No way would he, Orrin G. Summers, leave complex personal messages such as had formed on his tongue in the face of so canny an evasion as that.

Left to his own devices at a time when he really did need company (needed Eli's company specifically, for at The Club this sort of thing bore no discussion), Orrin indulged in a fantasy of exclusion where Eli and Marcy were pointedly avoiding him, taking refuge in youthful embraces, in laughter and handholding in the sheltered booths of small snug restaurants, not to mention the hours of intimate post-coital converse. Out of town!

Frankly Orrin was feeling a little loosely wrapped all week. He could attribute this in part to the mean climate of March, when a cold damp wind careened through Boston like an unpleasant child sustaining his tantrum for weeks. Whatever had made him unstable, though, Orrin knew that he was, and knew that this was a time for laying low. On the message pad above his desk, he had writ large NO CALLS TO FAMILY and just below it DO NOT HAS-SLE THEO.

A period of assessment, then, and maybe best to tone down the vocals at work too, lest in babbling he loose some thunderbolt of indiscretion upon Harris or the new one, Sinclair-Fugard from Cape Town. A white South African who had married a black South African and then fled to academic shelter in America (they both taught the philosophy of language, whatever that was), she couldn't stand her husband yet lived in desperate fear that he or anyone else should come to know it, and conclude it had a racial basis. So she was pitted squarely, hysterically, against herself.

Orrin always felt a twinge of guilt in billing out Cat Therapy as they called it; for dropping into a state of professional catatonia while one's patient flailed in confusion. Fortunately this one, Sinclair-Fugard, could benefit best from Cat, just bailing out bilge-water. In any event it was the only safe course for Orrin. GO CAT WITH THESE, he told his message pad to tell himself, until this crazy wind coursing through me dies down.

"Three hundred dollars a day just to turn the lights on!" Orrin had fulminated at a client once, in a time of similar unreliability. And the client, a very young man who shot rats in his Belmont cellar where according to the best researches there were none, had stood up and shrugged, "Hell, turn 'em out, then," and had never come back to conclude his treatment.

It seemed to be passing over. Certainly it was fine most of every day. There was one public occasion, however, which Orrin could not avoid: Air Force Two (opening for Warts & All) at The Rat.

For some reason he had pictured Elspeth and her band in astronaut gear, floating on a gravity-free platform as they clutched their flyaway guitars and drums. But the space programmers had just blown up The Lady in Space, a New England schoolteacher along for the ride. They blew her up over the Florida sea, actually, nowhere close to outer space, and for days it was all anyone could talk about. They showed the contraption explode time and again, in slow motion and stop-action, and they badgered little kids across America to venture forth and give expression to their pain.

Every station hired its own shrink to come on the air and explain America's emotions. Orrin, who had accepted such gigs in the past, the King and Kennedy assassinations, wondered privately if anyone knew where the emotions would go, now that TV was bringing us real violence as well as the unreal. How did lines get drawn? Most commentators were saying TV brought the disaster closer, made it immediate for the millions, an instant transcontinental trauma. Orrin suspected the reverse, that we were distanced from it, and from ourselves; from everything. That increasingly the national trauma was numbness, passivity. Certainly it was his own.

In any event he was forced to imagine a whole new look for Elspeth, and put her in a baggy double-breasted suit, doubled over a gleaming saxophone and wailing. (This image he drew from a new *People* magazine in his own waiting-room, a photo of another young lady who had been assailed by the blues in her suburban bedroom.) What he really needed was a look for himself, a disguise, as he would never plan to disport himself cognito at The Rat.

True, she might not even recognize him. She had not looked at him, *seen* him, in years. But there remained the chance that something in the features, or the manner, could trip an antediluvian trail of association leading back to him, and Orrin was not willing to risk it. Very dead set against a scene of any kind (steady-all-boats was still the prescription), he went to work in earnest.

The wig was almost enough. It snapped onto his skull in such a way that neither its own vile rubbery shell nor Orrin's barbered gray hair showed a trace. Instantly red-headed, newborn to a wild youthful exuberance, he looked in the mirror like Dylan Thomas coming through the carwash. What could he add? A cigarette, loose on the lip; dark glasses with the wraparound L.A. look; a seersucker jacket one size too small.

Given the late hour of this special occasion, and the unfamiliar locus, it seemed to call for the dulling of certain senses, consonant with the enlivening of others, a tricky job which Orrin trusted to Bushmills of County Cork, who surely had the expertise. There had been similar compromises earlier in the week, but the difference here was justification, and justification sped the benign essence through the system circulataire. Orrin could feel the flow inside him, could almost see it sailing along his bends and freshets like a sunny amber trout stream.

Flow gently sweet Afton/ Flow gently swee-eet Afton/ Flow GENTLY—and here he rose to full height, as he knotted his muffler and flowed down the staircase to the mirror-&-marble foyer. At the corner of Charles, he angled himself into a standing taxi. When the driver smiled and said, "What is this?", Orrin's confidence in the espionage aspect sagged briefly, but the river swept him gently round that small jut of rocky soil, like a piece of paper caught and then spun free, and he replied with charming unconcern, "Maid's night out." In a trice they were off for Kenmore Square.

Orrin once had a client who owned a gorilla suit. A sweet shy fellow who harbored within his bosom a vast exuberance for life that he rarely expressed, for fear of attracting notice. Inside that suit, however, the man could really cut loose. Dancing in the stands at football games, boldly approaching women in the street (with admittedly mixed results), working happily with groups of children. Orrin's getup tonight was just as all-concealing as a gorilla suit, and provided the same kind of shelter. It was like watching through one-way glass in a clinical observation room; the next best thing to being invisible. Totally unselfconscious, he filtered inside the club and down the curving stair to the cellar, mingling among the couples and clusters of young people. The place was lousy with pipes—half the plumbing in Boston routed through this Rat, miles of copper and cast-iron plus some outsized ductwork that alligators might easily negotiate—and thick with cigarette smoke and very dark, though garish lighting would flare up, flicker and bobble in irregular sequence.

Zap! it would spotlight a babyblue drummerboy, then Zoom! it would switch to a hot pink lady with a headdress of green feathers. Peacock? All the while the sound was mountainous, a squadron of planes strafing the room, but no one seemed to mind it, or even hear it. Orrin kept looking up, waiting to be engulfed, but all he saw was pipes.

He exchanged smiles with the lugubrious bartender, a tall young man with the posture of a discarded pipe cleaner, then turned his attention to a remarkable couple. They never spoke a word to one another yet clearly had a complete understanding, even though they seemed to belong in different magazines. The boy, swaying to the loud fast music as though it were a Chopin waltz, wore legtight jeans with torn pockets, and black boots with chromium buckles. Chains and bracelets on his arms and ankles, an earring with a long green tuft, and a simple discreet gold ring in his nose.

His hair-do looked a day's work easily, for on top it was shock electric, a comic-book Harold who has glimpsed a ghost, while down the back it fell in a queue, braided and beribboned like a turn-of-the-century Chinaman. And what made the effect so striking was the girl, swaying against him to the same secret rhythm, but totally without affect. Skirt and heels, understated co-ed makeup, dark hair brushed up neatly into two tortoise-shell combs. They did everything as a perfect duet, leaning together in their private dance, sipping beer from a single long-neck, even smoking on the same cigarette. It was the most concentrated display of oral activity Orrin had ever witnessed—until they went him one better with the single wad of chewing gum.

Then lightning struck the room—once, twice—and a crash of percussion occasioned deeper baths of blue illumination. For a moment all heads turned toward the band, who moved from this raucous transition into a blues number so soft and melodic that people actually listened for a minute. It was the lady with the feathers still, but she could sing, and in black spandex tights even seemed a little fetching. Orrin speculated that if she kept on peeling away layers of the rock-and-roll joke like a stripper, she might be quite something in the end. Might well provide another chance to confront and deny his sexuality, for the spandex really was a touch.

Then at last he woke to it. He had been killing time, waiting to see Elspeth, and he had nearly missed her clean. Right there on the drum he saw it, Air Force Two, but the blues had concluded and the band was unplugging, packing it in. Already the stage lights were down, as he searched for her and saw only thin boys snapping out jacks, reeling in wire, folding up cases. The girl in the headdress was Elspeth, he had seen her and he had not; had heard her without taking note. Shortchanged on this opportunity he had been hoarding up for weeks, Orrin charged past startled faces toward the dressing room door.

Then stopped. The bar was forty feet long and so was the mirror above it. Somewhere around the thirty-fifth

foot, he caught a glimmer of himself (warts and all) and hit
the brakes. This was not low profile; it would not do. He
wanted desperately to keep to the sane—to keep the joke a
little funny. He must not wreck Elspeth's evening, not to
mention his own teetering life. Orrin leaned on the bar,
softly humming a broadcast test signal until he felt composed. The bottles caught his eye, with just their necks
reflected, and brought him back toward the tangible. Must
be cool.

He could no more connect the character Elspie was
playing with the sweet daughter he knew and loved than
he could connect his own mirror image with himself. Too
many bridges to cross. It was getting hot inside the rubber
wig, but he would stay cool now. I'm cool, he told himself.
Be cool. Time to go, Daddy-O. Talking to himself, yes,
but just to set an inner rhythm.

Crossing Mass Ave., he started to sing a ditty his father
had always sung in the car—"Oblivion the gem *of* the
ocean!" This was the old man's running joke (it took a
hundred forms), with the mythical town of Oblivion,
Ohio always at the core. Sometimes in high spirits, the
whole family would try it together in shape-note har-
mony—"Oblivion the gem *of* the ocean!"—and John Summers would smile and shake his head with wonderful
meaningless irony and say, Oh yes, Oblivion was definitely the place to be.

III

The End Of The Thread

Volition, cognition, and perception were
like a tangled skein. One noticed this only
when one tried to find the end of the
thread.

—MUSIL

15

Orrin sat home in a bleak state of mind on the day after his fifty-ninth birthday. We think of our lives (most of us do) as being ahead of us—about to happen—even when we are not so very young. But there must come a moment, a sequence of years that breaks down toward an extended moment, in which this ceases to be true. Orrin wondered if that time had come for him.

He had been thinking of friends, and decided to make a list of his ten closest, to see where they all stood at this juncture. He could think of only seven, and three of them were dead. A fourth, Charlie Burns, was wheezing badly.

Fifty-nine years old! It was the ninth year of a decade that contained its end. People made much of turning thirty, forty, fifty. In truth the damage was done at twenty-nine, thirty-nine, forty-nine. The ninth was the killer year, the tenth was already the start of a new run. Orrin was as good as sixty.

He had no conviction that his life lay ahead of him. Even Eli's straw man, The Mean American Male, could look forward now to a mere dozen years of life—one brisk childhood!—and there remained the possibility always that one had less than an hour, less than ten minutes. Having recently pondered the state of mind of children on their birthdays, Orrin found the subject of older folk much less a conundrum.

Now Eli was back. He had been away so long this time that Orrin had ceased to expect him, but he burst in, dropped his briefcase and haversack on the sofa with a dusty splash, and clapped Orrin on the shoulder.

"How are you? Did you get my card?"

"Card? No. I don't think so. But it's nice to see you, Eli."

Paperman, spur of the moment fellow, appeared to have travelled. And Orrin was glad to see him, though he did not manage to display such pleasure as he bespoke. Mired so low in his chair that he might have been entombed there, his slow voice seemed to come from six feet under. In his birthday gloom, Orrin had pre-deceased himself!

Eli saw at once there was a problem, evidence of a binge lay all about the room. But what had been going on? Had Tia taken him up only to drop him so soon?

"O'Summers, you know I am no reformer, but I do see quite a few empties around the house."

"Oh don't worry, they *were* full."

"I'm sure they were. Did you manage this impressive project on your own?"

"So many bottles! I see what you mean."

Orrin seemed to come back from the dead, and to take note of the accumulated glassware as though for the first time. Despite the weight of gathering years, he was roused to life by the younger man's presence. Yet he was peeved with Eli too, with his absences and his insufferable vitality, and wrestled with this conflict not unlike a neglected lover.

"Looks to be an average of about one a day," said Eli.

"And it's all my fault. It wouldn't look that way at *all,* if not for me. I feel personally responsible."

Eli just kept shooting him the grin. He saw no sign of current drinking, no fresh glass at hand. The last thing he needed was a hassle, having overdosed on planes, trains, and taxicabs—even on work. He had strolled home from Government Center rather than take another change for Charles, grateful for the soft wind and peaceful evening light.

"Do we suppose I threw a party?" said Orrin, and his continuing disingenuousness briefly overcame Eli's craving for quiet.

"Too many bottles, O'Summers. It reeks in here."

"*Now* you are reforming. Open some windows if you like. Here, I'll open one for you."

"Sorry sorry. I didn't mean to sound moralistic—"

Maybe there had been a card—news from some coast or other. Orrin now wanted to believe in the missing postcard, one from *Minsk* for a change, full of good cheer.

"No, Eli, *I'm* sorry. Please excuse my state if you can, it's all too simple-headed. You see I have aged in your absence—a birthday, you know—and barely one-third of my immediate family thought to call and sing. Besides which, I didn't even *want* to age.

"So all this cheer was a birthday celebration?" said Eli, scooping loose bottles into a paper sack.

"Call it that, yes. I have been drowning in self-pity for the sheer glory of it. And know what else? I'd like a drink right now."

"Well at least it is the right time of day. We could both have one."

"Let's," said Orrin. He had thrown a test at Eli, a pop quiz, and Eli, perceiving it as such, had passed. To Orrin it meant his young friend cared after all.

"Well here's to you," said Eli, "To the birthday boy, skoal and banzai."

"Done."

"I hate birthdays too. I hate any holiday, actually. Any quirk in the calendar. Give me a good old Wednesday or Thursday anytime."

"To new legislation, then, calling for all days hence to be designated good old Wednesday or Thursday. And on the second day he rested, God bless his weary bones."

"The two-day week, skoal and banzai."

They knocked back in unison, then Orrin in bitter careless levity flung his glass at the mantelpiece in the grand manner. It didn't even break—nothing on the fastball! But his smile couldn't stay, and now he felt a deepborn sob jamming his gullet.

"What can a man say?"

"No need to say anything, Orrin. No big deal."

"But purpose, Eli, what's the bloody *purpose*. When your wife is gone, your kids are of course gone . . . and your work is what? A big sandbox. A shadow-box to play in, where you never produce anything concrete. All the breathing that goes on, and analyses of bloody analyses, my God what's to *show* for it. At sixty! Nothing. Bloody nada. Nujitsu. Zilchma."

"You make a life. You build a self."

Eli emitted this pearl with a nice conviction and may have even believed it. Hardly sentimental, he was a sincere man. Yet at the same time he was thinking; all this because the ex-wife neglected to wish him a Happy Birthday? And the rock-and-roll daughter?

"A pisspoor job I made of it, in that case. Face it—I've been facing it—there *is* no purpose. Even a pimpled adolescent can tell you as much."

"Leaving the complexion of things completely out of it, Doctor, I make a point of not going to adolescents for my slant on life."

"Rebut, then."

"All right. For the defense, then. Do you remember the film you saw, about an Austrian army man? Colonel Redl?"

"Redl, yes. Proceed, with the reedle of life."

"There's one scene where Redl is very depressed, disillusioned with all the political maneuvering, and his woman—blue-eyed beauty, wise and strong?—comes to him at the window and says, Forget it, it doesn't count, any of it. It only matters that we are alive. Do you remember the scene?"

"Actually I slept through a lot of that Redl film."

"Well that's it. That's the rebuttal. It *all* matters. Drop a stone in the water and you realize the splash matters."

"A splash? That's what she said, the blue-eyed beauty?"

"More or less, Orrin."

"Damn. And I come to such knowledge late in life."

But Orrin was grinning too, by now. And when Eli said the Defense would rest, Orrin said the Prosecution could use a little rest himself, and thanked Paperman for having made him feel better-already.

Which he did. Distracted and soothed. When the children were small, he used to walk them along Rock Creek and play countless games of Poohsticks off the old king-post bridge. And it was true, to a child the splash did indeed matter, very much. The literal visible splash and the different-shaped sticks spinning below the bridge on uneven curling currents.

It mattered whose stick came out first to the sunlight too, mattered tremendously. Redl's woman was right—the things that mattered were everywhere, for everyone. Only you had to feel it that way, or it wasn't so.

It was like old times next morning at The Paramount. Two newspapers, two coffees, two orders of the Hessian Eggs. And Eli restless, eager as always to begin the day's battles—this time an evidentiary hearing with the local school board that had failed a fourth time to hire a black headmaster in a predominantly black school.

"What I can never figure," said Orrin, smacking the paper with the backs of his fingers, "is whether there are two Stanley Ellins and one Stanley Elkin, or the other way around. Or are there two of each? And why the hell don't some of them change their name to Kluszewski, if you see what I mean."

"I've heard of Kluszewski."

"It's going to take me another shot of coffee to get to the bottom of this one, Paperman. Yourself?"

"No thanks, I've had enough. I've got to get moving in a minute. But maybe we can crack this Elkins case over dinner."

"You're on for the evening meal?"

"Absolutely. Though I might bring Marce, if she's bitter about last night."

"What happened, Eli? I thought you didn't see her last night?"

"Well that's what happened, of course. I didn't see her."

"Ah. But yes, bring her. You needn't ask, you know—it is your home too."

"Thanks, Orrin."

"Speaking of home, did you see your family last week?"

"I did. I even spoke with them though we were forced to converse in their language. I figure it's like getting by in Mexico with a small vocabulary—you're okay if all you want is coffee in the morning, beer in the afternoon, and tequila at night."

"You're too hard on them. I trust you are not so hard in their presence."

"No, there's nothing to be lost or gained at this point. It's odd, when you think about it—that parents and their children can be so different. And I suppose you probably do think about it."

"Not really," said Orrin, wondering briefly what ever became of Gail's "lost gain" on the old house. "What I have considered is how the tie that binds doesn't—doesn't bind, you know. Differences never surprise me, but I would think the common experiences, and the blood tie, would be worth something. I told you I saw her sing? At The Rat?"

"You didn't. I assume you mean your daughter. But listen, O'Summers, you and I are not speaking the same tongue either, it seems. First you tell me I never mentioned I'd be gone, and now you say you did mention this—"

"I'm never quite sure, you know. I mean to tell you something or other, but then you're off for a spell. It gets said out loud in my head and stops there. Let's agree the problem is mine—in a haze of alcohol and so forth."

"Too many bottles," Eli grinned. "So how did you find out?"

"About the band? Clyde told me at my grandson's birthday party. The group calls itself the Air Force, the idea being—"

"Air Force Two! I know their stuff. I mean, they have a disc out, Doctor, that's a very hot band. What an idiot I am. Your daughter is Elspeth Summers. Unbelievable. You have to introduce me."

"I'd love to, if someone will introduce *me* first."

"Orrin, she's *good*. She's a hot ticket, your little girl."

"I'm not sure I can think of her quite that way," said Orrin, which was so—though it had not been so last Friday night, in her spandex masquerade. (As for that, intimations of Electra, Orrin was hardly concerned: to him it was only close-up magic, the disappearing coin, the cap and ball.) "I'm not sure I can allow you to think of her that way, either, Eli. A hot ticket? Elspeth was very thin as a child, you know. Sweet and very skinny, with a wide gaptooth grin."

"Later. I'll want all the details, ancient and modern. After which I will marry her and call you Dad. What do you say to *that,* O'Summers. But look here, this has to be one of the wildest. MAN CRUSHED BY QUARTERS. Read it and weep, it's sad but true, page twenty-two."

"I don't know, Eli. It may make a funny headline, but the poor fellow is really dead, you know. And look, he has a family."

"I know, it's a terrible weakness of mine, headlines. But you'll have to cure me later, I've got to sprint now."

He sprinkled six or seven dollar bills onto the counter and flew into his parka. Before Orrin could do anything about the money, Eli was on his way, and though he had made a point to say he would be home for dinner, it would not have surprised Orrin to see him next a fortnight hence. He would bustle in, brimming over with cases and causes and half-told tales, and say he was back from the Gold Coast of Africa—certainly he had mentioned the trip, and hadn't he sent the air-letters from Yaoundé?

The man was a whirlwind, even unto himself Orrin suspected, and could no more be pinned down or accounted for than any other gust of air. No matter. Now that a new decade was under way for him, Orrin felt up to life again. How fitting it should begin with such a glorious heart-lifting day as this, warm air from the Georgia Sea Islands combining with dry air down from Hudson Bay. The park grounds were swarming with optimistic spring birds, flickering brown sparrows, huge zooming blue-jays—even the hideous twitching pigeons looked slim and sprightly in this Warm Dry Air. Yes; everything mattered.

Recently he had read a paper on the shock of waking. The slowed-down sleeping heart was not at all ready for harsh alarm bells or the ingestive jolt of coffee, much less a program of vigorous "setting-up" exercises. Best to pamper the heart until it was up to speed, to flatter it with a leisurely aristocratic start.

It made sense. Orrin had flattered his heart this morning, and now it responded with a clean steady beat that carried him to Beacon Street in perfect tune. Why doubt it would carry him into the future, as it had carried him unfailingly in the past? In the silvery plate-glass going in, he saw a dapper almost handsome man and it did not surprise him to learn that the man was Orrin G. Summers. He almost expected as much.

16

It was just as lovely strolling home that evening, Warm Dry Air now cooled by cottony sea-breezes. Orrin stopped by the lagoon to hear a girl in tattered antique dress sing "The Wild Mountain Thyme" in a haunting soaring voice. Enchanted and benevolent, he floated a fiver into her guitar-case before moving along. There was none of the usual fatigue as he hit the stairs at Filbert Street. He opened his own door as though unclasping a box of delights: faded light on the cherry table, rich aromas wafting from the kitchen, Paperman singing soul ballads in the shower.

So Eli made it. In fact he had been in production for some time; a stunning disarray of pots bespoke his high seriousness. It was Orrin's understanding that the best chef made the biggest mess. When Julia Child cooked on television she cut a swath like Sherman marching to the sea, and he always imagined an army of small men tidying up furiously in her wake. When *he* cooked, there was no detritus at all. Orrin heated food, primarily, at least that was his forte, whereas now the counter was littered with choppings—onions and cheese, red and green peppers, carrots and tomatoes—and the saucepans were thickly stacked, the spice-jars all uncorked. Mother Paperman's Hyperactive Chili!

When the chef himself appeared, Orrin was rinsing a Boston lettuce in the colander; he would contribute a nice salad to the feast. "Fine," said Eli, "but no need to rush.

This business needs to simmer another half-hour. By the way, I hope you *like* chili?"

"Well, Mother Paperman's *Special* Chili. . . ."

"Nothing too special. Chili's one of those things. You toss in the good fresh stuff and keep it bubbling. It's a can't miss, really."

"You say. And I say it smells—" Orrin paused, waiting for the appropriate conceit to present itself.

"—good enough to eat," supplied Eli, when the silence felt adequately elongated and no poesie appeared en route. "Orrin, I want to thank you for calling me out this morning—on that disaster with the armored-car driver."

"The Man Crushed By Quarters?"

"Yes. I spoke with his wife."

"You did what?"

"I got hold of the man's widow. I figured the least I could do was make certain the family was well fixed, so I did some looking into."

"Impossible," said Orrin, unable to forge a link between the squib in this morning's *Globe* and the movements of actual persons, such as Eli Paperman, and the coin widow.

"Five K, all in quarters, from vending machines. Needless to say, it should never have happened. All he did was hit the brakes. They will have to come through very large on this one for the family."

"Gee, I hope they don't pay up in quarters, it could prove traumatic."

"Hey, come on. You get to me on this and now you want to be making the jokes?"

"Not at all, Eli. I'm impressed—astonished, really—by the reach of your conscience and by your abilities. Who would conceive of such direct action?"

"Are you kidding? Plenty of my legal brethren conceived of it muy pronto—for a third of say two million buckaroos? There was a quotation on the desk of my favorite law professor: 'The law is a profession where much that is odious can be done without disgrace.' It's sad but true."

"But you got her ear."

"I did. By offering to oversee the settlement for no fee at all."

"Now what kind of a con artist is *that*." Orrin poked, but he did not wish to poke any more testy areas. He had instantly forgotten The Man Crushed By Quarters and had gone on down to the office to take six hundred quarters each from two unhappy women before lunch, and the same again from Sinclair-Fugard at two. Placing no limits on his self-indulgence, he had gone from there to The Club to read a few articles and sit by a birch-log fire with two sadistic young neurosurgeons, who were bitching about fees in the thousands per diem while Eli was out there doing good at his own expense.

Ted Neff had once had a conscience (in Orrin's version, May had simply confiscated it) and often said he still would if he had the time. What about Eli? What would he be up to in twenty years: good works, still, or golf on Mondays and Wednesdays? Did a good man slide inevitably toward mediocrity, his will and best energies eroded by all the quotidian setbacks and pleasures? By what Orrin's own profession (where also much that was odious could be done without disgrace) called "reality".

They had finished their meal and were cleaning up when Marcy arrived. Orrin offered to crisp up the salad, and hot up the bread, but Marcy declined all save a can of beer. Had this girl taken Bud in a can with her previous beaux? Could she be a typical mere chameleon? To Orrin, it seemed unlikely. She was attractive in a refined way (even laboring within the slight affectation of green corduroy overalls, she was) and had a charming sense of humor, deprecating and self-deprecating. When he passed along Eli's witticism about the lawyers, Marcy was ready with one of her own almost as good:

" 'The business of a solicitor is to conceal crime'. Oscar Wilde."

"We'd better make a list of these," said Orrin.

"Don't mind me," said Eli.

"You shouldn't feel badly," said Marcy. "Voltaire's rule of thumb was that all people use words mainly to conceal their true thoughts. Not only lawyers, Eli."

"I feel much better now, Marce. And it's all thanks to Voltaire's thumb."

But Voltaire! Some girl, thought Orrin Summers. This is not your average chickadeedee. Now her eyes were alight with merriment when Eli, in all seriousness, stated an intention to read more of the classic writers.

"Eli's reading habits are the most remarkable thing about him, I think. The way he *devours* things. He's sort of a benign monster. You know what he means when he talks about reading a book in one sitting?"

Orrin did not. Eli was shaking his head as Orrin, with a sly grin and a palm, gave her the floor in continuation.

"It means he goes to the john, takes a seat, and *reads*. A minute later you hear the flush and he's ready to read something else."

"A benign monster. I do like that, Eli."

Orrin was treading past a slight discomfort with Marcy's frank toilet talk. Plus it somehow had not occurred to him that she and Eli were room-mates too, more so in fact than he and Eli. He eased to the stereo and plucked Mendelssohn's Violin Concerto from the rack, and was monitoring the drop when he heard the telephone.

And here he realized something else for the first time. As rarely as it rang, the phone was never for Eli. Did he take his personal calls at Marcy's? Had he been doing so for long? Meanwhile he excused himself to take this one in the bedroom.

"Hello?"

"Dad, is it you?"

"Is it me? Well yes it is, whoever I am. This cannot be my daughter Elspeth?"

"Yeah, hi."

"Hello. Hello hello."

"Hi. I was talking to old Clydesdale and he said you were having trouble getting hold of me, so—I called! He said you came to hear us at The Rat, but I assume that's a gag."

"Oh no, I did hear. Or at least I did come. There were so many obstacles to hearing, you know."

"That's not the reputation, exactly."

"The volume was excellent, I didn't mean that. Or yes. But a very interesting experience. Very."

"Didn't like us, huh? Can't say I blame you. We were far from being sharp. Deado, in fact. That was consensus."

"Well I thought it was good. I wanted to hear the words, though, and I just couldn't catch many."

"Words can be tough."

"Yes. I thought so."

Orrin was dazed. Astounded. That she had called and that they were talking. Awkwardly, to be sure, gropingly—yet almost casually too, as though they talked together all the time. As though they were old friends, with familiar tones and timbres, easing past all intervening wounds and the measureless gaps in time.

"In a club gig," she was saying, "you don't really get lyrics as such. I mean, you aren't there for that, there."

"I'm sure you're right."

"What was it, though, did you want to analyze me from the lyrics—like, do an exegesis?"

"No, Elspie, nothing like that. Nothing to do with Jesus. I just wanted to hear what you were doing. I was

your father, you know, and took a kindly interest in your
progress. Remember?"

"Yes, Dad," she said, with the same weary irony that
had crept into her voice around fourteen.

"You would show me your science projects and I would
marvel at the achievement, and you would be simulta-
neously pleased and detached. More like that, what I had
in mind."

"Like, catch up on my work."

"Yes, exactly. And I thought, Who knows, maybe I'll
find I like it."

"No way, Dad. You don't like loud. No one did in that
house. Even old Clydesdale was forever upon my case
about the radio. This would be, like, prior to the onset of
walkman technology, of course.

"I'm sure you're right about the technology. But you
shouldn't assume I didn't care for it. I really might have. It
was hard to know. I was coping with a whole environment
too—that Rat, I mean."

"Not a place for the faint of heart. Anyway, Clyde said
you were trying to get me, so I thought I'd call."

"I can't express how glad I am that you did. But tell me
how things are with you. Maybe we should get together
for a bite to eat?"

"Now?"

Elspeth sounded truly alarmed at such a radical immi-
nence. "If you like. Or anytime. Whenever it suits your
schedule."

"Tell you what, Dad. Why don't I—when we get back—
see, we are going out on the road for a few weeks, starting
soon, and we are having to rehearse very heavily just now.
But when we get back, I get back to you and we make a
definite plan, to eat a bite."

Orrin could respond neither honestly nor with dishonest
assent to this transparent scrambling evasion. Slammed by
it, at a loss to mitigate or alter it, he stood listening to his

own breath in the receiver. What an extraordinary relationship, he thought: and how sad, for me. For her sake he
searched after any trite phrase of farewell, to let her off the
hook if that was what she needed, and yet when the power
of speech did return to him, he spoke with a gentle di-
rectness,

"El, doesn't it make you feel sad to be so far off, from
your mother and me? It's so unnecessary—" He faltered,
close to sobbing, and to the boundary of pure wordless
emotion. "—so unnecessary, you know. We really love
you, you know, and I miss you so very much."

Was she crying too at the other end, or was it only more
of his own distress echoing in the receiver? Once again the
absurdity of a life conducted over the phone! Was it symbolic of the age, that this was as close as he could get?

"Got to run, Dad," she finally spoke into the blooming
silence. Orrin knew he had blown it, had left her nowhere
to stand. What was she supposed to say—Oh yes, I miss
you too? Elspeth? Never. Nor could she hardline it and just
punch his ticket: hard cheese, old chap, good riddance to
bad rubbish. What *could* she do but cut and run?

"But I will be getting back to you as soon as we come off
this tour."

"To eat the bite," he said. In a pig's valise, he thought.
He was wearing the expression sometimes termed a shit-
eating grin.

"Yeah. Or maybe a few bites. Whatever, right? We'll get
together. And meanwhile take care, okay?"

Gone. As pleasantly impersonal as a cashier at the
Seven-Eleven: have a good day. Remarkable.

He sat a moment longer with the dead line, then stood
and wandered toward the bedroom door. He would wait
himself out, allowing the blood and air to make their way
around a few times, making sure the brain had cleared
itself for takeoff. Eli and Marcy had moved together on the
sofa and were talking energetically at close quarters, words

Orrin could not make out. The Mendelssohn had just concluded for in heightened sensitivity he could hear the gentle deceleration of the turntable to stasis, louder to his ear than the two ebullient voices.

Coming back now—reawakened to the world by his curiosity about their talk and by a fine needle of thirst in his throat which might require immediate attention. It was not his desire to make any mention of the call, except that Paperman put a finger right on it, unerringly: "Orrin, my man, you look like you just saw a ghost."

"More likely heard one," corrected Marcy, and while they quibbled good-naturedly about the specific gravity of clichéd phrasing, Orrin was quietly decanting a Fudd to the post-orbital torus and slapping it down.

"I did," he said.

"Gail?"

"No. Her daughter. My daughter."

"How nice. Unless there's some kind of difficulty?"

"No. No difficulty. She called to say hello—and not much else. God knows why tonight."

He did not even detect himself at topping up the glass, the call of this thirst being quite subterranean, like the functioning of unseen reliable glands.

"Marce, I have never properly introduced you to my room-mate here. You see he is Dr. Orrin G. Summers, as advertised, but he is also secretly the father of Elspeth Summers."

"You don't say. But who is Elspeth Summers?"

"The rock chanteuse. You must have heard Air Force Two?"

"Not to my knowledge. Can I congratulate you anyway?"

"On having a daughter, or on having a rock star in the family?"

"On getting a phone call!" said Paperman.

"Daughters are a world unto themselves. You, Marcy Green, are a daughter."

"Yes I are."

"But whose? If I may ask."

"My father's. Whoops—he got me, Eli. My mother's too. But I can stop being silly if you really want to know. My mother lives in New York and designs advertising layouts. My father lives in Connecticut and is a judge, believe it or not."

"You like him?"

"I love him."

"Because he is your father."

"I suppose that's where it all began. He is a very nice man, very considerate."

"He and your mother split, yet you find him considerate and you love him."

"Sure. But why do you assume that he left her?"

"I don't. Did he?"

"No. But you're probably right. I love him simply because he's my father. What the hell, I'm sure I wouldn't love him if he *weren't* my father."

"Yes, I agree, it's all pretty silly. I was just using available materials for a little spurious research."

The conversation drifted to other subjects and Orrin conducted it pellucidly despite the systematic dispatch of multiple Fudds. Something so deeply sobering had occurred that he might have diluted his blood by half and still glided through on cruise control. He was surprised when they suddenly got up to go—it had all been so pleasant, why cut it short? But he hid his disappointment beautifully, and took a hearty line as the night absorbed them: "Drop me a card from Yaoundé."

Such graciousness may have been necessary pretense and yet why not "improve the occasion" by getting on to the desk, tinkering together some of his notes on luck, or on habit. Though the theme of luck (along with its philosophical subtext) was more current, the topic of habit had become almost a habit with him, a fallback, ever since the time of his thesis. His conclusion then (that a habit was "essentially a self-indulgence which tripped stimuli to create a comfortable state of mind") seemed even at the time imbecilic, or sufficiently transparent as to require no formal statement. Yet he continued to get mileage out of that paper almost thirty years later.

He tuned the gooseneck, adjusted the swivel chair, shuffled and spread the note-cards, and then went quite blank. He had inadvertently absorbed enough hooch to stun a horse after all, and by now the rising tide of whiskey was going to erode the shores of intellectual ferment. Orrin rushed some strong French coffee into production and added it to the mix—too little too late.

The delayed effects were suddenly dramatic. He could see his hands fumble with a sheaf of papers but had to watch them helplessly, as though they were hands in a movie, shown closeup. He was leaning forward when his head cracked like a gunshot on the desk and for a time, maybe a minute, he just left it there, wondering why it felt wet.

When he finally touched his forehead, he found cooling coffee—or was there a trace of blood as well? Starting to the mirror to make sure, he hooked the jutting chairbase and went sprawling. Comedy, he thought, but not funny. Notes on Comedy? Notes on Notes and fuck-all-notes, he thought, and pushed himself on to a viewing of the coffee pompadour. The only blood was in his eyes, laced with the fine lines of a fury that focussed not on the problems of comedy, or scholarship, or drink, but on Eli.

Hadn't Eli tricked him? Conned him? Making such a big point about home for dinner only to outbail by eight, to be abed with Marcy's nice nice body by goddamn *nine*, leaving the old boy here to swim in the old black coffee sexual misery? Was that an evening at home or was it an eight o'clock date, con man? Conned him, and conned Marcy, and conned the bereaved widow of The Man Crushed By Quarters too, even if not to apparent advantage still a con job . . .

But this was unfair. This was ungenerous—a bad impulse—and possibly it was untrue. Orrin struggled desperately to clear his mind, to claw his way back to reality; he dearly wished to hold the line. Eli had met him halfway—by what right expect more? Why shouldn't the lad wish to be alone with Marcy Green, for goodness' sake? Unfair! the verdict; surely Judge Green the father would concur in Connecticut.

It was not Eli's fault that Orrin's powers of concentration had slipped, that his best ideas took such light hold of him. Not Eli's fault that Elspeth had called, that the call had upset him, that as a result he was currently sloggo. It was the call that had thrown him off his balance, and only because it was so unexpected. Seen in an objective light, the call was a good thing surely, it was progress of a sort.

Orrin was *doing* it, somehow he was holding the line. He got his teeth brushed, got himself into some fresh pajamas, and tuned in Jack-and-Liz, clinging to these icons of normalcy. He was sure Jack-and-Liz wore fresh pajamas every single night, and why not? Whatever they were paid, they were earning their money this time. He had never enjoyed them so much. Often buoyant, Liz was positively lit up tonight, looking forward perhaps to lobster and white wine after the broadcast, with a new romantic prospect? Yes, food and romance had lit up her evening, which in turn had forced Jack into that sly spectatorial role he did so well . . .

No, life was never easy, the smooth sailing was never forever. But balance was everything, control was the key, and Orrin Summers was determined to go to bed happy if it killed him.

17

Through days of slush and narrow morning sun, the season moved to spring. The calendar was a deceptive mode, though, for Boston was still a long way from lilac and apple-blossom time. After a few stanzas of deep blue sky, soft gray ice would again gush from above, and the cumulative blackened snows melted slowly, to reveal archaeological layers of swill and dog-droppings. (Dostoevsky once wrote of "the humiliating destiny of a potato"—what might he have done with the Gainesburgers of late November?)

So it was not the uplifting springtime of the Lake District poets, but Orrin took its best shots. He was trying on a new self-definition: he was now a survivor. The status went beyond simple breathing, though. You took the shots and you also kept probing to land a few of your own. He had given up on nothing—not Gail, not Elspeth, nor all the good work he had planned. It would all come to hand somehow.

He took steps toward survival. He retired Elmer Fudd, stowed him away on the topmost shelf behind the glass doors of the dining-room hutch, beyond reach, to shine forth as an emblem of his resolve. Of course some nights were longer than others and then the old patterns might have him briefly in thrall. But when he fell that way, he fell now with full awareness, and with the qualified optimism of the survivor. He might check the News or visit the nippery during work breaks, to take up the neck more from restlessness than from any debilitating thirst. This he likened to any small indulgence (salted nuts, thin mints) where you decide to have *one* yet inevitably drift back until the serving-dish is bare. Even a survivor was *human*.

If it happened to be a fine night (and there were many such, by one definition or another) he could stroll Charles Street and pick up a fresh bottle at McAllister's, in case company turned up unexpectedly. Then, refreshed by night air and a happy browse in the book shop, his limbs pleasingly sore from trudging over messy humps of half-baked snow, he might store a drop in his coffee cup as he worked—but keeping careful tabs, maintaining control, for there remained the possibility you could be nickel-and-dimed to death if you did not stay quite serious about your drinking.

Later on, before bed, it hardly mattered if you took a short one. It was almost medicinal, good for promoting sleep and for softening any annoyance at the Weatherbaby, under whose regime Orrin still bristled. Pacing back and forth past idiotic mockups of the winds in Wyoming and the rains of Ranchipur, the fellow seemed obsessed with upscale hobbies like flying and skiing. Fine *flying* weather? For goodness' sake, how many people were waiting to hear *that?*

And the skiing seemed such a sop to the puffy parka set, such a slam to the pale gray poor. Orrin imagined the poor, huddled in front of their endlessly repossessed consoles, taking in this jolly elf on the subject of base and powder, and was gripped by such moral revulsion as could best be eased by a short one.

He worried about Jack, who had been looking pallid and lumpy of late, big sagging circles under his eyes. Jack was so clearly a good egg—what would become of him if they took away his job reading the News? It depressed Orrin to think Jack might be forced to go into sales. He would switch over to see how Chet was looking on Channel Five and find him pallid and lumpy too, inside his banker's suit.

But Chet had always looked pallid and lumpy, it almost became him . . .

So it went. Slipping and sliding through to midnight, taking in too much bright light, doing his level best at sleep, often waking less than spry. But Orrin was fifty-nine, perhaps there was not so much spryness to be had. There were plenty of good mornings, certainly, but they only led him to believe that health departed in just that fashion, good days and bad days rather than all at once.

Nothing terrible, just a difficult passage, and the control was always there. If Sarah looked a bit concerned (at his appearance or his tardiness, he could never tell which) Orrin was quick to reassure her: "Oh no, I'm feeling very well, my dear. Fine flying weather over the next few days I hear."

He even planned a trip. Orrin rarely enjoyed travelling and he did not necessarily plan to *enjoy* it now. But to *do* it seemed right and timely; a week in the Great Elsewhere might very well do him the mythical wonders. So he settled on the idea of flying to the west coast of Mexico with Eli.

The case for going with Paperman was simple. He hated travelling alone, and he could not reach Gail on the phone, much less sign her to double occupancy. Eli would never lavish money on a frilly tropical vacation, yet he surely could use one, and deserved it. So Orrin offered to treat, and was more surprised than he ought to have been when Eli politely declined. Looking back over a fortnight in which Eli had averaged two Filbert hours per day on Orrin's new and absolutely reliable Papermeter, he might have guessed the younger man's priorities lay elsewhere.

Nevertheless, he went ahead and passed an hour at Crimson Travel with a pleasant southern girl, plotting daytrips out of Cancun and canvassing all the best places to stay. It was remarkable to Orrin that this girl could and unbegrudgingly would place a dozen calls to Mexico on his behalf. An absolute *genius* with the telephone, she could dial anyone anywhere and get through on the first ring. Watching her brilliant fingers at work, Orrin was tempted to ask if she would mind ringing Gail for him; it seemed it really might do the trick.

In the end he was forced to cancel. He was hardly about to pay the single rates (twice as high as the per person double occupancy!) and he could not supply the second occupant. It was one thing to fund a friend, quite another to piss away the money on unmunched salads or unindented beds. Orrin didn't really mind. As dull as his days and nights were, he was the happy willing slave of inertia. Beyond the obvious (that Gail might call in at any time) home was worth something to a man of fifty-nine years. Just to travel to the travel agency had been a little unsettling, sufficient adventure.

So he continued to tour only locally, in and out the small alleys and warrens of the neighborhood, like Lime Street, and Beaver Place. Lime Street, a nice address but *dank* ("Oh the sun never shines/ on Liii-iii-ime Street," he composed and sang), and Beaver Place, site of a small women's college ("I for one do not think a women's college should *locate* here," he commented in passing to no one in particular), and Whitefish Lane, where the Mayflower rats kept their townhouses.

Meantime, he had found it useful to redefine Eli too, or to hearken back to an earlier definition where his roommate was purely a boon. It was futile to ask of Eli more than he could give, and surely it was counterproductive to resent him, as had happened once or twice by chance. Moreover, it was unfair placing all the burden on Eli if it was social occasions Orrin sought. This was the reasoning which lay behind his decision to join Eli and Marcy at the Brattle Theatre in Cambridge late on a wet afternoon.

Carried practically door to door by the Red Line, Orrin ate his popcorn while Bogey smoked his Camels, then bumped into them outside, under the awning on Brattle Street. He offered a round of beers, and they all hustled through a silver slanting rain to the Wursthaus. There they drank not one beer but several, and laughed together for more than an hour.

They had filtered out into a now needling dark mist when he did make the one mistake. They were heading off and Orrin did try to detain them, suggesting they continue the party "back home" but also employing the delicate physicality of a lightly grasped sleeve.

"The doctor has just one question," he said, grabbing on. "Why does the lawyer never entertain the teacher at home?"

Cutting Orrin some slack, Eli gracefully transformed the indiscretion into a brief manly embrace and said,

"Partly so we don't impose on you, Orrin. Or vice-versa, I suppose. But we know you do work there at night."

"Sure, but it's your home too. I don't want you to think otherwise."

"No problem," said Eli.

In Boston, the expression 'no problem' had no meaning; it was for dead air, a filler. But it gave them a note to close. Eli and Marcy were welcome at Filbert Street whenever they chose to be there, and in the meanwhile they were guarding Orrin's privacy. Perhaps sensing that this was not quite enough, Marcy stepped forward and kissed Orrin on the cheek.

"Thanks for the beers. We had fun," she said.

"You're entirely welcome," he replied, and sensing the value of a clean clear exit, this time he made one.

But it was early still, and they hadn't eaten anything. Rather than forage far and wide, Orrin simply walked back inside the Wursthaus and ordered a corned beef sand-

wich at the bar, with one last glass of beer to rinse it down.
The place was filling up with its mixed clientele—couples,
groups of students, an occasional representative of the old
Harvard Square gentility—and Orrin cast an eye about the
room for familiar faces. Then he had an idea.

In the telephone cubicle, he looked down through the
Adamses, found no Tias or Dorotheas, but saw a D. on
Kinnaird Street and guessed it was the number he wanted.
Pushed in his quarter and carelessly dialled, without a trace
of nerves. Then heard a boy's voice. Mickey, was it?

"Hello. I'd like to speak with your mother, if I may."

"She's out."

"Oh, I see. Out on a date?"

"Who is this?"

"Just a friend—"

"Any message?"

"No, no thank you. I'll just—ah—try again, why don't
I? Tomorrow."

The child could tell as well as he could, Orrin felt, that
he would not very likely try again tomorrow.

He had to be careful, for pushing too hard did push Eli
away. It had done so the day of the Bogart film, just as it
had in relation to the Mexican excursion. Likewise he
discerned a trace of same at a now rare Paramount breakfast, when he offered to accompany Eli to the courthouse.
Another round of the political trial, charges of unlawful
trespass against the demonstrators at Brace Chemical this
time, and Orrin had an auspicious cancellation from Sinclair-Fugard, his hyphenated lady. Yet he was easy when
Eli balked. Not to press.

"But you will have to solve the problem for me. What is
the distinction between lawful trespass and unlawful trespass? In the eyes of the law-full?"

"A good question. Reminds me of all the references in

the basketball rulebook to something called a 'made basket'. Obviously it's either made, and therefore a basket, or
missed, and therefore not one at all. No?"

"I guess that sometimes language wants so badly to be
emphatic that it turns to redundancy for its effects."

"We'll have to start another list, won't we?"

Though Eli sometimes seemed a little distant now, he
never made any reference to Orrin's unpalatable lapse that
night in Cambridge. He had imagined Eli expressing his
annoyance, though, and had even gone so far as to imagine
Marcy's intercession, as they lay tranquil on her bed later
that night: "Oh Orrin was a little high and feeling lone-
some, why blame him for *expressing* it?"

Why indeed, and no one had. Getting away with things
was easy enough on the surface, not only because there
was always apology, but also because the bourgeoisie felt a
desperate aversion to social discomfort of any kind. Two
dozen indiscretions slid by, surely, for any one that was
called to account. But that was on the surface.

With Eli these days he felt almost on trial, somewhat like
a lover who senses that perfect balance shifting. At times it
seemed he had nothing to offer Eli except lodging, and
Marcy Green was providing rather a soft safety net on that
front. It was Marcy, in fact, who tended Orrin's needs
more than Eli now, by arranging an occasional threesome.

Not only did she include him, she flirted with him,
more or less. In the puerile mock debates he and Eli staged
for fun, she generally sided with Orrin. They might be
arguing the merits of day-old bread, or pornography as
free speech, or pure bred dogs versus the mutt. Whichever,
Marcy was apt to press her delicate blade of ridicule against
the Papermaniac position, and at such times she seemed to
edge closer to Orrin physically, often making a point to
rest her hand briefly on his forearm as she spoke. Was it his
cynical satanic imagination, or were these her instinctive
means of keeping Eli a little greedy for her, of bringing
him back to the mark?

In any event it was kind of her to include him, and Eli didn't seem to mind. He and Orrin had always had their best fun bantering, and levelled only the best-natured satire at one another. There were skirmishes, inevitably, for whether or not he was a reformer, Eli did seem to expect some kind of fealty to his decrees. Once or twice Orrin heard the iron in his voice (drained of any pretense at humor) on the subject of bottles.

No child at fifty-nine, sipping for simple relaxation within the walls of his own home, Orrin could sally back with a little iron of his own. One night he rolled an empty across his room-mate's threshold into the darkness beyond. This was *wrong,* he realized, yet no more so than Eli's presumption. The other side of the same coin, in fact.

Eli won this particular round by having the good sense never to mention the bottle at all, thereby magnifying the offense while at the same time reducing its perpetrator in size.

On the first day of April, Orrin left a whimsical proposition ("Come live with me and be my love") on Gail's whoosis. When she did not call back, he left a short sequel the next morning: "April Fool".

He was quietly in combat with her, a wrestle for dominion that was the less satisfying for her abstention. It was not so different in his relations with Eli, come to think of it. To an extent, Orrin could not avoid the adversarial aspects of dealing with affection at close range, nor could he lure his intimates as close to him as he was to them, quite. The best construction he could put on it was this: I try to be good to people and sometimes I fail. But maybe the same was true of them, in regard to him; maybe it was the essence of two versus the essence of one in a nutshell.

In the midmorning dark of April the fifth, Orrin endured a terrifying dream of suffocation, in which he felt a great weight pressing on his heart. Coronary, for sure!—

but it wasn't that. Bolts of firewood were raining down on him, hefty chunks of maple and ash like the ones his father kept stacked on the brick hearth at Grand Avenue. Several had already crashed against his rib-cage and now they were falling so thick and fast they obscured the sky. His bones, his whole skeleton sagged under the burden and was surely about to snap, dumping the wood onto soft aching organs.

Orrin woke shaking with horror, and came back slowly, after ducking his head under the kitchen spigot. Soon after, though, came understanding and compassion—for Eli Paperman and for The Man Crushed By Quarters. For that was the basis of course, and the dream did bring the poor wretch a continent closer. There were people on the surface of earth who had an inkling what that man had gone through—not just death, but the widening horror, the microquick flash of consequence as one foresaw the bereaved survivors, all the unfinished labors, and faced the stunning realization that death was more than possible, it was *now*.

Sweating in the darkness of his expensive bedroom, Orrin had become one of those who understood, not so much as a victim himself (MAN CRUSHED BY LIFE) but as one magically infused, viscerally linked to the rest of mankind. Paperman had this capacity, born with it apparently. He knew what it was to be poor, though he never had been. Knew what it was to be persecuted and felt a calling to address such instances personally.

Really Eli was more like a minister than a lawyer (Paperman's Hyperactive Conscience!) and like a minister might sometimes overlook the individual for mankind in the round. His concerns, as keenly felt as the weight of wood or the crush of coins, might necessarily preclude a few of the mundane bourgeois emotions. He could very well lack the capacity for an exclusive love and still remain an admirably affectionate man.

When Orrin posited that there were "two sides" to Eli

Paperman, he did not intend the usual dichotomy. He meant that there was Eli's side and there was Orrin's side. Eli would say "Enjoy your morning" (as he inhaled a blueberry muffin and bolted for Cambridge on his bike) and to Orrin it seemed the hollowest throwaway phrase. Yet Eli may have meant it quite literally: I hope things go well for you in the next few hours. . . .

Thus at his worst Orrin might find Eli cavalier, and confide to Marcy, "That lad of yours may rot in Limbo, if he don't do worse." But in brighter *concerned* moments he could tell her what a lucky girl she was, and mean it absolutely.

18

On the tenth day of April Orrin walked off to a late matinée, and walked back home in an unusually thoughtful state. Letting himself into the flat, he was distracted momentarily by the portrait of Paperman, casually reading on the couch. The apparition was so bizarre and unexpected that he thought at first it was a wax-work, some sort of a put-on.

Which it was, for Eli ostentatiously brandished a copy of *Finnegans Wake* and was simply awaiting Orrin's comment. It was not the practical joke that made Orrin smile, however, but the image it called up, of Eli speed-reading on the pot.

"A way a lone a lost a loved a long," said Orrin.

"Come again?"

"I guess you won't have reached the end yet. I was just quoting from your light reading there. And it's old and old it's sad and old it's sad and weary—"

"God, that's impressive! You've got it word for word."

"I've always had a faculty for remembering great poetry."

"Is that what this is? Marcy says it's a novel in the form of a dream."

"It's certainly not a legal brief, anyway. But Eli, if you don't mind, I need a minute or two in the study. Will you be around?"

"I was thinking dinner at The Bayou. Definite case of cajun fever tonight—blackened redfish and a bucket of beer?"

"Fine. I believe in obeying a whim. But I do need a little time."

Paperman could hardly overlook a pronounced sobriety in Orrin, not the literal absence of alcohol indicators but an oddly sombre bearing that he had not seen before. He could never have guessed the cause of it was a Hollywood movie, nor could he guess that Orrin had already begun to discuss this movie with him, aloud and gesticulating on the spongy greensward of the Common like some Hyde Park hobo blaring the Good News from within his narrow locked destiny.

It was a simple and utterly fabulous story about a tough Philadelphia cop thrown together with a lovely Amish widow. You knew there would be cultural conflict and you knew there would be sexual attraction. You liked the woman at once, slightly salty and ironic inside her cultural strait-jacket; you liked the cop better with time, as did the grudging Amish people.

The cop turns out to be a skilled carpenter. He goes about repairing bird-houses, fashioning elaborate wooden toys, and lending an expert hand at the community barn-raising. As a cop he appals the Amish; as a woodworker he wins their admiring nods and glances, becomes in effect one of them. Shameless Hollywood formula (the carpenter-hero rising on the heavy timber frame might as well be Errol Flynn clambering up the sails and rigging in *Captain Blood*) yet it works its way with the audience, Orrin included.

In fact it is a revelation to Orrin, fusing through him like fire racing down a roll of loose newsprint. The bare ability to do practical things that every country boy could once do—pound home a peg, trim off a tenon!—makes this man heroic. In our time of pushbutton everything, of dustbuffing professionalism, a hero is the man who can *do* something. Hollywood was clearly onto this. They had that awful Rocky boxer (even *that* worked) and they had the black man who knew all about cotton farming and saved Sally Field's mortgage . . . But it was no joke. However manipulative, it was not mere manipulation. It was felt.

We *are* the Hollow Men, Orrin thought, shivering at his desk, we truly are. Elspeth doesn't hate me, Gail probably doesn't hate me either, they just don't know I'm *there*. I don't exist anymore. And the clients, the lovely fundfilled clients, I could be the bloody wall and they would dole out their treasure to wail at it, just so long as the wall was listed at a good address downtown.

Was this the sort of epiphany that came unto suicides? This kind of terrible insight, so strong and obvious? Orrin Summers had known despair in many forms, but here was a different order of emotion, here was emotional *knowledge*. And what, at this point, could one do? Go out and start hoeing potatoes? How would he advise a client? Badly, was all he could think.

Paperman's voice jarred him from brown study. Collapsed on his elbows, eyes barely open, Orrin had risen to a slightly ethereal state in which the physical realities of the room (a voice, the light) seemed foreign. It had been ten minutes.

"Sorry to disturb you, Orrin. Should I tell him to call back?"

"No, that's fine, Eli. Thank you."

Orrin took the call, listless at his desk. He had missed hearing the ring somehow, and was immediately at sea with his caller.

"Report? What report? I'm afraid you have the advantage of me, sir."

"The information, Doctor Summers, that you requested."

"But I requested none. I am sure this is an honest mistake, Mr. ——?"

"Bemis."

"Yes. Mr. Bemis. But I am not the Summers you want."

"Then what are you doing answering his telephone? What's our little game here?"

"I regret this—truly I do. You say I asked you for some information?"

"That's correct. Information concerning your daughter, a Miss Elspeth Summers, address unknown. Information which I have gathered in this report."

"Now, Bemis, it occurs to me that this may all be a practical joke on my room-mate's part. Did you, that is, were you engaged by a tall young man with a full head of thick brown hair?"

"No sir, by a man of slightly better than average height, lean build, in his fifties I would say, with wavy gray hair neatly barbered."

"My God, man, where? Where did you see me?"

"Right here in this office, sir. You came here and you left a large cash deposit with me—though I may be brain-dead to remind you of it. Are you hurting here or is this a game of ours? Maybe you took a blow on the head?"

"To be sure I did, Bemis. But how do we conclude this business? Mail it? Can you mail it to me at my office?"

"You asked me not to, sir, but I can, if you will take care of the bill first. I have that ready also."

Shame had succeeded worthlessness in Orrin's orbit of emotions. He must have done this—hired a private detective to hound Elspie!—and he must have done it in a stupor so opaque as to obliterate all memory of the occasion. When could such a thing have taken place? The man Bemis alluded to the 30th of March but the day stood on his desk calendar as a perfectly ordinary Tuesday, with four regular sessions, no personal or social notations. Mystery.

Right now the thing was to pay the fellow off, incinerate his "information" (without so much as a glance at it), and pretend it never happened. To spy upon one's own seed! Such espionage was insupportable, frankly dishonorable,

and damned expensive into the bargain. This Bemis
wanted hundreds and he'd apparently had hundreds already. Man Crushed By Dollars!

Under siege at his own desk, Orrin suddenly smiled. He
tried to arrest this movement of his face and managed only
to modify the smile, make it crooked. So many odd fragments, though, in the puzzle of life, such messy little
shards of psycho-biography to sort and stack. Doodling
on the corner of his blotter that constituted the Papermeter, or Eli Log (In____Out____), he was suddenly fam-
ished, starving.

Oh crisis was rising on all sides for sure—he could hear
collisions in the air above him, could sniff the smoke of
roiling flames—yet he was desperately hungry and rushed
past Paperman to the pantry. There he ripped salty crackers
from a cellophane packet and plugged them into his mouth
by twos, dry, shaking his head and shrugging in lieu of
words that would be lost in mush.

Paperman naturally wondered what the phone call could
have meant, having seen it transport Orrin from unchara-
teristic gravity to a flat-out goofiness. Yet Orrin testified
that the call was "nothing at all, just some fellow I forgot
I'd ever met, actually", and his lightheadedness and con-
comitant lightness of stride was "chance, purely somatic."
But ordering a glass of *milk* with his redfish? Was that
somatic too?

"Just nod if I guess right," said Eli, settling in comfort-
ably behind a large plate of greens. "Or better yet—tap
once on the table if I'm right, twice if I'm wrong, and three
times if you just won the Lottery."

"It's nothing, Eli. I am unchanged."

"Gail called."

Orrin tapped three times on the table. Eli rolled his eyes.

"You really won't tell, will you."

"Nothing to tell. A man for whom I have no explanation called me on the telephone. And then I was seized

with appetite. That's it. I did see a film—disturbing and
not very good. What else can I tell you? Yesterday I don't
even recall: did it take place or was it rained out?"

"The movie was disturbing, you said."

"Did I say that? Well and it was disturbing—though only
to me I am sure. It was meant to be *fun*. Country folk
building a barn—"

"I've seen more disturbing stuff than that lately."

"—Religious farmers, taking their identity from what
they did each day, you know."

"Aha," said Paperman, organizing his fish onto a fork.
Do I sense an identity crisis here?"

"Well you know I always take these movies too much to
heart. But I'd say no, more like a crisis of self-esteem.
Divorce of men and means. Seligson."

"Never read Seligson," Eli smiled, mimicking the clip-
ped footnoting speech pattern that Orrin fell into sometimes. Orrin did often convey his thoughts in an academic
shorthand, as though making notes, because he reasoned
from situation to idea rather than idea to situation. That,
after all, was Freud's great error.

"No loss. Suffice to say the world is going to hell in a
handbasket, Eli. One psyche after another, tumbling like
autumn leaves."

"Come on. Because we aren't still attached to the *soil,*
this is? Is that what Seligson says? I mean, Orrin, there
isn't enough soil to go around anymore."

"Exactly. And so the world. A wasteland—and we are
the hollow men."

"Please. Those old soiled farmers would have given
every bushel of corn and potatoes for a Whopper-with-
cheese and some cable TV in the evening. They *do,* in fact:
check out Middle America some time."

"Mystery," said Orrin.

He felt no need, no desire to convince Eli of anything,
nor did he feel by now the crisis he was trying to describe.

He was just enjoying the fish and salad, and feeling mildly
surprised that one could have well-being without self-
esteem. But it was simple: add two, take away two, carry
the hyphen.

"What's new with you, Eli? How's Marcy?"

"Fine, she's fine. She tried to get you last night, actually.
We want you to join us for the weekend, if you're interested."

"The weekend?"

"We're going up to Killington to toss a few snowballs
and warm our toes by the fire. It's a dirt-cheap late-season
deal and she thought you might like to get away too. You
could view it as a Mexico-of-the-North."

The program of inclusion had gone too far. Yes, there
might be a slight temptation to travel in pleasant company,
but Eli could hardly want this and even Marcy was just
being a good girl. The threesome was a fifty-fifty proposition at best; gratifying as it unfolded, it generally left him
more keenly aware of his actual status than ever, for by
now Orrin was no longer denying his sexuality on principle, he was simply stuck with denial, as though holding an
outdated bank draft.

"A way a lone a lost a loved," he said.

"Is that a yes? You'll be very close to the soil, O'Summers. Less than two feet of base and powder, I'd guess."

"The thing of it is," said Orrin, not entirely apropos of
what Eli had just said to him, "I don't *do* anything. I do
exist, I suppose, and yet I *simply* exist. I pass the time, as
the French say. So I need someone to not do anything
with—to make the nothing into a little something. Or if it
doesn't, then at least you don't feel so personally that it
isn't. Am I making sense?"

"Not much. Better tell me the name of this flick,
O'Summers, I want to have it banned in Boston."

"It's an absolutely harmless trifle—guns and kisses. I
honestly don't recall the name of it. And I'm fine. But I
don't think I will ski Killington this time around, thanks.

Tell Marcy, and you too my friend, it was very sweet to ask. The truth is I hope to see my wife this weekend."

"Gail did call."

"No, no she didn't. But she always enjoyed The Rites of Spring Dance at The Club and I have hopes she will be joining me for it Saturday."

Hopes he did have, and perhaps Gail really could be enticed. So many nice memories, so many old friends— why not Saturday? It would soon be one year apart for them and if they passed that milestone Orrin feared the separation might stick. Right now was the time to get things straightened out; now or never possibly, for the Rites of Spring figured to be the best shot he would have.

Now as they sipped the strong chicory coffee and nibbled the rich pecan pie, Orrin was working on Gail, pressing his case, and it was remarkable how his expression could show a dreamy pleasure in the pastry while behind his smiling eyes bitter phrases crackled back and forth.

Eli knew he had lost him again (whether to Gail, the movie, or Seligson's crisis of self-esteem) and waited sympathetically. Poor Orrin really was on edge these days and his demands kept coming right to the surface as a result. Last week Eli had absently picked up the Papermeter (down to .80 hours per 24) and asked what it was all about. "Don't be disingenuous, Eli," Orrin had smiled at him, "That's my area."

The smile was hardly a nice one and Orrin's demanding, almost childlike candor made Eli a little nervous. But it was interesting. And Eli found it curious that at times Orrin seemed to be going mad—perhaps he already had— and yet a good attorney could argue that no pattern of behavior was saner.

Orrin dreamed again that night. He and Gail were in a restaurant arguing, and though their disagreement was soft and civil, it was at the same time implicitly painful.

Then he realized it wasn't Gail, it was Eli Paperman and no wonder he made the mistake: Eli now had the exact same air of disengagement that Gail had worn so often the last year at Acorn Street.

For all of Orrin's clarity and logic, Eli just kept staring at him as though measuring the criminally insane for institutional clothing. And Orrin was discouraged. He could see that it would only go on and degenerate. He was frayed by the tension between an irresistible desire to prolong it and the urgent need to shake off all the cobwebs that had so grotesquely ensnared him.

The real problem these days was that waking afforded little relief. It *was* better, like climbing out of a coffin each morning into a brighter, airier world. But the tension remained, dogging him through the day, and the ache had become incorporated, as natural to him now as breathing.

19

Bemis (more familiarly designated The Eagle Eye Security) was right there on Beacon Street, in the long block before Orrin's office. The second-storey plateglass with stencilled letters, the floral casting of the lintels, nasturtium tubs in front—Orrin had seen the exterior a thousand times. Once (apparently) he had gone inside as well.

Now he was inside a second time, but Bemis the man remained unreconstructed in memory, even when glimpsed face-on across a chipped white formica desk as barren as the Alaskan tundra. The lone object on this slab of real estate was a brown glass paperweight Buddha—or possibly, on second glance, paperweight Bemis. Small eyes in a smooth round head for each of them.

"Bemis, I have to say—with an eye toward your reputation—that this business of refusing to take a check does make it all seem a bit shady."

"You want to go modern, I told you I take credit card, Master and Visa. Plastic or cold cash, because anything else is not money."

"My checks are money. Besides, look how easily you could blackmail me if I welshed."

"I'm an investigator, Doctor, not a blackmailer. Is it such a bad idea to see my bill is paid? No. So thank you very much, here is your receipt, and here is your report."

"Page and a half? Bemis, yours is the life. Do you realize that at these rates, this sheet is worth a million times more than gold?"

"What'd Einstein's Theory of Relativity weigh?" said

Bemis, in concise defense of the value of words, or perhaps paper. Orrin pretended not to hear him, as he blithely fluttered the sheet of expensive sentences. "I'll run it down for you."

"Pardon?" He could act deaf to Bemis, or blind to the report, but it was awkward doing both at the same time.

"First of all, you got the address and telephone there, and that's plain enough. As requested. Now the apartment is rented by Commonweal Realty—who are biggies, owning quite a few dozen—to a Joseph Mirak. Mirak doesn't exist, as such. The real tenant, or the real renter is a Carl Bailey, who is living now in Roxbury and who sublets the place to your daughter's boyfriend. Follow?"

"Hickey."

"The boyfriend's name is not Hickey, as you had surmised, but a Genghis Ferguson, formerly of Roxbury. A drummer in the reggae band Bottled Spirits, but makes his living as a salesman."

"Seems unlikely, all of it. A Genghis Ferguson? And working as a salesman? I mean really, Loomis."

"I don't suggest the young man was born with the name, Doctor S., though among your black families you will find some colorful names tossed around. Your island people also—names you are hearing for the first time. And southerners, black, white, and mulatto, will go poetic on you with names. But hey, this was not a title search I did here—the man's friends call him Genghis."

"And what does he sell? Fuller Brushes or The Encyclopedia Brittanica? No, let me guess—*soft*ware."

"He sells cocaine, Doctor, like any other enterprising young businessman in this great land of opportunity. You can check out his incorporation papers for yourself, under Third World Apothecaries."

"Christ, Loomis, I hope you made sure he is an Equal Opportunity Employer!"

"Your daughter, you will see in the report, is not a user. Not at present or in anyone's memory. Clean as—"

"Your desk?"

"If you like. The driven snow, I was going to say, but whatever-have-you, Dr. S."

"The driven snow, Mr. L., is sadly no longer clean. I mention this only because I was discussing the inaccurate use of clichés just recently, with a friend."

"Whatever. She doesn't use it, he does. Will even free-base, though generally in connection with a sale. On his own he prefers just to smoke—the man also deals a little grass, you understand."

"Why does it say here Providence Hartford Worcester?" Orrin had glanced down chiefly to dodge the unwavering gaze of Bemis.

"That would be The Grand Tour. You wanted to know about the Air Force playing out of town? That's where they played. The numbers you see there represent the money."

"One thousand, six-fifty, eight hundred—this is what they were paid?"

"The money, correct. Per night. Providence was two nights. And they split even, five ways, though I must tell you that this daughter of yours deserves the lion's share. Writes the tunes, and does the singing, and I would venture to say she is the drawing card too. The band is strictly humdrum—screech screech bash crash type of stuff. But what the hell, that's democracy for you."

"Actually, that's socialism for you."

"Whatever. That's it, anyway. I can guarantee she has no inkling she was under investigation, as you requested. I use one young operative who has a rock-journalist-from-Jersey front going for him. A lot of it I got myself personally, the real estate and all. Now should you find you need further details—for example you asked me not to look into the sex life. . . ."

"Did I? Good for me. But no thank you, Loomis. This is sufficient unto itself. I thank you very much for your efficiency and for your confidentiality."

"A pleasure doing business. I enjoyed the music. And this Ferguson, I could add, is quite a nice fellow. I think you'll like him. Well-spoken gentleman, originally from Jamaica, came here at age three however and speaks the King's English to a tee. Sounds like a Harry Belafonte—*cultured,* I mean to say. Now this you won't find in the report so I just pass it along as a bonus."

Continuing along Beacon Street, toward the office, Orrin swung round to make sure The Eagle Eye was not following *him*—turned double agent! Had the man been angling for a tip with his bonus information? Did one tip a private eye fifteen percent? Must have a go at Amy Vanderbilt with that one. . . .

Meanwhile he pocketed the report and set about vacating his beleaguered brain for the Hyphenated Lady. In a sense they were renting his mind for the hour, and just as a landlord could not let a flat and continue to occupy it himself, Orrin felt an obligation to move out, with all his considerable furniture.

As it happened, he moved out so thoroughly, to such a degree of abstraction, that at lunch (which Sarah brought in, ham-and-cheese croissants from the upscaled Burger King) he could not recall a word Sinclair-Fugard had communicated to him. Had that been her in the red wool dress? His notes for the hour, recorded directly upon her departure, read in their entirety:

Hyphenated Lady? Hyphenated-Lady?

He did warm that afternoon to the new teenage suicidal, Seth Lowry, an absurdly goodlooking, well set up lad to be contemplating an end to it all. Orrin knew Seth would not *do* it, yet had to be concerned, for he believed that even to consider suicide signalled a condition that could radiate life-long. Of all the states it might indicate—unrequited love, self-hatred, hatred of family, fragility, Machiavellia, water on the brain—not a one was easily made over. Orrin liked this boy and felt a great patience with his pain; the boy liked him too, so it was possible he could help. What he could not do was to change the bad luck of the past, or dictate good luck in the future.

These days Orrin was not so confident that damage could be undone, or even that character was fate. Character and fate were chicken and egg, sometimes, and the human brain was hardly architecture. A damaged structure might be repaired and the damage soon forgotten; with human beings, the damage itself was necessarily the new foundation. How many times had Orrin seen memory rise up and shatter "reality" like a cheap toy?

Whatever, as Bemis would say. Bemis' report did not bother him. Really it was irrelevant. He could not begin dropping in on El and Genghis with beribboned boxes of chocolate-covered cocaine, or even ring her up about the grand tour. It was nice she had told him the truth there, and nice hearing she was "clean", but any contact must come from her. Bootless to pursue the standing of Third World Apothecaries on Wall Street, and Orrin didn't care whether the deadbeat Hickey or a bankable Ferguson stood by Elspeth's side, so long as he could too, now and again. He had only affection for her.

Seth left at four, then Sarah and Orrin closed the office early. He bought her a coffee at the corner and tried to listen to her chat until the bus arrived. Then he started walking. Pensive, rambling, he slid toward Kenmore Square, gravitated back to The Rat, curious to see it by daylight, minus all the rock-and-roleplaying—to see the soul of the place at rest.

The door opened on a small upstairs bar, empty row of stools, but the stair down was cordoned off with a velvet sash. Orrin started to unhook it, then chose to let it go. Just a room, presumably, with someone sweeping up or polishing glassware under a good old 75-watter. A room

that was deado, in El's argot, for it donned its aura by
night as surely as Orrin had pulled on that hideous red
peruke . . .

. . . As surely as Elspeth Summers (honor student, girl
wit of wide talents, healthy-looking lifeguard at Nahant
Beach) had donned a headdress of feathers and tucked
herself up somewhere with a Genghis Ferguson. Any reas-
surance he aimed to find down those dark stairs was purely
spurious. He did not wish to know that Elspeth was all
right; he wished to *know* Elspeth, whether she was all right
or not.

Away briskly from the shadow of The Rat, Orrin kept
going in the direction of a sudden uproar that seemed to
come from the artery bridge over the Turnpike. Of course:
today was opening day at Fenway Park and the roar he
heard was the sound made when 33,000 people willfully
suspend their disbelief in unison. Red Sox baseball!

The news item had glanced off him last night. It was
below 35 degrees at the time, after all, besides which Orrin
had ceased to follow sports this past year. Apart from the
obvious (that it was patently absurd to wax emotional over
the relationships of other men to a ball) there was the
reality: you either were or you were not emotional about
such things. Orrin himself had once smashed the legs off a
chair when his old Rochester Royals blew one in double
overtime to the Knickerbockers.

Here in the messy, familiar, festive air surrounding the
old ballpark, it was not 35 degrees but 60 and sunny, and
the expanding contracting hum of the crowd, the distinct
and perfect pitch of it, came wafting over on a breeze rich
with sausage and roasted peanuts. It was just right, this
magic they blended and bottled and brought out each year
with all its charms intact. Baseball, the eternal return!

These Red Socks—fifth place flunkies when last
glimpsed by the public—were in *first place* today. (Or tied
for first, with every other team.) It was tabula rasa for the

home team everywhere, congregations of forty thousand
bursting forth like daffodils, glowing against the cold.
Sometime between October and April (Christmas Day,
possibly?) hope had returned. A brand new season.

Orrin could see it was pointless to envy the entire Socks
organization, but perhaps it made sense to envy an individual sock, a Clemens, or better still, Oil Can Boyd.
Because Boyd had fallen apart last year, lost his composure
when things went badly for him, so that they went to
worse. Really he'd had a baseball breakdown. Yet here he
stood, at zero wins and zero losses, with a shot at a solid
18-win season.

Nothing for and nothing *against,* nothing to hint at the
sad horror shows the man staged last season. You couldn't
catch a break like that in real life, which incidentally did
not pay as well either. There, your losses stayed with you
to the end, the mistakes and the inevitable compoundings:
you never got back to zero and zero. Orrin would not envy
the 18 victories, should they occur (all power to the Can),
but he did resent the tabula rasa.

Outside the ballpark, souvenir men fussed with their
stock. Kids were scattered in every direction and running.
Behind the smeary plateglass of the corner sub shop, a
teenager ducked down to corral a strand of pizza cheese. A
peanut vendor on Landsdowne gestured Orrin to him with
a subtle inclination of the head.

"Ten bags a buck," he confided in almost a whisper.
"Bargain."

"I'm afraid I don't like peanuts."

"Feed the birds and animals, then. Feed the brats on
bicycles, feed the homeless and hungry—Live Aid, governor. A real killing at ten bags a buck. Clean me out,
prevent waste, maybe your last chance at prosperity."

The voice had stayed soft, but the engine behind it was
idling higher. Orrin marvelled at the sheer generation of it.

"All right, then, I'll take a hundred."

"A hundred bags?"

"Yes. Ten bucks."

"Guv, I haven't got that many. I got maybe thirty. But hey, for the ten I'll toss in a hot tip on a pooch at Wonderland tonight."

"A racing tip, on a dog?"

"You got it. But cast-iron, a lockup."

"I don't gamble on dogs," said Orrin, who had not gambled a cent on anything since the days of penny-ante poker in college, three bumps and a dime high.

"Gimme a break! You don't eat peanuts, you don't play the dogs, what the hell. Better watch yourself, guv, these are patriotic times we live in."

Baffled by the implications of this, Orrin nonetheless held out a five-dollar bill. The vendor let it hang there a second, like laundry, then snatched it and handed Orrin his remaining stock in a green plastic bag.

"Sold to this gentleman right here. Now listen careful, this one is ears only. The pup you want is Tokyo Joe. Fifth race, tonight, at Wonderland. The price will be nice."

"Tokyo Joe."

"You got it now."

"Thank you."

Slinging the garbage bag over his shoulder Santa Claus style, Orrin wondered if he owed the man five dollars (ten bucks for the tip) or the man owed him two (ten bags a buck).

"Have a good one," said the vendor with a wink and one thumb up. Was it the out sign? A cheer came soaring over the Fenway walls, then waned comically like a balloon losing its air. When Orrin turned back, the peanut man was gone, his shell game concluded.

Orrin retraced his steps back through Kenmore to Mass Ave, where he tried without success to attract a taxi. He blamed the garbage bag for this and strolled up to Newbury's with a mind to unloading it. Fast friends at the bar, the regulars cheered him when he sowed the mahogany

with bags of free nuts, booed him when he resisted all
libation, cheered him again as he threw them a Lone
Ranger salute and left.

Somehow it served as a pit stop. Even without libation,
he felt distinctly refreshed. There was a nice bite to the
dinner-hour air, a cool restorative dampness grafted onto
the gentle zephyr. The older brick structures, mostly Vic-
torian, were awash in a moist light that brought out the
architecturally irrecoverable beauty of their hue, alongside
which all latterday bricks were inevitably tacky. He had
been thinking this was especially true of Gail's building on
Marlborough (where the bricks were flecked with black)
when he chanced in sight of it, and stopped to confirm the
details. And at that very moment a woman not unlike Gail
was letting herself into the foyer.

Cautiously at first (lest this prove another case of mis-
taken identity), he began trotting, but hurrying pro-
gressively, as though the suspect might dive through a rear
window and vanish in a maze of alleys. He ran not for a
reason but simply because his legs had begun to do so,
crossing Marlborough under a hail of hornwork and squall-
ing brakes. Though he called an apology back over his
shoulder, a few unappeased trombonists harassed his wake.

But wasn't this a piece of luck, spotting Gail! Now they
could talk about Elspeth, and settle up about the Rites of
Spring in advance of Saturday. Gail was not one to buzz
people indiscriminately, however, so he elected to go with
Turner, O'Brien and Wallstein, a denominational cross-
section that yielded an instant flurry of results. He was in.
To catch his breath he took the elevator up (mild breach of
the fitness program) and soon enough stood tapping at her
actual door.

"Who is it?"

Definitely, definitively Gail Summers. And why not
Gail, really?—her very own door.

"It's Orrin."

"No," she said, flat as the Sahara.

"Gail, be reasonable. I just want to talk to you."

"Orrin, no. I won't have it. You cannot start showing up here at odd hours and expect to be warmly received."

"Receive me coldly, my love, please feel free to receive me most frigidaire. Only open up, people are listening to us."

"You've been drinking."

"Not a drip!" Orrin protested, thinking how very unfair it was when he had been so specifically not-drinking. "Not a drop."

"Shall I call the police?"

"For what for? Goodness, Gail, why be crazy? I'm standing here as calm as a chrysanthemum for Christ's own sake, what more can I do in the law-abiding way?"

"You can go. Go away right now. Please, Orrin."

How to proceed? On the one hand, Gail was *right there,* the closest she had been since last summer. On the other hand, she seemed bent on avoiding him—yes, clearly she was. But it was so silly for her to avoid him at this point. Pressing his head against her door, he calculated they were barely two inches apart. How absurd for this shabby neoteric slab to obstruct a relationship so vital that it had survived wars, the raising of children, menopause, the passing of three dogs, each one dearly beloved . . .

"I know what you are thinking, that I want to put pressure on you about Saturday—"

"I'm not thinking anything, Orrin. Please believe that. I am going away from this door now, going back to the kitchen, and I won't be able to hear a word you say from now on. Goodbye."

His ear pressed to the panel, Orrin knew she had yet to move foot one. He could even hear her breathing when he interrupted his own.

"Saturday would be nice, I'm sure we could enjoy it a great deal, but I have no desire to pressure anyone about any—"

"Are you mad?" she burst out. "I am not subject to your pressures any more, Orrin. Whether you desire or don't desire, do you see? I am not connected to any of it any more."

"Disconnected," he murmured.

He might have argued the point (we will always be connected . . .) but his instincts were good, he hung fire. Let her boil it off. In the calm to follow, there would be time to air the true issues.

"Now," she said (but sounding calm already, sounding dangerously *disconnected*), "I am going to the kitchen this time, Orrin. If I come back in ten minutes and you have not gone, I will simply call the police."

Simply, no less. Could it really be simple for her to have the constabs haul him away? She went now, clicking across some hardwood, then a rug, after that a door softly latching. Could she really go compose a salad—one of her best, olives and mushrooms and the thin strips of prosciutto—with Orrin stranded unhappy at her very portal?

They needed to discuss their mutual daughter, he had come a long way to do so . . . and yet it was true there was nothing much to discuss, true that he had not come such a long way, half a block and across the street really was all. . . .

"I just love you," he said. "Is that such a terrible crime?"

I love you all, he thought, I can even learn to love a Belafonte Ferguson if I must. But the pain and absurdity of his position somehow cut through; there could be no dignity this side of her door. Orrin knew his eyes and face were wet, and that he was breathing as though he had the bends. Rapture of the deep. This was a fork in the road, no question.

"I do love you," he said, then wiped his face and re-gathered himself for the finishing kick on his constitutional.

20

The weekend went badly. More rain, empty rooms, forced abstention from the rites of spring. No longer could Orrin say with any conviction that he had hopes for Gail.

The week got off to a bad start too, when he tussled with Eli. Eli had punched in at 6:26 ("How nice of you to grace the chambers") and was hurtling back out at 6:42 ("Y'all come back") when he realized he had better say something about this nasty little skit.

"What is it, Orrin? What's up?"

"Nothing," said Orrin. "Nothing I can explain." (And this was true, for what a monumental sophistry it would take even to mock explanation.) "Why don't we talk of other matters."

"Fine," said Eli, though they had not as yet talked of any matters at all.

"Red Socks holding up so far—get it? Tokyo Joe sixth in a field of seven. That's the sports and meanwhile the weather is in a wetting trend, or on a warming bend—something. . . ."

"Tokyo Joe? Racehorses, Orrin?"

"Dogs, actually. I received an indoor tip, a lockup, and the price was right. Except that Tokyo ran slowly—relatively speaking, you understand, sixth in a field of seven."

"You lost a lot of money?"

"Me? Not a red centavo. I felt lucky enough just deciphering the doggie page in the newspaper. I *should* have bet my entire fortune on him, though it's true I would have lost."

"So the fact is, you *saved* a lot of money."

"Yes I did. Such a deal. But tell me how you have been. And our Marcy."

"Fine, we're fine . . ."

Eli considered saying more but left it at that, lacking his usual confidence in Orrin. And indeed, Orrin now gargled a good slug of whiskey, wiped his lips with the back of his hand, and asked if the young bride of The Man Crushed By Quarters was anything to look at.

Eli could only blink in disbelief. Had Orrin really said that? So callous and petty, aggressively uncouth? It was too much for Paperman, who was already an hour behind schedule. He left without speech or ceremony at 6:48 (thus concluding the only twenty-two minutes on the Eli Log since Tuesday last) and in the ensuing void Orrin was certain he had behaved badly, and counter to any purpose he might consciously have conceived.

But patching it up would not prove easy. No answer all that evening at Marcy's, and after yet another night of shivering and tossing, he was stonewalled next morning by Eli's receptionist, no longer his confidante. Heavy laden, he appeared at the Cambridge YMCA during Eli's basketball hour, but Eli was cold to him there. Orrin readily conceded they had bickered without cause and the fault was all his; Eli nodded, emitted the blankest of thanks, and walked onto the court.

That afternoon, even Clyde snubbed him. Or not snubbed but *failed* him, cancelling a dinner date because both boys had the China Flu or the Swine Flu—some highly subjective germ. Orrin dragged himself to The Club instead and tried to raise the old tones, but it was tough sledding. One was paying for a mantle of self-esteem and a sense of belonging there, but too often Orrin felt like a straggler at The Club these days, an outsider.

Faced with the endless weekend (not to mention a virtual institutionalization of the wetting trend) Orrin was

prepared to make it official: he was depressed. In com-
memoration, he fetched down the jellyglass and reprised
the old anatomical criteria for decanting—Fudd's Eyeball
generally, though there was one bottom-of-the bottle con-
figuration that by chance could only be Fudd's Privie Parts
and hence gave rise to a nightcapping toast to "the dark
side of Disney", albeit Orrin knew that Walt Disney technically bore no responsibility for Elmer Fudd, who was
after all a Walter Lanz creation. But Bacchic license, this.

His sleeps were shallow and dreamless, unsatisfying,
and he ate poorly, dining off canned soups and salty nib-
bles, in a behavior gleaned from clients over the years. Not
that it was all negative. Certain mornings the dehydration
of hangover left him oddly trim of intellect, throbless and
unmuddied of mind, as though the froth had boiled away
and only the essence remained: in short, he did some
thinking. But on one such morning, with just such searing
lucidity, Orrin suffered a painful epiphany.

He was tying his shoes that day when he stopped,
strands-a-dangle, to record the trivial overwhelming insight he had. Which was this: no matter the variables (day
or night, boaters or brogans) Orrin always did up his left
lace first. He had in stock no old home movies to prove
this, yet he knew it was so (and it *was* so) and the force was
not in his having such a habit, the force was in his absolute
lifelong obliviousness to it. How could he dodge the conclusion that he was equally unknown to himself in many
other ways as well? What if Bemis *were* to shadow him
now, hovering by, making purely objective notes on
Orrin's appearance and behavings. Would Orrin even recognize himself in the resulting portrait?

He could recall inviting Paperman into his life as a
perfect stranger—no, *because* he was a perfect stranger—
and now in the clear dry light of his blood he saw a larger
truth; that they all were perfect strangers. Not only Eli, a
truly random sampling right off the rack, but Orrin's own

family, son and a daughter, wife of three decades, in the
end mystifying. And himself as well. "It's only the truth,"
he exclaimed aloud, after Elspeth, who at the age of nine
would use this expression to firm up her most heartfelt
allegations. "It's only the truth!"

"Don't you even know the first thing about yourself?"
Theo asked not long ago, and Orrin had cavalierly dis-
missed the remark. Not now.

He cancelled two days' worth of appointments (giving
as his excuse to Sarah the Swine Flu) and saw too much of
McAllister and McAllister's pale son. Pale and shaky himself, he did what he could at this time. Took the improving
May air along the beach at Hull, feeling lonely, very lonely,
yet genuinely touched by the beauty of this world. And he
pulled hard for Oil Can Boyd out in Cleveland and De-
troit.

Had Eli come back at any point during these eight days
in May, the outcome would have been about the same.
Unconsciously the depression was tailored to last precisely
until he tripped the Papermeter and unwittingly sublet all
of Orrin's disappointment. Consciously Orrin was thinking that things would not improve until he had squared
matters with the younger man; until the resumption of
domestic tranquility at Filbert Street.

He had begun to wonder if the chance would ever come.
Never had the Papermeter gathered such dust, never so
long between the minimalist perfunctory punch-ins, Fudd
and a Bud. From behind the high windowless walls of his
despair, each day could feel like a month, each week seem a
whole era. Orrin could believe that sweeping changes had
taken place: Eli and Marcy married, already the parents of
auburn-haired children, inking a purchase-and-sales on a
ticky-tacky in Belmont . . .

Unbeknownst to him, Eli and Marcy had troubles of
their own. Marcy had decided to lay down a rule or two,
like the one limiting Paperman to three nights a week at

her apartment; she must begin to rebuild her private life, after all, if he did not seriously wish to share it. Faced with this manifesto from Marcy, and having seen about enough of Orrin's shenanigans, Eli had been browsing for alternative lodgings and now needed to know the final score with Orrin. Orrin would either make it perfectly possible or perfectly impossible—clearly he was a master of each mode.

So there Eli was, suddenly one night, and Orrin did not so much as glance up from the TV, or speak, though even as he sat there he realized this was an odd, arbitrary and counter-productive fragment of behavior. Certainly it had nothing to do with Jack's update on the baggage handlers' strike out at Logan, and yet still he did not turn, or nod, or wave, or speak. And as the seconds gathered, he began to experience a verbal gravidity, an inability to raise sound from his mouth, though by now he was trying in earnest.

"Orrin?" said Paperman cautiously. "Are you—in there?"

"Eli! I thought I heard you come in."

This was lame, but at least it got him off the schneid. He was vaguely aware of wishing to project an aura of coziness, of a household so rife with warm, simple pleasures that intrusions from without were at best marginally perceptible. In truth, he had just walked in himself: flicked on the Jack-and-Liz and sunk straight to the bottom of the man-eating "Depression Chair", an unnaturally square severe armchair which stifled all save the most vigorous movement.

Extricating himself from it now, Orrin selected a subtle offense; to play the host. "I should offer you something," he said, precluding the possibility that Eli might simply make himself at home. But Paperman refused to take the offense to heart. True, Orrin was complaining again, but Eli was prepared to acknowledge he had not been a good friend of late. Between the stickiness with Marcy and the time press on all sides, he had definitely let things lapse at Filbert Street.

"The place is looking good," he said. "New plants. The bay looks downright lush."

"No name-calling now," said Orrin. He was smiling, but teeth first. "It does add something, doesn't it? McAllister down the hill carries a few houseplants and it seemed worth the small investment."

He had purchased the plants on consecutive occasions during the official depression, times when he required a second bottle in a single calendar day. To ward off implications, Orrin had sprung for the coleus, the spider, and the swedish ivy.

"Definitely," said Paperman. "We should have done it sooner."

Eli's use of the word 'we' tasted unfortunately bitter to Orrin but he worked his way past it. He refueled, counted ten, and plunged in on his long pent-up apology:

"Eli, I hope you know how very ashamed I am for my behavior the last time. Inexcusable, though accounted for in part by the devil in the bottle. I was on the occasion not uninebriated. Was *influenced,* in short."

"Not uninebriated? I believe I may have just heard the world's first triple negative." Maybe it was only two negatives, but he had no real response to these inevitable retrenchments of Orrin's.

"I'm very serious, Eli. I want you to know I am deeply sorry for what I said. For *whatever* I said, you know."

"Are you, Orrin?"

This was a slip. But having made it, having lapsed from repartée, Eli saw that it was just as well. Walking on eggshells had begun to pall quickly this time, and it was silly to prop up a relationship on lies and evasions.

"Am I sorry? I am *telling* you that I am sorry. That is what I am telling you precisely."

"But is it such a wonderful thing, this being sorry? Should we celebrate it by closing the banks and the schools?"

"You are rude, Eli. Really you are."

"I don't mean to be rude. I just want to say that being drunk isn't an excuse for anything, and being sorry isn't an excuse for being drunk, and furthermore that I'm not sure you really are sorry. Though you may really be drunk."

"That is not a cutting remark, Eli. What makes you think it is such a smirking laughable matter, your rudeness?"

"Orrin, come on. When I first knew you, you would have laughed too—at my calling out your bullshit. Relax, man."

"You arrogant shit!" said Orrin, turning sharply away. Paperman simply gaped. Orrin tried to collect himself by stealing a peek at the television, a few scattered clouds out over the Cape and the islands . . .

"Orrin, really—don't you think you might need some help on this," Eli was saying softly, ingratiatingly, as though addressing a child. Not meaning *his* help, though, not offering companionship, but meaning to suggest Orrin was bricko, crackers. Some help.

"How much? A pint of help or a whole goody gallon of it? What's prescribed exactly?"

"Oh Orrin."

"*Damn* you. You damnable shit, Paperman. I know what you think. I am a boozing old over-the-hill fool of a human, so useless and you so very able. You think I was never worth a goody goddamn but I will tell you this—"

"No need."

"—An old boozing neutered goat, but I will tell you that I am not, was not that, no sir! She loved me *plenty,* and we did what people do. We did it plenty. Did it up against the wall, did it hanging over the edge of the bed, *cantilevered* goddamn your eyes! We did it from here to Timbuktu and you—"

"I don't need to hear this, Orrin."

"You don't need to, *you* don't need to. But maybe *I* need to *say* this, Paperpig, because we would be doing it still, do you understand, it isn't physically impossible to keep it, it's just the bloody baggage of life that stops you. Jesus! Do you see that, *can* you see that, Paperpiggle? Because you would if you ever *loved* anyone in your miserable half-baked life!"

Orrin spun to laser Eli's eyes, to fucking-A *nail* him, and saw there a detachment so bland, a withdrawal so complete that it made his own face bestial—gums flaring, blood pounding—and he spun back only to find the Weatherbaby every bit as goddamn blithe, cloud fucking ninety-nine as usual, and went after him with the high hard one, fastballing the Fudd right between his eyes.

"Jee Zuz!" emitted Paperman, as the TV flashed and fizzled in a hail of electronic fire and webbed glass.

The thing was still sizzling and tinkling to rest and here came Paperman, shaking his head gently, frowning his damnable liberal frown, moving forward to take Orrin in hand like a bloody child. Orrin braced himself physically. He heaved a big right hand, fanned on it, then came back with a flurry of left hooks, because the right shoulder was really hanging after hitting 95 on the radar gun with no proper warmup.

The lefts did nothing inside Eli's clinch, so he pushed free and shot out a toe-kick that caught solid shin. Now Orrin circled, his hands milling karate-style, in an unconscious parody of Peter Sellers doing the bumbling French inspector, but neither man was close to laughter.

"Stop yourself, Orrin. Just stop yourself. Look at this place."

"Why should I? Why can't I do as I like with my own television set? And why can't I defend myself in my own bloody home?"

"Oh Jesus."

"Stop my self. You told me my self was my greatest creation, remember? I built a self, you said, and now you want me to stop it. Then what? *Then* what?"

"Just do me a favor, Orrin. Don't apologize for this. Now or ever. Give me five minutes to pack up and do not apologize, that's all."

Things had gotten out of hand. Eli was shaking, visibly upset, and Orrin's only need now was to see to him, to say soothing words of apology and comfort. But he was forced to stand fast and do nothing. He was forced to sit, as the raging blood subsided, and he did sit, inside the ululating silence. He sat for hours without moving, like a tree on a windless day, and the more he sat the more he did sit.

When he stood again, hours after Eli had gone, he went instinctively to search for Jack-and-Liz inside the shattered machinery. All the king's horses, he couldn't help thinking, as he scanned the rubble for their broken faces. And he saw no reason to deny himself the long thin nasal laughter that came keening from the depths of his disturbance.

IV

THE OLD REALITY

"I understand nothing," Ivan went on, as though in delirium. "I don't want to understand anything now. I want to stick to the fact. I made up my mind long ago not to understand. If I try to understand anything, I shall be false to the fact and I have determined to stick to the fact."

—DOSTOEVSKY

21

Clyde had taken over. Alarmed by the call from Eli Paperman, he came prepared to buck his father's will if necessary. As it happened, nothing extreme was needed, because Orrin appeared at his own front door around midnight in a state so sodden and disoriented that he believed he was dreaming the mere sight of Clyde. Gliding along with the dreamwork, he went easily, almost light-heartedly, the short few blocks to Massachusetts General Hospital.

There, in the frankly elitist Waldo Emerson Ward, Orrin's ailment could be loosely diagnosed: it might be the ticker, or the great gray brain, or even just a touch of the old rheumatizz. They gave a lot of leeway at the Emerson—much the best setting for any painless debility, a glorified spa, really. As far as Clyde was concerned (and this both for public consumption and his father's) the program would be "a few days' rest for overwork and fatigue," plus of course the slight "concussion" they had concocted, knowing Orrin would want something solid and a tad dramatic.

So he woke on Saturday morning to a view of sun-tipped sails on the bright choppy Charles River. He was in a private room with two high windows delineating the water—not too shabby for a midnight arrival. Starlings darted across his view, and the enveloping whiteness of pane and counterpane almost convinced Orrin he was waking amongst the angels, in heaven. The advent of the breakfast tray soon enough brought him back down to earth, and he was picking it over with limited interest when he glanced up to find Clyde and Phyllis framed in the doorway.

"Advance, children. By all means, do advance."

Phyll was gripping a mixed bouquet, iris and jonquils, and Clyde held a clutch of those detective novels he was always recommending as great relaxation. Orrin could never fathom his son's craving for relaxation. Between his cushy, almost squushy life (a two-course teaching load and the nearly overlapping sabbaticals), it seemed all Clyde ever *did* was relax.

"So how are you feeling?"

"Not bad. How am I supposed to be feeling? I tried to debrief Nurse Wretched there about my symptoms—so I could proceed to limp on the correct leg, you know—but she was as closemouthed as a priest in the box."

"You *sound* like yourself."

"Thank you, Clydie, you sound like yourself too. But what am I doing here? Why the Mass. General?"

"Just a few days of observation and rest, Dad. You know you hit your head pretty hard last night. In a bar-room dispute, apparently."

"If it happened in a bar-room dispute, it seems more likely that someone else hit it. I do recall engaging in discussion with some younger fellows in a drinkery. Possibly one of *them* hit it—though I must say they seemed very civil to me."

"Well, the details are hazy. Possible concussion, at any rate, hence the observation and rest. It's not such a bad spot to be in, Dad. I could almost envy you."

"Yes," said Phyll. "We both thought it was so cozy and cheerful in here. You have the nicest room, Orrin."

"First class," added Clyde. "And by the time you get out, the lilacs will be out too. . . ."

"That's silly. I can't stay in here to be *observed*. I don't *like* to be observed. They must know already whether I have a concussion, and frankly I don't feel the least bit concussed. I can rest perfectly well at home."

"It's all covered by the insurance. Why not take advantage of it for a few days?"

"We'll see." said Orrin, glancing toward the closet to see if his clothes were visible. He could simply dress and leave, after they had. Ever since the events of last evening came back to him, he felt a powerful urge to rush back home and sweep up the broken glass, to quick replace the busted TV with a new one exactly the same. To restore order, as it were, before the disorder could take root, or appear meaningful.

"This one looks possible," he said now. He had been turning the paperback mysteries over in his hand, pretending to peruse the dustjacket blurbs.

"Tell me about this fight in the bar," said Clyde. "In the drinkery."

Clyde knew there had been no fight, of course, and no concussion. But he wanted to be gently on the offensive. He was banking on his father's insobriety and shame, for Orrin would not be certain what had happened and would accept some direction rather than appear the least bit unknowing.

"It was nothing. A discussion, as I say."

"A concussion, you mean."

"Discussion. And on a fairly high plane at that. I was bitter about the Red Sox, you know, about the way they get a clean slate every spring. They have no *past,* Clydie, they hibernate and wake up in first place."

"You don't believe that. The Red Sox? Don't you know they carry the burden of history with them on every turn around the bases?"

"That's what the fat one kept saying! The same words, burden of history. Can you believe it?"

This last he addressed to Phyllis, who could only shrug and say, "Well, it hardly matters."

"It does matter, though. Do either of you want this apple juice, by the way? Phyll?"

"No thank you, Orrin."

"No, Dad, but let's not lose the thrust of this. The Red Sox have a team character, and character is fate for them too. It's true of every sports franchise with a past."

"Phyll, these are very lovely. Shall I ring the nurse for some kind of vase?"

"Why don't I take care of it, Orrin. You two can talk."

Phyllis was always stealing off to let them "talk", as though they had secrets from her, or would turn to some manly tone of address that must naturally exclude her. Was this a form of polite respect, or was it merely a form of escape for her?

"Seriously, Clyde, I want out of here. I have so much to do at home."

"They definitely won't let you go yet. No point tussling with City Hall."

Clyde was determined to pin his father here for at least a few days, to take better stock of the problem. The lawyer Eli Paperman thought it went beyond drink—that something had really snapped in Orrin—and had urged Clyde to disregard any charming disclaimers. Orrin meanwhile felt oddly cleansed, and had begun to worry about neglected work, about Sinclair-Fugard, and the gifted lad Lowry, and the notes on self-knowledge . . .

"There is simply no way I can fail to be in the office first thing Monday, son. That's for starters."

"Okay, that might be possible. But let's do be realistic, Dad. Be professional with yourself. You've been under a mighty strain, you've been unhappy—"

"Not at all. How measured? And by whom?"

"—and doing too much drinking—"

"Now how can you sit out in Lexington and know a thing like that, for goodness sake? I am a realist, Clyde, and I know you mean very well. But tracking the old reality is sometimes not so easy."

"Forget the old reality—it's the weekend. And it's pleasant enough here. You can catch up on your reading."

"I just want you to understand that I am all right. I appreciate your taking such trouble over me, I'm touched by it really, but I'm sure you have better things to worry about."

"Not a one, in fact."

"Now tell me: is your mother the source on my alleged drinking? Because I know she took a wrong impression one night—"

"It doesn't matter," Clyde shrugged, replicating his bride's tone of voice precisely. He was not about to name his source.

"You know, when your mother was still in the house— and you may say or *she* may say she wasn't really, but really she was, you know, physically there—and you and I would get together occasionally for lunch? Back then, it was just last year really, it seemed to me that Elspeth was the aberration, and by her own choice, you know. We were still there, as a family."

Clyde was casting about for a soothing response to this sudden spillage when the nurse came in with a black blood-pressure cuff and merrily bound up Orrin's arm. He ignored this, speaking and gesturing with both arms despite the loose band flapping.

"And then there was this *slight shift* and suddenly it seemed clear that *I* was now the aberration—though I had done nothing differently, nothing at all. But I was the aberration and I couldn't get back because now there *was* no family anymore. But so *suddenly,* so mysteriously, you know."

"Please be still for just a moment, Mr. Summers."

"It's very sad to me, Clyde. Very sad."

"I understand, Dad. We want to do what we can to help. To—" Clyde paused and with surprising force in his eyes caused the nurse to cease, desist, and leave the room. "—to remind you that we consider you an important part of *our* family too. The boys are so fond of you, and I'm sure in time you and Mom will be on better terms too."

"Does she plan to visit? Does she know about my near-fatal concussing?"

Clyde hesitated. There were strategies to consider. His father might lie back and act the proper invalid if he had reason to expect a visit from his mother. But there was the old reality to ponder, those late returns from the outlying precincts. For Clyde knew there would be no visit forthcoming.

"I hope you don't mind her knowing. I did tell her how the situation stood, and she asked to be kept up to date . . ."

"Do you suppose she would come if you reported I was on my deathbed? That I was weighing out the cadences of my final words?"

"She might, Dad. But then if you failed to kick off, she would never take the bait a second time."

"Right you are. Better not to chance it," said Orrin, smiling back at his son, as Phyllis returned with a plastic water-pitcher, hospital green, for the flowers.

Clyde must have moved in to the hospital too, for he kept popping up every few hours. Ted Neff ducked in after lunch (somehow finding the time to "crosscheck this rumor they had slowed your stride") and he was extremely kind. Ted was a man, Orrin felt in watching him, who might have been happier as a failure. Success had not spoiled him, but it had somehow disoriented him, shaken up his ditty bag and left him with a jumble of loose emotional change in lieu of true feeling. But then maybe all lives were sad, or seemed sad, once they began winding down. . . .

This Orrin was not quite ready to believe. His afternoon was both busy and slow, sociable and yet agreeably private—like the sick days he would take in grade school, alone with his mother in the Grand Avenue house. She would take those days off too, and she would set him up with puzzles and comic-books and lemon custard, and take his fever down with orange-flavored aspergum. Sleep was there at the welcome moments when it simply took him.

By dinnertime (his meal catered in by Phyll against the hospital fare, which even in the Emerson was pretty unpalatable) Orrin was convinced he must really have been ailing, since he unquestionably felt a great deal better. In the lounge room after dinner, it was downright festive, as Theo found the time to return and this time brought along a few faces from The Club.

They worked through the jokes about mortality, and the Red Sox of course, and then took up the unfortunate extent to which madness was taking root among the *poor,* so that clinics and halfway houses were overflowing, the streets were teeming with borderliners, while along Carriage Row a mild recession had set in. "Human frailty just ain't what it used to be," lamented Barry Grimm, dismissing from the category human anyone earning less than sixty-five thousand per annum.

By the time the pipe smoke had risen and all the trivial banter trailed away with it, Orrin was pleasantly exhausted, and eager for a perfect sleep. Had he fallen off straightaway, he was good for the duration, till the powers-that-be came in to draw his drapes and unveil the bright blooming banks of the Charles. Once or twice he narrowly missed: the full flavor of sleep was right there on his palate, only to vaporize in a mistwist of the neck or a voice adrift on the ward. After a time though, the twists and discomforts multiplied and the unfamiliar sounds grew more rampant and sonorous by the minute. As sleep became less possible (and Orrin concomitantly more deeply exhausted) he began to contemplate escape. At three a.m. a nurse actually flickered on the overhead fluorescent to *see* if he was finally sleeping and there was no longer any question: a hospital was the last place on earth where a person could expect to get any rest. He endured another half-hour of it (arhythmic hum of traffic on Storrow, arriving sirens, scuffle and clatter in the overbright corridor) then rang for the nurse to let her know he would be checking out.

"I'm sure if you are feeling up to it, Doctor will let you go home tomorrow."

"Tomorrow is out of the question. Besides which it *is* tomorrow. Has been for hours, unfortunately."

"No one can leave the hospital before Doctor signs a release, sir—you can understand that."

"Well then, get me Doctor. Please. I'll see the night man."

"I would have to wake him up to do that. And this is not really something I can't help you with myself."

"Fine. Help me with it, then. I'll put on my pants and you put on my shirt."

"You can't leave, sir."

"Then I insist on seeing Doctor. Why shouldn't you wake him up, he is being paid to take care of business all night. I happen to know he is being paid by the hour and paid plenty, and I for one would like to see him earn it. What's he done so far this hour?"

Would she return empty-handed with a lame excuse, or with some young fool sleepily in tow? Orrin was dressed and brushing his teeth when there appeared at his elbow a fellow younger than Clyde, blonde and bespectacled, sleepsoaked yet stethoscoped: Doctor.

"I understand you are having some difficulty sleeping."

"Unlike yourself, my good man! But seriously, Doctor, I am. And luckily for us, I'm well enough and close enough by to stroll home and sleep the sleep of the just in my own soft bed."

"That's fine, sir, and I hope you understand we will need to decide it in the morning. For now, it's best you get some rest."

"My whole point. Not getting any. Therefore not best!" The sleeping prince had somehow failed to grasp the issue.

"Please be calm, sir. We're certainly not going to discuss anything at all with you acting up."

"Is that what I'm doing? Do you really think it so crazy that a man in perfect health wishes to leave the hospital?"

"No, I don't. I didn't say the word crazy."

"*I* said the word crazy. You said the word acting up, but it was two words, so I condensed. The point is I feel fine— or I would if I were asleep."

"How do you know?" said Doctor, stopping Orrin cold. The young fool was entering into the spirit of things!

"Excellent point, Doctor. Allow me a rephrase: were I asleep, I would not *care* whether or not I felt fine."

"Maybe not. I'm not at all familiar with your case. As I say, it's a matter for the a.m."

Thus concluded Doctor's brief foray into metaphysics; he was headed back to bed. So Orrin could march (out the door, down the vile corridor, and out under the May stars) or he could capitulate. What held him, really, was Kafka. Orrin knew as well as anyone that a medical bureaucracy could swallow the key. And any words he spoke could be used to bolster their case, for such statements at such times were as minutely flexible as pipe-cleaners. He could see the Kafka plot already unfolding, what with Nurse loading one up on the sideboard, a hypo to stun a hippo, "a little something to help you rest. . . ."

Orrin declined the shot and swore compliance. He thanked Nurse for her valuable time. But it went beyond Kafka: he was determined to prove his sanity. And his reward for such good intentions, (surprisingly) was sleep, though not for very long. Apparently they did not prescribe too *much* rest here, and certainly none past 5:45 when the ward was nudged back to life by the first flock of chirruping nurses. Astounding to think they would jar a man, presumed ill, from a shallow two-hour snooze to inquire did he wish prunes with his breakfast!

"I don't even want breakfast with my prunes!" he stated with some exasperation, then clamped both pillows to his throbbing skull. Somehow, in the midst of ward life, he managed to drift back and latch onto a pale washy dream, shot through a summer evening lens, in which Eli came grinning to the portal with flowers and said, "Top o' the mornin' to you, O'Summers."

Clyde appeared there in fact—no Phyllis and no flowers, but he did come bearing potable coffee, croissants, and the Sunday papers. Almost at once, with the first long swallow of coffee, Orrin came sidearm with a question he had not premeditated:

"Did I ever strike you? As a child?"

"I don't think so, Dad. Why in the world do you ask?"

"I must have *spanked* you."

"Not really. Nothing that hurt enough to make a memory, at least. Nothing worse, certainly, than the thump I gave Corey last night."

"What about your sister?"

Clyde did not know that his father had struck Eli Paperman, and Orrin did not know that Paperman had spoken with Clyde: they were both fencing in the blue here.

"I really don't think so, Dad. You seem to have this idea that Elspeth hates you but she doesn't, at all. There is no explanation, nothing to be explained about her. She is just

out there on The Precipice, as I may have already mentioned?"

"Your mother isn't on The Precipice. Why won't *she* talk
to me?"

"I don't know. She must have told you?"

"Nothing. Not a word, believe me, Clyde."

"Well but the point is, I suppose, it doesn't matter why.
You can see that."

"I did strike your mother once. Did you know?"

Clyde shrugged, conveying an unwillingness to acknowledge such unpleasant truth, or a reluctance to med-
dle; at the very least a desire to keep things *rest*ful here in
hospital. But he had misunderstood and when pressed
admitted he did know it; Clyde was recalling a specific
occasion, where Orrin had not been referring to one.

"Because we saw you."

"You and El?"

"Yes."

"A long time ago?"

"Yes, Dad, it was a very long time ago. It was not a very
big deal."

"Tell me everything you remember about it. Everything. Please."

Clyde kept it spare. No adjectives, no emotions. He at
fifteen and Elspeth at ten had watched their father push
their mother onto a bed in a hotel suite in New York City,
and place his hands briefly on her neck.

"And you hated me."

"Of course not."

"But they do. Why of-course-not? Why shouldn't you?"

"It just isn't so. No one simplifies that way. I wasn't a
one-year-old. And no one age fifteen expects a parent to be
perfect."

"Ah but they do expect that, Clydie."

"I assure you, my dear concussed father, that this was

not the all-informing trauma of anyone's vita. Really. El and I are both happy, healthy, productive people, with nice little lives. Relax about all this stuff."

"Everyone tells me to relax. I don't *want* to relax. I want to—whatever the opposite is—*live*. One more thing, though. Did you, did your mother realize you had seen?"

"Yes. And maybe I was angry in a way—or not angry but guilty about it, guilty for not helping Mom. Because she did try to smooth it over for me."

"Tell me everything. Exactly as it happened."

"She said you were sick—"

"Sick?"

"Physically sick. And you'd had a bad reaction to some medicine you'd been given."

"It was a lie."

"I suppose it was. I guess one knew that even then. But it did the trick. She was okay if we were, that's how it was, so of course we were and it all got lost in the shuffle. Honestly I remember the rest of that day much more vividly—Rockefeller Center, Radio City Music Hall. It was the first time you took us to New York and I am positive that Elspeth also recalls the city more clearly than she does that silly scuffle."

"A nice word for it, Clydie. You have a nice way about you, and you're nobody's fool, either. But really now, if you venerate the old man at all, spring me from this place. God knows I have had my rest."

"Soon."

"*Now.* Let me go home and I'll swear a vow to avoid the rowdy set. To drink up my usual thumbnail in the soft safe bosom of The Club, and to sneeze politely into my hanky. I mean it, I'll swear to it. Just do spring me from these sallow walls."

Clyde did drive him home that afternoon, though Orrin

had stated categorically he would prefer the walk. What he really sought to avert was having his son bear witness to the wreckage of Jack-and-Liz, or see the remains of The Weatherbaby as widely scattered as his distant cousin Humpty-Dumpty. Luckily there were no parking spaces along Filbert.

"I can get out here. I haven't got any luggage, you know."

"Are you sure?"

"Go have what's left of your Sunday with Phyll and the boys. You've done more than enough for me, and I'll feel worse—maybe even terrible, Clydie—if you try to do more. I can feel a secondary concussion coming on."

"Well all right. But I'll call tonight."

"My parole officer? It's not necessary. I do want to thank you, Clyde—for everything. And I want you to know that I am feeling extremely sound just now."

"That's right. Nothing like a few days in prison to teach a man the true meaning of freedom."

"Exactly. I stand deterred, certainly I do."

Orrin walked up and let himself into the flat, and at first he was visually confused, caught in a time warp; the rooms were as orderly as a museum corridor. Every hair in place, somehow. And for an instant he felt he really might be starkers after all. Then he spotted the note, and knew without reading it that Eli the relentless liberal had come back to deal with the mess.

Had *vacuumed* even, and set two new plants on the dining table, flowering gerania. Between the two was a bottle of Bushmills, or a Bushmills' bottle as it turned out, filled with sparkling spring water and labelled "the choice of reformed tipplers worldwide." In the note Eli said he was sorry it had not worked out and that he would be by to visit in the future. He supplied the June rent check, in case Orrin had trouble getting a replacement on short notice.

Orrin might have bristled at so much patronization from Paperman, except that he was weary, and drained of strong emotions. The truth was Eli had cause, and moreover had done all this with a touch of class. He could not see Eli as the sort to visit his own past and yet maybe even that was for the best. Orrin was pointing toward the future, eager for life-after-sleep, and particularly eager to see each of his clients, to be their doctor.

At the Mass. General he had felt a compulsion to replace the busted TV at once, to conceal the damage as it were. Now he saw there was none extant. The damage was history, like every Red Sox fifth-place finish. But the hospital had served a purpose. The hospital had galvanized him, shocked him back to sense and purpose. It was a hinge to swing open new doors of perception.

He would replace the idiot-box all right, but not with another of its own ilk. Instead, on the Bombay table where late the sweet box sang, he was envisioning one last houseplant, something vibrant, a lush red speckled begonia. The whole room would definitely be better for it.

22

When you split an apple with your thumbs, or struck a bolt of ashwood with a maul, there was a grain that could only be guessed at from the surface. You might slice down four clean quarters, or alternatively tear off some crazy shapes: every log was a sculpture of unforeseeability.

It was no different with people. When trauma came, they broke according to the grain. A man abandoned by his true love might hang himself from the nearest chandelier or he might prowl the backstreets with murder in his heart, and do murder. Sit helplessly whimpering in his chair, or rush to solace in another woman's arms. For Orrin's money it made a wash of all reductive thinking, and put the pressure on every therapist every day. No longer content to go through the motions, he applied himself with a fierce high seriousness at work.

Seth Lowry was his favorite. He enjoyed the boy and reveled in Seth's trust and affection. (Of course the boy had nothing to say at home; his parents suffered through meals like monks under a vow of silence.) Orrin liked being brought up to date on adolescence—having recently wrestled with the symbolism of shoe-lacing, he was charmed to learn that a whole generation of boys did not tie their laces at all. But he had yet to uncover the grain of this perfect boyhood in crisis and until he did, until they did, the crisis would not truly have passed.

Sinclair-Fugard was easier to understand, yet even harder to help. She was what they call in the trade a help-rejecting complainer; complaint itself was perhaps her therapy. Orrin offered to meet with the husband gratis, but this, she told him, was impossible. With his fierce foolish black African pride, Winston put no stock in therapy, and with her weak foolish white African guilt, Elizabeth had not even admitted to him she was seeing a therapist.

Orrin secured the pro bono case of a young black man who had raped and killed his first cousin. Twice weekly he listened to the schizoid monologues of Kenny Fellows in a chill, cramped parody of a dingy institutional room at Walpole. Half man and half infant, viciously aggressive and pathetically vulnerable, perpetrator and victim, Kenny registered 50/50 on every test Orrin ran at him. He loved and he hated everyone close to him.

Orrin had been frightened by clients before, yet never while being so thoroughly charmed. Did Kenny know right from wrong? Orrin was supposed to determine if the young man felt remorse, but the young man refused to discuss it until he'd had a chance to research all the legal implications. And he could not be fooled. Though he would not soon be free to publish it, Orrin wrote the case up, and polished it down to a trim readable forty pages.

Meanwhile Clyde kept after him, half nursemaid half parole officer, and Elspeth did call, a month after Bemis the Shamus had filed on her. She couldn't eat a bite (not a good time for her) but she was sending a cassette on which her lyrics should be perfectly audible. El said she wanted a copy of his exegesis and would be happy to eat the bite at some future time that was better for her. Gail did not call and Orrin called her just once, to record the message: "No messages. Doing well, hope you are too."

As May was ending in a procession of resplendent blue skies, he hired a car and treated himself to a quiet weekend in Truro. The main house was still shuttered, but Theo gave him the key to the tiny cottage and the boathouse. Out on the Pamet River in the floodtide at twilight, Orrin considered the lives of the saints and watched gulls wheel like boomerangs in the paling sky. He read volumes of lyric poetry—Yeats, Hopkins, Larkin—and ate the fettucini at Napi's, in Provincetown.

He remembered thinking how difficult it would be to find a suitable woman for companionship, and how simple to find a man. Now how much simpler still to seek and find no one at all? To take the universe as he had entered it, one small creature adrift in a limitless splendor. At North Truro in late May, lyric poetry made great sense to him.

Back in town, he worked and walked, attended parties and shows. One afternoon he slipped into the King's Chapel, wondering if he might add a strand or two of church feeling to the strength of the lyric poetry. A pleasant caretaker defined for him the architectural niceties of the building, all terminology and time-frames, but Orrin could barely see past the outsized white pillars and was nowhere close to focussing on such divine energy as may have been present. Too bad, for God would have been a nice help; luckily, Orrin did not need the help so much as he would have enjoyed having it.

He was asked to dinner and he went, and ate, although privately he felt put off by the smugness and pallor of his generation. Knowing he had been no better (and probably a deal worse) one year ago, Orrin thanked his stars for the bliss of personal difficulty. MAN CRUSHED BY LIFE, YET SURVIVES! Wishing to settle all accounts amicably, he courted good will everywhere, though it was futile to explain the thing to Gail and he lacked the courage to try with Eli.

He craved Eli's reaction to Kenny Fellows, wanted updates on the Baker 27 and the real Man Crushed, but he did not quite trust himself with Paperman. A number of times he spotted Eli in the street, but it was never really him; always a perfect stranger in fact. Spotted him twice in one

day in Cambridge—even went so far as to address one of
him—and found it was only sleight-of-eye. Until the second week in June, he made no attempt at direct contact.

Even this was accidental, almost—roundabout, certainly. It was a Sunday and Orrin had eaten his own
concoction of stir-fry vegetables on rice, then taken the
train to Cambridge to see a film. It was a warm, flawless
night, dim dusk when he emerged at nine o'clock, and
strolling under the stars soon realized he was just blocks
away from Marcy Green's apartment. As good a time as
any. If Eli and Marcy were disinclined for company, they
wouldn't answer the door. If they did answer it, then
perhaps the dynamics of the threesome could ease them
past any lingering tensions . . .

Two young women—one in windbreaker and shorts,
the other in a thick bathrobe—sat drinking coffee on the
railing of Marcy's porch. Tenants in the building, presumably, they chatted with a conspiratorial delight that Orrin
envied. And though they took no notice of him, their
presence made him self-conscious as he rang the bell. Too
late to chicken out, however. He took the dirty winding
wooden stairs two at a time up to Marcy's door, painted a
pale blue, with the numeral four mounted in brass. The
door swung open.

"Orrin," she said, peering past him and then back to
meet his eyes. Marcy was informal, to say the least, in a
cotton gown worn extremely thin. "Would you like to
come in? I mean, of course you would—here you are,
really."

"Yes, here I am. So a fairer question is would you like to
have me come in. I should have phoned, of course, but it
was a spur of the moment thing—just a hello to the two of
you—not *stay* at all, you know."

He glanced at his watch-wrist, to mime a punctuation.
(This was an odd habit, since he wore no wrist-watch on

his watch-wrist, but it did help to orient him at times.)
"Please say no if it is even the slightest imposition."

"No. That is, No I'm glad to see you. Come in. But Eli
isn't here, if that's what 'the two of you' means. There's
only one of me."

"Oh well. Just estimating, you know."

"I haven't seen him in a month. And wasn't really expecting to, though I confess I thought you might be him.
Since no one else arrives at my door out of the blue like
that."

"Sorry. And sorry to disappoint."

"So am I, then. Shall we commiserate over a beer? Or I
have some Daniels if you'd rather?"

"Maybe just one. Thank you, Marcy."

He spoke in a courtly, almost fatherly way as he took in
the rooms, and accepted a glass. In the aftermath of the
barroom brawl (as he had come to think of it), Orrin had
been almost a teetotaler, but not out of principle.

"You're deciding whether to ask *why* I haven't seen
him—or how to ask it."

"Not at all. Quite blank, to be honest—a little surprised
to find myself here. Did you know I hadn't seen him
either?"

"I guess I figured it out. But you look very well, Orrin."

"The good weather helps. I dare not say, in mixed company, how well *you* look, dear girl."

"You dirty old man," she said, smiling and covering up
more conscientiously. Her cotton gown was worn through
in one spot, where lamplight glanced off a shiny hip. But
Marcy was much less surprised by Orrin's remark than he
was.

"A clean old man, I'm afraid. Sorry if I couldn't help but
notice. Tell me how your work is going, with the young."

"Oh I love it, Orrin. I'm almost sorry summer is coming. Right now, I've got to decide about the summer

program—it would be four weeks, so I'd still get a nice solid vacation . . ."

"Sounds ideal. I'm glad the whole thing has worked out so well."

Marcy might not have been 'good enough' as a dancer, by someone's standards, but her legs were surely good enough. As lean and shapely as legs can be, thought Orrin, and there was a distinctive beauty to her foot as well, in the strong delicate arch. Fragments of this girl's anatomy seemed to turn inevitably to fetishes—the neck and now the feet—but Orrin could reckon for himself the truth, that he was isolating the parts to block a reception of the whole. Originally in keeping with the policy of denial, this was now perhaps a little trick for simple self-preservation.

"I just got back an hour ago," she was saying, apropros of nothing. And then in a curiously absent voice, "I was about to wash my hair."

"I'll go. No reason not to wash it on schedule."

"No, no," Marcy said, brightening. "It's nice to have some company for a change. It's not like I *needed* to wash my hair."

"I find it hard to imagine you anything but besieged by company. Have you been off on one of your skiing weekends?"

"Orrin, it's June? You might notice such details?"

"Oh well, I've been off Weather for a while. *Water*-skiing, I must have meant."

"I was down in New York for the weekend, actually. Helping my mother move into a new apartment."

"That's nice—your mother. You get along together?"

"We have fun. But this apartment is an amazing dump. Roaches the size of my hand. Mice the size of rats—I'd hate to see the rats! We hauled away a junky old mattress and a billion fleas jumped us—and moved right into my socks."

"But you called this fun."

"You had to be there. We took some sandwiches to the

Park and sat near a couple of Noo York ladies—fur coats in June and little white poodles on leashes? And those poochlets were so irresistible—"

"You didn't?"

"We did. Our fleas had found a new home."

"Your *mother* participated?"

"My sainted mother? Mothers are just old girls, Orrin. You should meet my mother. But yes, for sure she did."

"Ah the spirit of evil is in it, Marcy Green."

"That's what we thought, too. But it seemed to us that the alternative was a rather *dispirited* moralism in which one refuses to contaminate the sweet doggie doggie."

"And continues to itch oneself."

"There's the rub! And one never wants to be too dogmatic either, if you see what I mean."

They were doing fine now, feeling chumly. The trouble was that whenever Marcy rose, or shifted her weight, what he saw was too much thigh, and one time a soft shadow where the thighs intersected. For Orrin, not currently in training for the incursions of casual lust, it was quite literally dizzymaking.

"But enough about these fleas. What have you been up to lately, Orrin? How have you been feeling?"

"Feeling human. Doing I can hardly remember. But it's been very pleasant lately, very positive."

"Another drink?"

It occurred to him he might be missing a cue. On the lookout for his hint to go, he never considered a signal to stay. But Marcy was two drinks ahead of him, making herself high—goading herself to it—and it began to seem a seduction was possible. Overwhelmed by the mere possibility, blasted from monasticism in the presence of the shining flesh, Orrin fell back into polite weak-kneed confusion. So young and so lovely!

"I'd better not. I have to negotiate my way back to Boston soon."

"Suit yourself," she said, leaving the bottle for him. It was incredible, nothing less, yet he was now certain Marcy was moving her body (not by parts but as a concerted choreographic entity) in ways meant to shock him into action. Pulling her legs underneath her on the chair, she left him to stare at (or broadly stare away from) a parabolic slice of thigh rounding into buttock.

Hardly in condition for this sort of thing, Orrin didn't want to blow it either; did not wish to play the fool, or even simply miss a cue. He stood, without a plan in mind. Options included the bottle, the bathroom, the gate, and Ms. Green.

But when she stood too, facing him, the matter was clinched. Not at all certain which he feared more, acceptance or rejection, Orrin took her shoulders and leaned forward to attempt a kiss.

Marcy attempted it too, briefly. Like Orrin, she was wrestling mostly with herself. And just as he was impelled forward out of the awkward bind, she was in the end impelled backward.

"Wrong," he said. "Right?"

"Right, yes, but not your fault, Orrin. Mine."

It was true, Marcy had been engaged in a seduction; seducing not Orrin but, again, herself. Only at the last had it gone bust.

"It's just a situation," she shrugged. (To this meaningless attempt at good will, he could only muse, and shrug back, And what isn't?) "Don't feel badly," she tried again.

"Don't you. I'm a big boy. But maybe I would accept that drink now . . ."

Orrin swallowed, breathed; swallowed again, breathed again. A sort of boy-scout-pace for social survival.

"Well it *is* just a situation, isn't it?" he could now concede, though he saw that she had turned more somber.

"Both of us lonely—and fond of each other, too. It's so *trite,* Orrin. But I think that loneliness is like a job description, either it fits you or it doesn't."

"Certainly a mystery to me."

"I mean some people can't be lonely. They aren't lonely even when they're alone. Consequently they aren't alone very much."

"Consequently, eh? I wonder who you can be thinking of."

"It's true, though—the things that make Eli happy on his own are the things that make him so appealing to other people."

"Oh I know. I really did come here looking for Eli, by the way. I insist on your believing that."

"Of course. And really, Orrin, it would have been perfectly all right if you had come just to see me. I won't even die of your kiss. I didn't hate the idea, it was just—"

"Wrong."

"Right. You know why."

Orrin did know why, of course; the girl was in love with Paperman, and reasonably enough. There was nothing reasonable about any visions of himself in the rare embrace of this sleek, witty, green-eyed creature. Unfortunately it was not his reason but his unreason upon which she had almost inadvertently laid a claim.

Mere chance that he found her, and mere mischance to find her in a state so vulnerable, so readily intimate. Moons in Jupiter, or something. But after an excessively civil leavetaking, and an extremely long walk home, his senses still brimmed with her: the soft lips, hard muscles of her arms, sweet bourbon-flavored breath.

He was overcome with a panic made visceral—unless he could touch her again soon, he might cease to exist. This was wild, sudden, excessive, but it was there, sapping him like fever. He could think of nothing else.

Something kin to this panic had come over him once before in his life, long ago, in May of 1949, when Gail accepted a weekend invitation to Cornell in order to "broaden her experience." Orrin took it to mean that after three wonderful years she was done with him and he waited out the weekend like a shock victim, a vacant husk.

But Gail, the love of his life, and Marcy Green, a lovely girl he barely knew? It was blasphemy to consider the two together. He was reliving an emotion, that was all, a terrible emotional drowning. And however unexpected or unwarranted it might be, it was the same tonight as it had been then. Emotion, Orrin knew, was not always imprecise.

In May of 1949, Gail had come back embarrassed, and vastly relieved. Grateful for his familiarity, their familiarity, so that very soon they were talking familiar family talk again, naming their prospective babies. The Cornell man had never even kissed her.

Why this searing sense of loss now?—and loss of something he had never considered having? It could not be love. There was Gail, for one thing, and there was also the fact that it had not been love just prior to his arrival at Dana Street. It had not been anything at all.

But it was something now. Intoning her name like a lyric, invoking the merry green eyes and the sweet jughandle hip, Orrin was in straight adolescent meltdown. Shaky in the legs, hollow in the gut—all the clichés applied, and there was nothing he could do except try to intellectualize.

Thus he ransacked the file cabinet for an ancient paper on the chemical basis of love. In it he had discussed the extent to which love was something "real" versus something "constructed", and at what point the imaginative construct might become objective reality. There had been a lengthy section, closely argued, on the chemical aspect of "love at first sight", Orrin recalled, but he could recall none of his conclusions. He had proved something in that paper, but what? More mystery.

Now he turned to reductive thinking, so freshly discredited. If this phenomenon was not love, then it could only be lust or illusion. If illusion it would be gone by morning, or by the next time he and Marcy met. If lust it showed what a powerhouse Orrin was, for sexuality was strong enough to do this to him and yet *he* was strong enough to deny it. And here, finally, at four in the morning he had drawn a conclusion worth drinking to and he drank—just the one—and either the drink or the consoling knowledge it celebrated gave him ease enough to sleep at last.

Even there, however, he dreamed a dream as direct as a bullet, in which he ravished Marcy Green and she ravished him back, in the chair she had earlier occupied, in positions inconceivable, time and time again, to the violins of Mendelssohn, with her tracery of cotton gown shredded like kleenex and her head tossed back to show the regal pulsing neck.

23

Orrin was not exactly surprised, three nights later, to see Marcy come in smiling from a dense yellow rain. He had fantasized the sight of her so relentlessly that by now she was purely an adjunct of his own thought. Of course he never expected her to materialize, but that assumption evaporated to complete insignificance once she simply and magically had.

Nor was he surprised when with no salutation beyond the smile she commenced peeling away layers of clothing—the faded silk kerchief she had bonneted on her head, the sweatshirt and canvas sneakers—since they all were soaking wet. But it did leave her in quite apparently just two more garments (white cotton top and red flannel sweatpants) that were similarly drenched so as to be uniquely formfitting. And tugging now at the drawstring of her sweats, Marcy was taking the sequence to a consistent if not exactly proper conclusion.

"Whoa," said Orrin. "Hadn't I better go fetch a nice big towel or blanket at this juncture?"

"That would be nice," she said, though when he returned with the towels she was standing there in her skin; skin that appeared astoundingly dry and smooth and luminous. The skin took his breath away, for all the clichés still applied.

"Marcy, are you trying to tell me you've had a change of heart?"

"Me?" she grinned, wrapping the tan towel around her waist steambath style and winding the green one on her head like a turban. Her gleaming white breasts, the nipples bunched dark and grainy as red briar, were impossible not to touch. And touching them, he could feel his pants lift in response.

"But you see," he managed, "I know this whole scenario. Soon you'll start to tremble and heave miserable sobs—"

"No, Orrin, don't you worry. I've been thinking this through for days."

"Oh so have I, make no mistake. I'd almost finished rationalizing it, in fact—decided the point was in my making the attempt, in *wanting* to, you know."

"If you wanted to, Orrin, why don't you want to now?"

"Not so fast. You didn't want to then. So why *do* you want to now?"

"Yak yak yak," she said, and Orrin blushed more at this accusation than he had at her dazzling anatomy. "Don't you feel ridiculously out of place standing there with all your clothes on?"

He certainly did, by this time.

Orrin was not surprised he could love her like a man, nor did Marcy seem to expect anything else. To Orrin, an easy accustomed dreamer, it seemed entirely natural they should fit a bed so well, fit together so easily and so often. They conjoined throughout the night, as young lovers do in songs, only at greater and talkier intervals, and to varying degrees of conclusion. That they both were happy with it all there was no denying.

"At my age," said Orrin, "one is glad just to have it happen."

"I'm glad to have it happen, too. I don't think we want age to be a topic here."

"Why not?"

"Because you're not old, you're you. Besides, I like older men. I liked you the first time we met."

"That can't be true."

"Why can't it? You seemed handsome and wise. And you had a sense of humor."

"Did I? I sound almost perfect. It's amazing you could resist me. Don't these ever get soft?"

"You should talk. But I couldn't resist you, as it turns out. I just had to *schedule* you. It's very inconvenient meeting two men you like, after you've gone a year without meeting any at all."

"So inefficient, you mean. But shouldn't you have scheduled us in reverse—elders first? According to my doctor, I may have only thirty more years to live.'

"Now you're talking."

"Wait, though, Marcy. You are the one who called me a dirty old man."

"It was just wishful thinking at the time. You'll have to drop this complex about age, because what I really hate is neurosis."

"Oh dear, in that case I'm afraid I may have to refer you."

A week later, after one night at her place and one more at his, Orrin grew bold with her. "Would you have any interest in renting Eli's old room?"

"I don't think so. But thanks."

"If I were to give up on Gail—just hypothetically— would you have any interest in renting *my* room? Say half of it?"

"No thank you, Orrin."

"Really not? I could offer you a marriage of convenience."

"Aren't we better off with a non-marriage, of inconvenience? I don't love you, Orrin, and you don't love me either. You love Gail."

Was this so? If it was so, this bilateral absence of love, wasn't it okay anyway? Wasn't it what made a marriage of convenience convenient? Orrin was framing this little joke when a stray thought intruded on him:

"You love Eli."

"I told him so, for all the good it did me. But it wasn't spoken lightly. I can't retract it just because he ditched me."

"So why are we here, then?"

"Because life goes on. And this is what life gave each of us next. Because it's good for us and can't devastate either one of us—"

"Since you love Eli and I supposedly love Gail."

"Supposedly? Let's be serious for a minute, Orrin. Would you seriously want to be hooked up to a young thing on the rebound? It's so trite. Think how your friends would all nod sagely and say Oh yes, another aging shrink taking up with a younger woman—"

"They wouldn't understand."

"Sure they would. And they'd be right, probably."

"Well goodness, Marcy, I don't care—really and truly I don't—about trite. I'd be proud to show you off at my Club or anywhere else. Is that so terrible?"

"It depends. Let's say that for now I find it flattering."

"But you categorically reject my hand in marriage?"

"I think it will be for the best."

Orrin was continually reminded of something he had known from the start: having turned thirty-three, Marcy was younger than he was, but she was not actually young—or foolish.

"Maybe you're right," he said. "In the long run, we'll be saving the price of a postcard."

"Pardon?"

"Nothing. A silly inside joke, between me, myself, and I. But I do have a dream to relate."

"A new one? What are you waiting for—tell me."

"The night before last. I dreamt you turned me down flat. I said, you know, come live with me and be my love, and you called me a fool and walked away. I closed up shop and left the city. Bought a vast estate—in Transylvania, from the look of it. A cobwebbed stone castle with raging fires in a dozen great hearths—called Madlands. There was a painted sign between two granite columns, swaying on chains, like some old medieval inn."

"And you lived there in splendid isolation?"

"I don't know. I dreamed the *place* very vividly, but I never did see myself there, nor anyone else."

"Not even the house-servants laying the fires?"

"No, nothing but the architectural detail."

"So what do you think? Defiance? Or a craving for some solitude—you could be sick of me already."

"Madness would be my guess. Trying to *contain* madness, you know."

Orrin was never surprised to see genuine force in Marcy's affection—physically she held nothing back—nor was he surprised to discover rigid lines where the affection left off. In fact, he believed that nothing would ever surprise him again. (He even believed that this was itself an illusion, so that he would not be surprised when something did.) He did understand that Marcy Green was an impermanent star in his firmament, and yet by the time she left him Gail might be ready to return. Indeed it would not surprise him if Gail were ready now, or whenever she learned about Marcy, though it would be no *more* surprising should she prove altogether and eternally indifferent.

He even expected Elspeth's packet, though it was the first piece of mail he'd had from her since summer camp in 1974. Her cassette was entitled *Sluggish Plumbing*. The front showed El in her feathers and the band in black leather; on the back, there was a photograph of the Madison Hotel imploding. Orrin wasn't surprised to find the music crisp, or the lyrics tough and rich. All songs

were copyright Third World Music and the best cut by far
("Bottled Spirits" by Summers/Ferguson) played a lilting
calypso verse off against a harrowing vision of political
smash and batter in the chorus.

Still he was surprised (if only momentarily) on a Saturday night in July, while dressing for The Midsummer
Night's Bal Masque. The windows were wide open, the
air benign with distant ringing bells and long-fallen
blossoms. On a night just like this one, Orrin reflected, he
had moved into these rooms last summer. The year was an
immensely flexible measure: so short and at the same time
so very endless.

For simplicity's sake, Orrin had chosen to go as himself
tonight ("No one will recognize me!") and to defuse her
first appearance at a Club function Marcy would be The
Younger Woman, herself as well.

"You're going to hate this, you know."

"Oh I hope so," Marcy replied as the doorbell was
sounding, "but I never like to *count* on anything."

A confusing moment, doorbells mingling with the
churchbells, plus the idea that "they" had a visitor. It could
only be Eli, or so Orrin feared in a searing vision of all his
joys disbanded. "Take a guess," he said bravely, then saw at
once that Marcy was shaken by the same supposition.

"Gail," she guessed.

"I say it's one of my children. I'll guess Clyde."

It was not Eli Paperman. Instead there stood before
them a messy, mismatched couple, like a practical joke, a
facialgram meant to parody the two of them in some
obscure fashion. It occurred to Marcy they must be chums
of Orrin's, arriving in costume for a drink before the
dance.

Orrin meanwhile suffered a moment of total blankness,
followed by a brief nervous impulse—flickering genuflection to forgotton notions—and then achieved a wonderful
smile, his best in decades, a smile that welled up from an

enormous reservoir of new calm and pleasure. And extending both arms to embrace P. Jones, he confessed he was surprised, though happily so.

"Come in, my friend. Come in, Mary. You two must be thirsty on a night like this."

"Thank you, Orry. And how are you tonight, young lady?"

"Pigford, Mary, may I present my friend Marcy Green. Marcy, Pigford and Mary."

"Sorry I never came by sooner, Orry. Things come up, you know how it is, and before you know it the time slides away."

"Of course, but you mustn't overlook the plight of the homeful. You've been well?"

"Plus ça change, Orry. I'm still me. It's a dog-eat-dog world and I just have no taste for dog. Never had it, really."

"Fair enough. Try this stuff, if you'd like."

"I suppose there was a sort of a *class* thing, too, if you know what I mean. Happy to see you down at The Dog & Cat anyoldtime but to come up here without an invite—"

"I'm so glad you finally overcame your reluctance. Something must have inspired you. What?"

"He's a sharp one, The Doctor. I told Mary you would read my mind right off the bat. I guess you know"— Pigford now addressed Marcy—"that Orry here is a famous headshrinker."

"I want to see your sliding scale," cackled Sad Mary.

"Her idea of humor," said Pigford. "Talks of it now and then, like it would slide down the hill, see?"

"Let's see it," she giggled again.

"The truth is this, and best taken straight out front—we came by hoping for a smallish loan."

"Small enough and I'll make an outright gift of it."

"Oh no. It's got to be a loaner."

"A scholarship, then. What's our ballpark here, how large a sum are we discussing?"

"Well I did a little work for the city, two months aboard the S.S. Sanitation. We got some clothes out of that, and we have the loose change in savings."

"Yes?"

"The idea is to go on vacation, All-American style. Ride the bus down to the Cape for a weekend of surf."

"The crowds are awful," said Marcy.

"Sure they are, and we might have more fun at home, like any vacationer. But I convinced us that we earned the right to find it out."

"Except you haven't. Literally earned it, that is."

"See! Right with Eversharp, Orry. We've got a hundred twenty and are looking for the balance. Busfare, motel, plus the necessaries. What do you suppose it would take?"

"I wouldn't cut it too close. Err on the high side. You get your tickets and pay for the room, and then be sure to have a hundred fifty for each day you are there."

"One fifty per diem! Gawd, no. Ten will be good for that, surely?"

"Pigford, no. Don't get caught short. If you spend less, you can always return the balance and shrink your principal on the loan. But the money will be there if you need it."

"You never know what can come up," said Marcy.

"*She* knows," Sad Mary agreed—fellow females these.

"Anyway, consider it done. Happy to come to terms, Pigford. I am a great believer in loaning a good man money—once."

"That says it all. The Once."

"But listen, here's another proposition. We were just stepping out to my Club, not far from here. There's a shindig on tonight—moyles and moyles of food, and a bottomless well of pedigreed booze. Would you consider joining us?"

"We are hardly presentable, you kind man."

"But you are. It's a masquerade, you see, so you can come just as you are and be—what?"

"Street-life," said Mary.

"The Man in the Street! And the Woman. I am going disguised as Myself and Marcy as The Younger Woman. Among our party, we are bound to take a door prize."

"That is good, as yourself. So we would be as ourself too, wouldn't we. And she *is* a younger woman—than you, Mary."

"She's a good gal, though," said Mary.

"But let's run," said Orrin. "It's getting late, and I think we are all ready?"

"I don't know about this one, Orry."

They were halfway into the corridor as Pigford expressed his hesitancy. Back inside the flat, Orrin's phone was ringing, but he waved it off and snugged the door behind them.

"Oh come on, Pigford, what the hell. If we're not enjoying ourselves, we can always just go somewhere for a drink."

Foliage À Deux

(envoi)

The world is sometimes quite
unsteady even when one is not drunk.
—MUSIL

Three months later, in October, the Boston Red Sox were playing for the world championship in New York. There was wide disagreement in Boston as to whether they overcame the burden of history by going so far, or whether history rose up and overcame them—for naturally, they had victory in their grasp and failed to grasp it.

Orrin Summers was not watching. He and Marcy were just back from a weekend in Fitzwilliam, New Hampshire, and when he read that Oil Can Boyd was being yanked from the pitching rotation for the decisive seventh game, he boydcotted it. The manager, McNamara, had told the press throughout the Series that he did not intend to tamper with a lineup that had won all year simply because logic might appear to dictate such changes. Then he yanked the Can and explained that the change was dictated by logic. This was a logic Orrin felt he had seen before in Boston sports.

But he was two-faced, too. The irony was not lost on him, for he had invited Marcy to fill Gail's spot in the lineup on the annual Foliage à Deux excursion and it seemed to him in doing so that nothing was sacred now. It seemed that way to Tony, the innkeeper, too, although he kept his tightened twisted mouth shut about it.

Orrin wanted to explain to Tony that it was not his choice, that it was not what it seemed. Less than a week earlier, he'd tried to convince Gail they really ought to tough it out together for the sake of the children and, laughing almost in the old way, she confessed she hadn't thought of that angle. "I would have gone on," he wanted to tell Tony, "if only for the sake of little Clyde and Elspeth."

As badly as he felt about the roster change, Orrin could not (or at least he did not) resist it and much of the bad feeling proved sadly hypothetical. For the meals were as delicious as ever, the sugar maples had never flared a more sultry red or radiant yellow, and the Ashuelot, the Contoocook, and the old Souhegan rippled happily still through the inflamed forests. And though Tony had stuck it to them, he was sure, with the most prohibitive hay-rack of a bed (out of a touching loyalty to Gail) it was nonetheless impossible for Orrin to deny his sexuality in Fitzwilliam, or repress a single note of any song.